JACK PICKLEWICK XIII

AND THE

HANDS OF TIME

HARRIS & NEEDHAM

HARRIS & NEEDHAM

First Edition

Published in Great Britain by Harris & Needham

ISBN 978-1-3999-2945-5

Also available as an eBook

Book design by LightField London

www.harrisneedham.com

You are given it every day, yet fail to appreciate it. You can use it however you choose but don't always do so wisely. Most unforgivable of all, you wish it away, but when it's too late, realise you never had enough of it.

Time is a gift. Use it wisely.

Your forever faithful horology enthusiast,

Maxamus B. Moretimer

December 1899

CONTENTS

For Jersey, Liberty, Hugh, and George.

PROLOGUE

*F*ATHER Time and Mother Nature: two of many roles created by the Order of Foretellers when they oversaw the formation of the universe.

In the Realm of Time, the first Father, Solomon Solstice, crafted a device so powerful, so enduring, it would function for all eternity. With the Hands of Time, he provided life with a never-ending blank canvas on which it could paint; the capability to remember the past, to live in the present and to dream of the future. This was his gift to the universe and from that moment, whatever else happened, time was exactly as the Order of Foretellers had intended it to be: **constant.**

In the Realm of Earth, Mother Nature gave birth to the sun, sea, and sky. The natural world blossomed as mountains were raised from the depths of the oceans, great land masses formed from rock and forests exploded from the soil. She gave life a platform from which it could spring and thrive. This was her gift to the universe and, from that moment, whatever else happened, nature was exactly as the Order of Foretellers had intended it to be: **beautiful.**

Eventually, time wore out Solomon Solstice and he could no longer keep up with it. He believed it necessary to pass on the role of Father Time to another who could dedicate as much passion and energy to it that he once had. A tradition was born and whenever a serving Father felt his time was up, he would bestow the honour upon another who would then be responsible for keeping time the way it was intended to be. Mother Nature was different; the natural world bloomed throughout the years and the constant change ensured she fell in love with the beauty of her creation over, and over, again.

For centuries, the serving Father Time and Mother Nature lived alongside each other in harmony, the keepers of their respective realms. However, as the Hands of Time ticked on, Mother Nature grew to resent Father Time for there was one flaw with his incredible invention.

The creation of time brought with it the coming of age.

Mother Nature, so obsessed with physical appearance, was condemned to watch her creation grow old, wither and eventually, if nothing was done about it, die.

Eleven Fathers succeeded Solomon Solstice and the time of the Twelfth had begun. Mother Nature sought him out and pleaded with him, but the great wizard stood firm: *time is constant.*

Enraged by his stubbornness, Mother Nature unleashed her wrath; wind, rain, thunder, and lightning became her weapons as she tore through the Realm of Time in search of the one thing that could restore her creation to the way she had intended it. Unable to compete with her fury, Father Time took the Hands of Time and fled to the one place he thought she would never destroy - that which she was trying to preserve: the Realm of Earth.

Once Mother Nature had completely scoured and destroyed the Realm of Time, she returned to the Realm of Earth and, just as Father Time had predicted, her anger subsided. Through fear that she would strike again in the future, Father Time built a shield between the two realms - the Meridian - a magical divide that would keep Mother Nature confined to the Realm of Earth. For years, the Meridian served its purpose and time remained just as it had been intended. Father Time hid right under Mother Nature's nose in the Realm of Earth, crossing the Meridian whenever he could to rebuild the Realm of Time. He chronicled the history of everything; major, world-changing moments to the smallest, incidental events. All were recorded and stored in a vault high atop the Evercanever; a huge mountain which ascended for miles into the stratosphere of the Realm of Time.

Happy in the knowledge that the Meridian would keep history safe, the Twelfth Father remained hidden in the Realm of Earth. But, as with time comes the certainty of age, age can also have its own side effects, such as, in the case of the Twelfth Father...

...forgetfulness.

- I -

THE PREPOSTEROUS PICKLEWICK

'STEP right up, folks, step right up; you won't believe your peepholes! You'll ooh, you'll aah, you'll be amazed by the brilliantly bizarre as the world-renowned, Preposterous Picklewick makes the impossible possible.'

World-renowned was a stretch by anyone's imagination, but there was no doubt that Jack Picklewick was quite the showman. Despite looking better suited to sweeping chimneys, the scruffy twelve-year-old commanded his wooden bushel box stage with the presence of a professional magician. Armed with confidence beyond his years, sleight of hand that Houdini would envy, and charm that could seduce any snake, Jack was missing just one thing:

An audience.

The London streets bustled with punters but this morning, just like every other morning, Jack found them a tough crowd. Rich factory owners marched by his upturned flat cap which laid on the cobbles for tips that never came. Even his fellow street peasants and beggars, who surrounded him on all sides, paid his impressive card shuffling no mind at all. The only thing that seemed remotely interested was the scruffy teddy bear which guarded Jack's personal belongings: a battered wooden stick, on the end of which was a cotton sack stuffed with a few dirty clothes, and a well-thumbed copy of Jules Verne's Twenty Thousand Leagues Under the Sea. Despite his age, Jack took Edgar everywhere, but he would not have been surprised if his stuffed companion got up and walked away from him as well, the way things were going. 1899 had not been a great year for the aspiring trickster but neither had any of his previous eleven - the ones he could remember, anyway. Suffering with amnesia, he knew nothing of his life before the day he awoke on the cold, hard cobbles but he possessed a picture-perfect memory of his time since then, most of which had been spent begging, sleeping rough and perfecting his wasted magic act. When he came to, the only possessions he had were a single photograph and the teddy, which he promptly named given that no one else seemed interested in being his friend. As he approached his thirteenth birthday, Jack lived in hope that a day would come when he would perform on the biggest theatre stages in England, giving him the financial means to get a roof over his head and track his family down, if he even had one. If today was anything to go by, that day was nothing more than a pipe dream.

Just as Jack was about to pack up his act and try his luck elsewhere, a pompous, self-important gentleman swaggered towards him. Jack's silver tongue worked its magic and reeled off his introductory spiel once again.

Success!

His eyes widened as the gentleman's hands reached into his deep pockets.

A couple of days-worth of bread here we come! The gentleman walked straight past Jack and tossed a beggar a single coin. 'Oh, come on,' yelled Jack, 'his only trick involves drinking himself unconscious!' The gentleman carried on his way, Jack's protest falling on deaf ears.

Well, Edgar, no one can say we didn't try the honest way.

Evidently, magic was not Jack's only talent. As he scurried off in pursuit of the gentleman, he pick-pocketed the morning commuters, slipping in and out of crowds, ducking beneath arms and sliding between legs. The way he saw it, if they were lucky enough to have anything in their pockets, he wasn't taking anything they would miss. Despite his cavalier attitude, stealing wasn't something Jack was proud of, but, on the dog-eat-dog London streets, wrong and right looked a lot like life and death, especially for homeless twelve-year-olds.

What surprised Jack was how easy it was; it amazed him how blissfully unaware people were when they were otherwise occupied. The more he thought about it, the more it seemed that robbing somebody blind had striking similarities to performing magic; distract then deceive. It was certainly more fruitful when he made a few bob the dishonest way, but, if he got caught, the only audience he would find himself in front of would be a jury. A performance in a workhouse had much less appeal than one in The Adelphi.

That won't happen, I'm the world renowned, Preposterous Picklewick.

Jack acquired enough coins that he wouldn't go hungry at least for the next day or two. He gave up his pursuit of the pompous gentleman, but, as he skipped away across the cobbles, a young lady with her nose buried in the morning newspaper trundled towards him. She ranted and raved to herself about something or other. Jack weighed up his options and looked to Edgar for approval.

One more won't hurt.

This was the habit of a lifetime for Jack. Curious by nature, he always pushed things that little bit further when enough should have been enough. He worked his magic as the lady rushed by him then opened his hand and revealed his takings.

Not worth the risk.

A pen, inscribed with the letters V. FLEMMING, sat on Jack's palm. On reflection, it was better than nothing and might bear fruit at some stage, so he shoved it into his sack as he legged it around the corner and out of sight.

The rest of the day unfolded the same way it had started with Jack's magic show falling on blind eyes and deaf ears. To make matters worse, a storm brewed on the horizon and the sky was almost entirely blacked out by dark clouds.

Suppose I better be calling it a day.

Jack bought as much bread as he could afford with the stolen money. Even the shopkeeper ignored him, so he just left the coins in place of the bread and off he went. He coped surprisingly well with being homeless, but the recent erratic climate had made things that little bit more challenging. Despite it being summer, the weather had become completely unpredictable, and Jack was more desperate than ever to switch the cold, unforgiving streets for a warm, appreciative stage.

When the rain came, it came hard, bouncing off the ground, soaking anyone and anything who was daft enough to stay out in it. Jack took shelter beneath a bridge but did not want to stay there all night, despite the guaranteed refuge from the elements. By nightfall it would be crawling with starving peasants, all desperate for a bite to eat. Jack had witnessed first-hand how desperation could cause even the best of people to commit the most extreme of acts and it wasn't unheard of to find bodies floating in the River Thames. Higher, more open ground was much safer, but the bridge would have to do, at least until the rain subsided. He sat down, propped Edgar beside him and stuffed his face like he hadn't eaten for days.

Beneath the bridge, on the opposite side of the river, a young girl, no older than Jack, shivered in the shadows as she curled herself up into a ball on the ground. Jack glanced at his evening meal and then back at the young girl. His stomach groaned but he felt a niggle inside that didn't quite sit right. He gathered his belongings and made his way across the river. By the time he got there, the young girl was fast asleep. Jack looked at her; skin deathly white and filthy with cheek bones that protruded like knives.

She was in much worse condition than he was. He glanced at the half-eaten bread roll in his hand and sighed. Around the girl's neck was a heavily torn scarf, the only thing keeping her warm. Ignoring his bowel's pleas to reconsider, Jack wrapped the bread in the scarf and placed it down beside her.

We're all in this together.

Looking out onto the street, Jack could see the rain had not subsided at all. It was heavier than ever, but night had fallen, and he didn't want to take any chances. Get soaked by the rain or get soaked when a fellow peasant mugged him and threw him in the Thames; it hardly took a genius to work out the better option.

He took flight and weaved around shadowy corners, sprinted down foggy side streets and scaled weathered buildings until he reached the rooftops. Rain soaked him to the bone, but he carried on regardless and leapt from one rooftop to another. The London streets below were intermittently lit up by frequent flashes of lightning as he ran by. Up here, Jack felt happiest - the stars within his reach and the world at his feet.

How it will be, one day.

The storm subsided as quickly as it had begun and revealed a perfect, full moon. It was mild in temperature in contrast to the extreme weather that had beaten the city for the past hour or so. Jack arrived at his destination and set up camp on a terraced rooftop, directly opposite Big Ben. Painted by the moonlight and cloaked in the evening fog, the huge clock had a creepy, gothic feel about it.

Jack loved to admire it and he often wondered how long it would take him to build something as grand and impressive.

'We need to think bigger, Edgar,' said Jack, sitting the teddy bear beside him so it could also enjoy the view. 'That's what will get the punters coughing up. Folk want illusions, not card tricks. We need something unique for the twentieth century, something...,' Jack racked his brain until he found the word he wanted.

'Real.'

He laid back and gazed up at the stars, insignificant in size compared to the darkness of the night sky which surrounded them but shining so bright they stood out to anyone who cared to look. He tucked Edgar up beside him and removed Twenty Thousand Leagues Under the Sea from his sack. He opened the book and removed a photograph, which made quite a handy bookmark. For a moment, Jack put the book to one side and stared at the photograph. His family were wealthy, that much he knew. The house in the background certainly proved that. It looked more like a mansion than a house. Everyone in the photograph looked happy; his mother and father had great big smiles on their faces, as did his younger sister. Even he was smiling, ear to ear, all dressed up in nice clothes with Edgar dangling by his side, as always.

Why would they abandon me?

Was the photograph just for show?

What if something happened and I'm the only one who survived?

These were just some of the questions that haunted Jack every night, and, so far, he was no closer to finding the answers. A sudden gust of wind blew the photograph from his grasp. He leapt to action and slid down the roof, snatching it out of the air just before it got swept over the edge. In his rescue attempt, Jack knocked his sack and stolen coins rattled down the roof, eventually lost to the streets below. He looked back at Edgar, the bear expressionless, as ever. 'Don't look at me like that. We can replace the money.' The photograph was the only thing Jack had that linked him to any sort of history, his only clue to times he remembered nothing about. As he settled down for the night and read the next chapter of Captain Nemo's adventures aboard the Nautilus, Big Ben chimed to signal midnight.

As one day ends, another begins.

Jack's eyes grew heavy. He drifted off to sleep and dreamed about a past he could not remember and of a future he hoped he could belong. In reality, the time that was about to come would be something far, far beyond any fantasy he could ever dream of in his sleep.

- II -

JACK'S NIGHTMARE

*Z*ZZZZZZ!
Mouth wide open, Jack snored as he laid asleep on the rooftop. A tiny fly landed on his face and crawled into his mouth, which made him cough and woke him from his sleep. He cleared his throat and checked he still had his possessions. Satisfied Edgar had done his nightly duty and kept him safe, he admired his family photograph, clutching it firmly between his fingers as he stared at it. The morning scene was very different to the one which he had fallen asleep to; scorching rays of sunlight blasted out from between the clouds and warmed his face. He felt a tickle in the back of his throat and coughed again.

Stupid fly.

The feeling didn't go away, and he coughed some more until he felt like he was going to vomit. He fell to his knees and clutched his stomach. A stabbing pain built deep within his core which got worse and worse until he coughed one final time.

Something shot out of his mouth and splattered on the rooftop a few feet away.

A cockroach.

On closer inspection, it clearly wasn't the familiar household insect, at least not one Jack had ever seen before. About three times the size of the six-legged pest, it was jet black and had two sharp fangs which resembled the hands of a clock, one shorter than the other, protruding from its mouth. It also had twelve legs, which Jack counted one by one to make sure he wasn't seeing things. He admired the strange creature but, as it scuttled towards him, he suddenly felt terrified. The closer it got the more panic gripped him. Faster than a steam train, the rays of sunlight fizzled out and the sky filled with black clouds. The photograph in his hands disintegrated into black sand, grain by grain escaping between his fingers. Jack leapt to his feet but everything around him - the roof top, Big Ben, even Edgar - disintegrated too. He found himself standing in a hellish, barren land, surrounded by nothing but darkness. In the sky above, three black holes appeared, swirling side by side, huge voids surrounded by fire that got wider and wider the more they rotated. Suddenly, the middle void morphed into the shape of a demonic face. It chanted and muttered words in a language Jack did not understand. One word was uttered, repeatedly.

Makutu, Makutu, Makutu.

Jack screamed and ran away across the never-ending black dust-covered land that carpeted his feet. As far as it felt like he ran, he was never any further away, the demonic face always the same distance behind him, babbling and chanting. Dust twirled around Jack and wrapped itself around him until he crashed to the floor, dizzy. It held him prisoner as he writhed and struggled to free himself. No matter how hard he tried; he couldn't break loose. It was hopeless.

The demonic face, bigger than ever, circled like a typhoon until it was sucked back into the black hole in an explosion of fire. From within the void, a monstrous black hand with huge, razor-sharp claws reached out and descended towards Jack. No chance of escape, Jack scrunched his peepholes shut and prayed that when he opened them everything would be back to normal. Despite his calls to the almighty, when he opened his eyes, nothing had changed. The monstrous hand was upon him, inches away, each claw easily twice as big as himself. The cockroach-like insect leapt from one of the claws and scuttled up Jack's leg, settling on his chest. In a desperate attempt to knock the insect away, Jack wriggled but, unable to move any part of his body, the creature remained glued to him. Doom impending, the monstrous hand wrapped its fingers around Jack as the insect plunged its fangs deep into his heart.

CRACK!

The biblical thunder strike woke Jack with such a fright that he almost fell off the rooftop. He was sweating profusely and gasping for breath. When he looked down at his hands, black veins throbbed and pulsed beneath his skin then gradually returned to normal. It had happened so many times before that it didn't faze him as it once had. Even though he wondered what it all meant, he had grown used to it. The same nightmare plagued him at night, every night. At first, he didn't remember it when he woke but, recently, it was much more vivid.

Just like in the nightmare, the London skyline clouded over at an oddly rapid pace which sent a chill down Jack's spine. Thunder cracked again, much closer this time, accompanied by an impressive display of forked lightning.

'Looks like we need a change of scenery.'

He tucked Edgar beneath his armpit, gathered his belongings and slid down a drainpipe all the way to the cobbled street below. The weather had been awful in recent weeks and was always extreme; if it was hot, it was enough to roast a turkey. If it was cold, it was arctic-like and, much like the storm that rapidly approached, if it rained, it was a monsoon. Being homeless was hard enough but the conditions made circumstances a lot more challenging, and Jack was desperate for a roof over his head.

As the rain poured, Jack sprinted towards a door. He hammered on it like there was no tomorrow which, if he kept getting soaked every time there was a storm, it would only be a matter of time before he caught pneumonia and croaked it. After assaulting the door for what seemed like an eternity, a snooty looking fellow whipped it open and stuck his big nose out. 'Please, Sir, any chance of a bed for the--' Before Jack could finish his sentence, the man slammed the door shut in his face.

People can be so horrible to each other.

He had often wondered why this was. In his mind, everybody was in the same boat; just people trying to survive. Granted, there were different social standings and levels but, when everything was stripped back to the essentials, everyone was just skin and bone. Would it really kill someone to give him a bed for one night? He could even do them a magic show as payment in kind. How many other beggars could do that?

Jack ran to another doorway and bashed on it. Same result.

Three doors later, Jack gave up and came to terms with the thought of a night dicing with death beneath the bridge.

'Well, Edgar, if we're face down in the Thames tomorrow morning at least we won't have to worry about the weather anymore.' Icy winds bit Jack's face as he sprinted down the cobbles in a useless attempt to warm himself up. Just as he reached the end of the street, the loudest crack of thunder he had ever heard erupted above in the sky. It rattled around inside Jack's chest and unbalanced him, making him lose his footing. He tumbled to the ground, and with a sickening thud his head collided with the unforgiving street beneath a mucky puddle. Completely helpless, Edgar watched on.

Jack's eyes rolled back in his head as he lost consciousness.

- III -

TIME IS NOTHING BUT A DEATH SENTENCE

$\mathcal{S}$PLASH!

The construction worker's foot stomped down into a puddle of dirty rainwater as he dashed away from the building site and into the surrounding forest. It was either that or take a bone numbing night swim in the River Thames that ran alongside it. Already cold enough and shivering to his core, the worker fancied his chances more in the overgrown woodland.

Dirt, grime, and terror all over his face, he stuttered and stammered as he glanced over his shoulder, the pouring rain obscuring his view.

'Oh, God, please, no!'

Even though he couldn't see it, something was there, he was sure of it. The same thing that had already abducted several of his colleagues chased him.

Hunted him.

Fog as thick as clouds swirled up to his knees, and the further he waded through it into the forest, the more the natural light of the moon faded, masked by thick tree branches that formed a canopy of foliage above. The only light came from the candlelit lantern he held in his heavily calloused hands, the flame of which flickered and danced inside the glass. The jingle-jangle of keys which dangled from his belt was the only sound that could be heard as they rattled with every panicked step he took. Exhausted and soaking wet, he stopped for breath.

It was eerily silent. He could hear the tick-tock of his watch accompany the pitter-patter of rain, which the sheer volume of surrounding trees provided him shelter from. The refreshing peacefulness disarmed him for a moment; it was a far cry from the noise and filth of the building site which he had grown accustomed to. When the foundations had been laid for Alfred Threadbare's latest industrial monstrosity, nature had been shown no mercy as endless trees had been chopped down to make way for it. The corpses of fallen trees laid on the bank of the River Thames, undeniable evidence of a human crime against nature. The location was no doubt the reason why Threadbare had selected the area to develop. It would be easy for boats to transport large shipments of material in and the resulting products out of the factory rather than navigating the slow, busy city streets. In other words, it would ensure Threadbare's bank balance increased at a faster rate whilst Earth's natural beauty was ravaged as a result.

The construction worker held out the lamp in front of him. He could barely see a thing, sweat and rain had washed muck into his eyes and blurred his vision. A humming sound, like a woman singing in beautiful, songbird-like tones filled the air everywhere. A gust of wind extinguished the candle, and the worker was left in total darkness as the singing abruptly stopped.

'*Murderer.*'

The whispering voice shocked him. He ran for his life once again. Where he was going, he had no idea, but he had to get away. He lost count of the number of times he fell, face first into the dirt of the forest floor. Nettles stung his skin and tree roots tripped him, like the forest had decided to punish him for his part in its destruction. As he pulled himself from the dirt, he heard something. The faint sound of a wind chime. Fireflies, hundreds of them, appeared, flickering in the air, and illuminating the area. The worker was in a clearing, deep in the heart of the forest. It was a perfect circle, with trees surrounding him on all sides. He strained his eyes and in front of each tree there seemed to be the outline of a person. Maybe it was his work colleagues, and they hadn't mysteriously disappeared. They were all just hiding in the woods, playing a joke on him.

'C...c... come on, lads,' stuttered the worker, to no one in particular. 'It's hardly the t...t... time.'

'*Time, my dear, is nothing but a death sentence.*'

The whispering voice sounded again, and the worker felt something crawl over his feet. He looked down and saw tree roots slither and wrap themselves around his ankles, like snakes. The fireflies in the air burned brighter than ever and he saw them; his missing colleagues, staring back at him through lifeless eyes, their bodies petrified within the tree bark, like wooden statues.

THUD!

WHAM!

CRASH!

All around him, one by one, trees were sucked up and swallowed into the ground. The fireflies extinguished themselves and he was left in darkness. He tried to run but his feet were anchored to the ground. Crouching down, he hammered and tugged at the tree roots that held him prisoner, but they did not budge. In blind panic, the worker scrambled around in his pocket until he found a box of matches. He re-lit the lantern and held it out in front of him but was met with the sight of nothing. No trees, no forest, just him and the vast emptiness of the night sky. He was completely alone and defenceless, trapped at the mercy of his hunter. Other than the sound of his heavy breathing, all was silent like the calm before the storm.

Frozen by fear, the worker trembled. Just ahead of him, he thought he saw something.

A hooded silhouette, masked in shadows.

The worker gulped as he addressed the apparition before him.

'Wh... who...wh... what are you? Wh... what do you want?'

The whispering voice answered.

'Change.'

The tree roots yanked the worker down and he screamed as the Earth swallowed him whole.

'For the better.'

The lantern was left sitting on the ground.

Something else sat beside it, glimmering in the candlelight.

His watch.

The big and little hand ticked on as the candle wick melted down into a lake of wax, the flame in the lantern extinguished, the watch consumed entirely by darkness.

- IV -

A STORM IS COMING

*T*HE storm was in full flow when Jack woke. His pupils dilated as he opened his eyes then quickly closed them to protect them from the unrelenting rain. Still groggy and with blurred vision, he sat up and rubbed the back of his head, which was covered in sticky, matted blood. From the position of the moon in the sky, which was just about visible between a rare break in the cloud, he guessed that it was probably about three in the morning. He checked his pockets and belongings. Surprisingly, everything was accounted for.

From out of an alley up ahead, a glorious flash of light illuminated the rain-soaked street, flickered, and then faded away completely. Jack rescued Edgar from the puddle and cleaned him up as best he could. 'Did you see that?' The teddy bear gave Jack its usual silent response. 'Maybe I hit my head harder than I thought.'

Jack dragged himself to his feet and stumbled up the cobbles until he reached the alley. A street sign, nailed to a building above a padlocked, rusted iron gate, identified the alley.

Jubilee Walk.

Jack had knowledge of the London streets which would rival that of even the most experienced tour guide, but he had never noticed this one before. It wasn't anything to look at and blended in perfectly with the rest of the city, which was probably why he had never come across it before. Incredibly narrow, even by London standards, it was just about wide enough for two people to walk down, side by side, and the buildings that ran along each side of it were so tall it created a very claustrophobic feel. It wouldn't have been far-fetched to think that somebody might wander down it, get stuck and never be found. If anything, Jubilee Walk was a street that people probably wouldn't want to venture down, even if they noticed it in the first place. The sharp spikes that ran across the top of the gate and the padlock told late night passers-by that they were not welcome.

However, most late-night passers-by were not the Preposterous Picklewick.

In normal circumstances, Jack would have just taken his chances and climbed over the gate, but he was still unsteady on his feet and lightheaded from the bump to his head. Instead, he approached the gate and studied the padlock. It was extremely difficult to pick such a thing, but Jack was well versed in the art. He took a small piece of shrapnel from his pocket and tinkered with the lock. After seven minutes of pure dedication to the task, the padlock clicked open. He glanced down at Edgar, who somehow managed to look as though he disapproved of Jack's intentions.

Beggars can't be choosers, Edgar.

Jack heaved the gate open then clanged it shut

behind him.

The street slalomed and snaked, side to side, up and down, seemingly going on forever. Only a sliver of moonlight was allowed to creep in between the rooftops of the adjacent buildings. Mounted to the walls, the odd gas lamp flickered and provided just enough light for Jack to see what lay ahead of him. Other than those, there was nothing on Jubilee Walk at all. No doors, no windows, no shops.

Nothing.

The flash of light had to have come from somewhere, but Jack had seen absolutely nothing. About to abandon his little adventure, he heard something.

CREEEEAAAAAK.

He heard it again, coming from further down the street. Reinvigorated, Jack picked up the pace and continued. Eventually, he saw the source of the noise.

A signpost swung slowly above a doorway.

An eerie, flickering glow came from a glass window front beside it. It looked like a shop but, if it was, the owner had zero advertising expertise.

Who would open a shop all the way down here?

Jack snuck in for a closer look and confirmed it was, indeed, a shop. On the door were three bronze Roman numerals.

XII.

Other than those and an ancient looking door handle which looked as though it might fall off if anyone touched it, that was all. No knocker or letter box, it was a door that seemed to want no visitors or correspondence passing through it, only those who had been invited.

If this is number twelve, then where are one to eleven?!

Jack glanced down the street, which continued much further beyond the shop.

Nothing.

Number twelve was the only shop on Jubilee Walk.

The rusted tin signpost which stuck out above the doorway and into the street contained a small clock which, despite looking incredibly old and battered, still worked. The glass which covered the clock face was cracked but the time was still visible. Beneath the clock, mounted within the frame of the signpost, was a rotten piece of wood with the shop name nailed onto it.

Mr. Moretimer's Timely Creations.

The letters were worn and some of them hung on by a thread. If it wasn't for the protection the narrow street provided from nature's elements, Jack was certain they would have fallen off with even the slightest gust of wind. The eerie glow was provided by three candles behind the shop window front which flickered and gave the ancient looking shop a warm, cosy feel.

Like a curious but incredibly wet cat, Jack pressed his nose up against the window and peeked inside.

If the Nautilus was a shop, this would be it.

Completely enchanted by what he saw, Jack lifted Edgar up so the teddy bear could share in his amazement. The window display was stocked full of peculiar timepieces, glamorous watches, and bizarre clocks, all of which looked incredibly rare.

Which usually translates as valuable!

Jack's peepholes grew bigger than his belly.

Something appeared behind the window, above the display. Like the trail of light that a sparkler leaves behind as it is waved around, a tiny gold line of glitter, only a couple of inches long, appeared and twinkled like fairy dust, in mid-air. Mesmerised, Jack couldn't look away. It hung there for several moments until there was a ripping sound, like fabric being torn at the seams. The glimmering line expanded into a tiny hole, no wider than a small coin, like it had just been torn open in the nothingness of thin air. Jack pressed his face closer against the glass as something burrowed its way through the hole and dropped down onto the window display.

A cockroach!

Jack stumbled away from the window and fell onto his backside as the insect scuttled across the display and then disappeared, leaving only the strange tear it had crawled through hanging there.

Maybe I'm still unconscious and this is just another nightmare!

Jack pinched himself to make sure.

'Ouch!'

He was awake, no doubt about it. A shiver ran down his spine as his nightmare flooded his thoughts and pushed everything else from his mind. He crouched down beneath the window and curled up into a ball, clutching Edgar to his chest.

WHAM!

The shop door swung open. Jack crawled into the shadows and hid, but, in his hurry, dropped Edgar. The cockroach scurried out from the shop and onto Jubilee Walk, pursued by a cloaked figure. No taller than a child, it wobbled out of the shop and onto the soaked cobbles. Before Jack could get a clear look at it, the figure snatched Edgar up off the ground and ran off in pursuit of the cockroach. Despite being extremely unsteady on its feet, it moved with alarming speed. The heavy clunk of metal on stone echoed down the street with every step it took. Eventually, it caught up with the insect.

CLANG!

The sound echoed all the way along Jubilee Walk as the figure squashed the cockroach beneath its foot then returned to the shop. Once it had disappeared inside, Jack sprung from his hiding place.

Don't worry, Edgar, I'm coming for you.

Lifeless teddy bear or not, Edgar was Jack's only friend in the world, and he wasn't about to abandon him. He plucked up all his courage and tip-toed towards the shop door, which had been left slightly ajar.

He peeked through the doorway but couldn't see anything.

'Edgar?'

Jack opened the door a little wider and slipped his head through the gap.

'Edgar?'

SLAM!

The shop door slammed shut behind him as

Jack was dragged through it.

- V -

VIOLET FLEMMING

'CALL this a story?'

Violet Flemming chuntered away to herself as she trundled down the street.

'Could write better with my eyes closed. Complete overuse of adverbs, from a so-called professional as well!'

It had long been the ambition of the twenty-year-old to become a journalist but picking apart the columns and articles of the city tabloids was as close to it that she had got so far in her life. Finding fault in the headlines had become part of her morning routine. It made her feel better for a little while before the mind-numbing reality of her actual job set in.

Completely engrossed in the news and prioritising it above all else, if she had paid more attention the previous morning, she might not have had her favourite pen stolen from her by a pickpocket. Violet stuffed her face so far into the paper that the print dominated her sense of smell which, in fairness, was an improvement on the stench of early morning London. Both smells would soon be overwhelmed by the all too familiar whiff of dry cotton and fabric

when she reached Threadbare's factory.
All it will take is one great story, then I'll be out of that death-hole.

Her place of employment was a workhouse in all but name and there were beggars who would rather stay on the streets and starve than be employed in one of Alfred Threadbare's factories. One of the richest men in the city, he owned three, soon to be four, factories and had vast amounts of his bottomless fortune invested in all sorts of dodgy dealings overseas. Threadbare was a man loaded with resources but lacking in humanity.

The newspaper crumpled against Violet's face as she bumped into something. 'Watch where you're...' Violet's words trailed off as she realised who she had collided with. 'Mister Threadbare, I'm...'

'Late.'

The bluntness of Threadbare's observation hit her in the face like a hammer.

'Again,' he added, taking a second swing.

Before Violet could respond, Threadbare shoved a pocket watch in her face. A stickler for perfection and with zero tolerance for anything, or anybody, he regarded as slack, Violet had been on the wrong side of Threadbare far too often.

'You shall make the time both guillotine and executioner less you pay more attention to it.'

Preaching from his high horse was one of Threadbare's less- appealing qualities, not that he had many appealing ones to start with, and Violet hated being talked down to.

Bite your tongue, don't give him an excuse.

31

Threadbare snatched the newspaper from Violet and continued his lecture. 'Journalism is the profession of someone from much better stock than yours. One would suggest your leisure time be better spent improving your punctuality.' The pocket-watch almost took the end of Violet's nose off as Threadbare snapped it shut.

'Consider this your final warning.'

He tossed the newspaper into the dirt and marched into the factory. Violet salvaged the paper, dusted it off then dragged her feet behind him.

The freezing cold factory was a hive of activity. Rows of women sat side by side on stone slabs and sewed like their lives depended on it. It was through fear of Threadbare that they worked their fingers to the bone. Many of them had husbands who also worked but times were so hard that the pittance Threadbare paid them was a necessity. Violet lived alone and with no significant other to help pay the rent on her dingy little bedsit, she would be out on the streets if she ever lost her job. The consequences didn't seem to bother her one bit as she regularly threw caution to the wind in her cavalier attitude towards Threadbare. Truth was, Violet's head was so high up in the clouds that she couldn't see how thin the ice was below her.

'He's watching you like a hawk.'

Connie was Violet's best friend in the factory and had always looked out for her. Violet approached and dropped the newspaper on her workspace, ignoring Connie's comment. 'All doom and gloom out there.' Violet gave her usual morning outlook, a reflection of the depressing stories that filled the pages of London's press. 'It'll be doom and gloom in here if Threadbare catches you again,' replied Connie. 'That podgy pig couldn't catch the plague.' Violet plonked down beside Connie, who chuckled at the accurate observation. Threadbare glared across the factory floor directly at Violet, who deliberately took her time to settle into her work.

'I wouldn't be so presumptuous,' said Connie, 'he'll have you out on the street if you're not careful.' Violet smiled the fakest smile she could muster and threaded cotton through a needle as she shouted across to Threadbare. 'Just getting the magic fingers ready, Sir.' Threadbare stomped away and nit-picked the work of every worker as he passed them by. 'See,' said Violet, 'he knows where his bread gets buttered.' Violet sewed at a pace much faster than anyone else in the factory and her work was always of the highest standard. She was a real perfectionist and stickler for detail, both skills she knew would aid her well in her future career as a journalist. In short, Violet was a factory owner's dream. Motivated purely by money, this was the only reason greedy Threadbare had tolerated her lateness for so long.

'Anyway,' said Violet as she worked, 'I'll be out of here soon enough, you'll see. The winds are changing.'

'The weather has definitely been strange as of late, I'll give you that,' observed Connie, 'but, come on; you're living in dreamland, and you know it. Why don't you concentrate on your actual job? Heaven knows you're the best seamstress in here.'

'Look around,' replied Violet, directing Connie's attention towards the thirty or so women who all nursed sore fingers as they worked them to the bone for the man who would replace them at the drop of a hat if anything unfortunate happened to them. 'Is this really where you want to be every day for the rest of your life? We're both better than this, working our socks off for some scumbag who could afford to pay us far more than he does.' Connie knew Violet was right but there was one difference between the two friends that made all the difference; Connie was comfortable and accepted her situation.

Violet wanted better.

One great story, that's all it will take.

- VI -

MR. MORETIMER'S
TIMELY CREATIONS

*T*ICK-tock, tick-tock, tick-tock...

Jack opened his eyes but this time his surroundings were infinitely nicer. The constant **tick-tock** filling his ears was strangely relaxing despite him not having the foggiest where he was. It was the comfiest he had felt in a long time, and he didn't want to move. To be perfectly honest, he couldn't have cared less where he was, but his curiosity didn't allow him too long to make the most of his new-found, comfortable position. He rolled over onto his side and rubbed sleep from his eyes, his location revealed.

A bedroom.

Not just any bedroom.

Surrounding Jack on every side were walls covered with clocks. Old clocks, very old clocks, new clocks, futuristic clocks, ancient clocks, weird clocks, funny clocks, strange clocks, and downright bizarre clocks; a collage of timepieces that completely covered every inch of every wall from top to bottom, leaving no room for anything else. Every single clock tick-tocked in perfect unison, none so much a millisecond out of sync. Jack rubbed his head which had been bandaged,

his wound cleaned and stitched. He hadn't even the slightest semblance of a headache. He had accumulated a colourful collection of bumps and bruises over the past two years and, just like those, the knock he had taken the previous night hadn't caused him any discomfort. It was nothing short of a miracle that he wasn't in any discomfort, but he possessed an incredibly high pain thresh-hold.

Where am I?

It was clearly morning as the sun shone into the room. Jack slipped out of the bed he had been tucked into and ran towards the window. It was closed and wouldn't budge as he struggled to open it.

Houdini couldn't get this open! It's like it hasn't been opened for centuries!

After some serious effort, the window gave way. Jack heaved it upwards and stuck his head into the world outside. He could barely believe his eyes. Jubilee Walk was a hive of activity, like it had become the centre of the Earth and people from all four corners had descended upon it. They weren't run of the mill Londoners either; everyone looked important, regal even, and many looked like they had travelled from other countries judging by the strange yet unique clothing they wore. He instantly remembered where he was.

The Nautilus!

He instinctively looked for Edgar.

Edgar!

The memory of the night before returned.

Where was Edgar? Who or what had taken him? Jack popped his head outside the window once again. A queue had formed outside Mr. Moretimer's Timely Creations that stretched as far as

Jack could see down the winding street. Everybody there must have been present for one reason only: to see Mr. Moretimer, whoever he was. There couldn't possibly be any other reason. There was nothing else there, after all.

'They say he is over three thousand years old!'

The absurd claim made by the very wealthy looking gentleman at the front of the queue was quickly shot down by the woman on his arm. 'How much wine did you drink last night, my love?' Jack yanked his head back inside the window frame.

Three thousand years old?!

Who could possibly live to be three thousand years old? Was the gentleman referring to Mr. Moretimer? Could Mr. Moretimer have been the cloaked figure who had kidnapped Edgar? Jack had so many questions he thought his head might explode. He ran across the room towards a door he fully expected to be locked. To his surprise, when he twisted the knob, the door clicked open. He tip-toed out onto a very dark, creaky landing which made his attempts to mute his footsteps pointless. Everything around him was old.

Very old.

Possibly ancient.

A thick dust hung in the air, highlighted by thin beams of light which sneaked through tiny cracks in decrepit walls. What he could smell was also old.

A damp, fusty stench that diffused from the rotting roof beams high above. Jack pinched his nose as he crept along the landing in the hope it would protect his lungs from the stale stench which assaulted his nostrils.

The landing was lined with lit candles and grandfather clocks on both sides. Oddly, instead of just standing on the floor, the grandfather clocks were mounted all over the high reaching walls, like a portrait would be. Some small, some tall, some ordinary, some peculiar, all of them old. Just like the clocks on the wall in the bedroom, every grandfather clock was perfectly in sync with the rest. Jack admired every one of them. No two of them were the same. Accompanying the symphony of tick-tocks that the orchestra of clocks performed was a scratching sound that came from deep within the walls. Jack tuned his ears out from it, not wanting to entertain the possibility of what might be causing such a sound.

I've seen enough insects for one day.

At the end of the landing was a winding, wooden staircase which spiralled down onto the shop floor. On the top step was a bucket which caught droplets of water that leaked in from a hole in the ceiling. It wasn't a big hole, in fact it was tiny, but since the bucket was about to overflow with grubby water, Jack judged that it must have been there for some time and the necessary maintenance neglected or completely forgotten about.

He heard voices from the shop floor below.

Desperate to see what was downstairs but not

wanting to be caught eavesdropping, Jack tip-toed down the first few steps until he was able to peek through the staircase spindles.

What he saw was quite a sight.

Beside an immaculate, shiny grand piano, a phonograph played classical Baroque music. All manner of vibrant clocks, hourglasses and timepieces filled the room, floor to ceiling, on shelves, behind glass cases and randomly scattered across the floor. Right in the middle of the room was a huge grandfather clock. The room itself was big, but due to the sheer volume of clock-based clutter which filled it, it was impossible for Jack to make out the shape of it. Parts of the ceiling were high and other parts were much lower which restricted his view and there were many different alcoves, crevices, and doorways, all filled with clocks, clocks, and more clocks.

Aladdin's cave of wonders has nothing on this.

Laid on the floor was a Persian carpet, very bright and intricate in detail. It was the only thing that didn't have clocks or watches on it; a much needed, obvious path for customers to tread. Subtle candlelight provided a dim glow which lit the room. Jack traced the carpet with his eyes all through the organised mess as far as he could. Impressive as the timepiece collection was, it was the wrinkled man with long, lightning white hair hidden away, right at the back of the shop, behind rows and rows of clocks, who Jack was most drawn towards. Garbed in a long red robe, he stood at a watchmaker's desk which was raised up on a podium, three steps led up to it on each side and long, fully drawn red curtains provided a grand backdrop behind it. Right beneath his Adam's apple, the Roman numeral **XII** was scarred into his leathery skin, which was completely covered with weird markings, a cross between Egyptian hieroglyphics and the drawings cavemen etched onto the walls of their dwellings. He wasn't sure the old man looked three thousand years old but, then again, he had never laid his peepholes on anybody that old before. One thing was certain; time had not been kind to him.

It must be him. That's Mr. Moretimer!

And it was.

Mr. Moretimer examined a pocket watch in painstaking detail as three completely identical, suited, and booted men looked up at him from the opposite side of the desk. The Von Karger brothers were triplets, identical in each and every way. Even the manner in which they each rolled their thin, handlebar moustaches between their fingertips was the same. The only way they could be told apart was the way each angled a bowler hat on their head. Artemis wore his perfectly square, Boris angled his to the left and Chlodwig perched his to the right. All three smoked cigarettes, inhaling and exhaling at exactly the same time. They stood with such self-importance that Jack thought they might have swallowed the silver spoons they had been gifted at their birth.

With the enthusiasm one might expect from a child on Christmas morning, Mr. Moretimer leapt to life, revealing various trinkets and pocket watches hanging from his belted waist.

'Totally tantalising tick-tockery!'

With each word that left his lips, he became more and more excited as he waxed lyrical about the pocket watch he held in his palm.

'After all these years, a genuine Maher-Schmidt seventeen-ninety-eight, right before my very eyes! Simply exquisite.' The old man studied every aspect of the timepiece, multiple times. 'Very clever Mr. Maher, oh, and Mr. Schmidt, don't think I don't see your craftsmanship too. Out of a million, this truly is one.'

The Von Karger brothers yawned and checked their wrist watches simultaneously as Mr. Moretimer continued his appraisal, talking directly to the watch. 'You seem to have slowed in your age, my remarkable friend. Not to worry, though, I shall have you ticking with time in, oh, I'd say, five hours and forty-two minutes; approximately.'

'We don't want it fixing,' quipped Artemis in a heavy German accent.

'That shan't do,' added Boris.

'Does he not know who we are?' questioned Chlodwig.

'As the respected antique dealers that we are, we have journeyed here to have our palms well laced for this incredibly rare antiquity.' Artemis eyeballed Mr. Moretimer closely as he spoke. 'Now, are we to do business?'

'Or not?' chimed Boris.

'We will, if he has even half an idea who we are,' Chlodwig added.

Jack found the brothers quite comical with the way they spoke in such quick succession and in the same order. That aside, there was something sinister about them which unsettled him.

Mr. Moretimer sat back down in his chair and gazed at the pocket watch like a parent would a newborn baby.

'Absolutely, without a shadow of a doubt...'

The Von Kargers smiled, lips curling upwards in unison.

'Not.'

Mr. Moretimer's answer was clearly not what the brothers had been expecting and Artemis, as always, was first to respond.

'We have travelled all the way from Berlin, across land and sea, through this un-Godly weather I might add, and you are to make our endeavour a fool's errand?'

'He must think we have nothing better to do!'

'He definitely does not know who we are!'

'Simply wonderful as this is,' replied Mr. Moretimer, 'I already have one in my collection.'

The Von Kargers cackled like a coven of witches.

'Your own words betray you,' said Artemis as he snatched the pocket watch out of Mr. Moretimer's grasp. 'This, as you say, is one in a million.'

'The rarest of rarities,' Boris added.

'Do his eyes not work?' mused Chlodwig.

Mr. Moretimer wandered around the desk and put his arm around Artemis.

'My friends, this is indeed one in a million; I just happen to have the second in two.'

The Von Kargers were not impressed.

'The people we represent do not take kindly to having their time wasted.'

'Most certainly not.'

'Does he not know who they are?'

Despite the veiled threat from Artemis and his brothers, Mr. Moretimer politely escorted them to the shop exit. He hobbled along on weary legs and grabbed anything he could to maintain his balance, his body clearly wanting to do more than his age would allow.

'My fellow chronology enthusiasts, there is no such thing as wasted time.'

The triplets muttered away to themselves as Mr. Moretimer ushered them through the door and out onto

Jubilee Walk. The line of eager customers, all with their own items to be appraised, surged forward.

'Friends from near, halfway and afar,' announced Mr. Moretimer, 'my cogs require a quick service, so I shall reopen when it is time.'

'When the bloody hell will that be?' said the very wealthy looking gentleman at the front of the queue. Completely ignoring him, Mr. Moretimer slammed the door and locked it with a key which hung from his belt. 'Now, where was I?' Mr. Moretimer scratched his head and shuffled back to his desk. 'I really should start writing things down.' He continued rambling to himself as he slipped between the long, red curtain and disappeared.

Jack bounded down the stairs like a kid let loose in a candy shop.

Edgar! Where are you?

Jack searched the shop from top to bottom. Along the way, he helped himself to as many watches and time pieces as he could until his pockets bulged at the seams. A scratching sound grabbed his attention and brought his daylight robbery to a halt. It came from the towering grandfather clock in the centre of the room. As Jack approached for a closer inspection, a cockroach buried its way out from the woodwork.

Ah! This place is infested!

He leapt back away from the clock and kept his eyes fixed on the insect so he could see where it went. The longer he looked at it, the more he thought it didn't quite look like a normal cockroach. Jack counted twelve legs in total, just like the cockroach from his nightmare. Two fangs which resembled the hands of a clock protruded from its mouth. To Jack's horror, the insect turned its attention towards him and scuttled in his direction. In a blind panic, he dashed across the shop, bundling into shelves, and knocking all manner of priceless clocks from the wall. He looked over his shoulder to see if the creature was still in pursuit. It was still there and showed no signs of giving up.

THUD!

Jack bumped into the grand piano and crashed onto the floor. The insect took advantage and crawled across his chest. It reared its razor-sharp fangs directly above his heart, his nightmare about to become reality. Gripped by terror, Jack couldn't even move his arms he was so scared. He scrunched his eyes shut and screamed for help.

SPLAT!

Something splattered across his face. He convinced himself it was blood.

His blood.

When Jack opened his eyes, Mr. Moretimer stood over him, the creature impaled on the end of a fire poker, black liquid seeping from its body and dripping onto his face.

'By the sands of the hourglass, roach-proof the longcase, that was it!' exclaimed Mr. Moretimer. 'Two days, three hours and fifty-two seconds I've been looking for that little pest.' Mr. Moretimer helped Jack to his feet.

'Approximately, of course.'

'What was that?' gasped Jack.

'What was what?'

Jack pointed towards the end of the fire poker 'That!'

There was nothing there, the creature had vanished.

'Such a wonderful imagination,' said Mr. Moretimer as he ruffled Jack's hair. Before he had chance to unleash a barrage of questions, the old man caught Jack off guard. 'I would say thank you for refreshing my memory, but it seems you should be thanking me for all those watches you have in your pockets.' Like a naughty schoolboy caught red-handed, Jack avoided the old man's gaze. 'Put them back and we shall say no more about it.' Jack blushed as he emptied the stolen loot from his pockets. Mr. Moretimer glanced at the time on the pocket watch

which dangled from his belt. 'And three, two, one...'
The old man unlocked the shop door.
'It is time for you to be on your way.'
'But...'
Mr. Moretimer showed Jack the way out.
'Fear not, you leave just as rich as when you entered.' He winked at Jack as he handed him his sack of belongings...
...and Edgar.
Jack's face lit up, but his joy was short-lived as Mr. Moretimer bundled him through the door and out onto Jubilee Walk. The line of customers surged forwards as they pushed, shoved, and bickered like an unruly mob to get into the shop.
If he won't give me answers, I'll just help myself.
Jack opened his fist; no longer secured on the old man's belt, the key to Mr. Moretimer's Timely Creations laid in the palm of his hand.

- VII -

LATE...AGAIN

*T*HREADBARE'S factory had always been a miserable place to work, constantly cold, dirty, and dark. Tiny, grime-stained windows, inches thick with cobwebs and muck, served little purpose as they allowed in very little light and certainly no air. The workers had offered to clean them on many occasions but Threadbare threatened to sack anyone who tried to do so. They gave the place "character", he believed.

Around London, there was a saying amongst the common folk; if you were employed by Alfred Threadbare you went home with the pay of a seamstress and the lungs of a chimney sweep. Connie found the words of wisdom worryingly accurate. On several occasions, people had stopped her on her way home and asked why, on God's green Earth, a young woman would choose to work down a coal mine. Usually, she humoured them with a witty comment about how she enjoyed the heavy lifting but, more recently, she just ignored them and instead reflected on the sadly true observation that the Earth wasn't particularly green anymore.

Thanks to the industrial revolution, London

had become a stinking cesspit, polluting the skies with soot and drowning rivers with slurry. The benefits to industry, engineering and technology could not be questioned; these areas had grown and developed at an incredible rate but the knock-on effect on the natural world was evident, visually and via the nostrils.

Connie slaved away amongst rows of seamstresses who all worked like donkeys. Threadbare stomped out of his office and onto the factory floor, the empty space beside Connie could not have smacked him in the face harder if a heavyweight boxer threw the punch.

'The dizzy wench clocked in?'

Connie pretended she didn't hear and got on with her work. Threadbare marched over and grabbed her by the scruff of her neck. 'Your worthless backside will feel the cold of the cobbles along with hers if you do not give me an answer.' Connie lied but was far from convincing. 'She had to nip to the loo, Sir.'

'I ain't seen her all morning, Sir,' another seamstress piped up. Right on cue, Violet trundled into the factory, newspaper rolled up beneath her armpit.

'Sorry, Sir, had to nip out for some fresh air.'

Violet's excuse was poor, considering the air outside wasn't much better than it was inside. 'Won't happen again.'

'That, I am quite sure of,' said Threadbare.

'You're sacked.'

Violet was taken aback, as if she never really

expected the words to ever come out of his mouth. Unsure how to react, she turned on Connie, blaming her. 'I thought you were covering for me?' 'I was, I mean, I did,' sputtered Connie, 'but, like I said, sometimes it's good to have allies.'

'Not to worry,' said Threadbare, snatching the newspaper from Violet and tossing it out of the door.

'I am sure this will all make a great story, one day.'

Violet resisted the urge to swing for Threadbare and slumped out of the factory. It wasn't worth the argument. Despite Threadbare's many undesirable attributes, he was a man of his word and once his mind was made up, he was as immovable as a statue. Connie got back to work but Threadbare wasn't finished with her either. 'Punctuality is one thing, but trust is another.' Before Connie had a chance to respond, he dragged her out of her seat and shoved her down the same path as Violet.

'Get out.'

'Sir!' Connie's protest fell on deaf ears as Threadbare turned his back on her and marched back to his office. 'Let that be a lesson to the rest of you,' he barked at the rest of the women. With no support coming her way from the other seamstresses, Connie slumped out of the factory.

As she set foot on the street, her upset turned to anger. She stormed after Violet, the target of her justified frustration.

'You just look after number one, don't you? Not a second thought given about anybody else. You're selfish, Violet, always putting your own interests first. Some of us have other mouths to feed.'

Violet didn't even apologise, too wrapped up contemplating how she was now going to afford to pay the rent on her bedsit and make ends meet.

'The winds have changed now,' continued Connie, frustrated that Violet didn't seem to care, 'I hope they blow some sense into you.'

Connie bawled her eyes out as she ran off down the street in despair.

That night, Violet sat in the tiny, cramped room she called home, only a bottle of red wine for company. Hardly homely, it was barely big enough for her which was just as well since she had nobody to share it with. A small window allowed her a glorious view of endless forked lightning bolts which attacked the city outside and illuminated the room with each strike. Stray dogs barked on the street outside. Violet couldn't tell what was louder; the thunder cracks or the angry arguing of the couple next door that she had to put up with every night through the paper-thin wall. She turned her purse inside out and a single coin clattered onto the floor, nowhere near enough to keep up with her spiralling debts and rent payments.

Not a regular drinker, the bottle of wine had been a gift from years ago that Violet was saving for a very particular special occasion. She had contemplated selling it, but it would have only been a drop in the ocean and since it now looked like the occasion would never come, the wine looked much more appealing after the day's events. Popping the cork from the bottle, Violet turned her attention towards the only decoration she had in the room; a framed photograph of herself and a young girl, no older than four, arm in arm. The young girl had the look of Violet, of that there was no doubt. Long, beautiful jet-black hair highlighted her otherwise pasty features and she had the same gritty determination in her eyes that Violet possessed. A crack of thunder stole Violet's attention for a moment. Never in her twenty years had she heard thunder quite so loud. She glanced back at the photograph as she pressed the bottle to her lips and reminisced of days gone by when she was together with the only thing she cared about.

Her daughter.

My beautiful Eve. I'll never get you back now.

- VIII -

MIDNIGHT SHOPPING

*S*TOLEN key firmly in one hand and Edgar dangling from the other, Jack crept down Jubilee Walk towards Mr. Moretimer's Timely Creations. His mission had been planned with two objectives:

Number one: find out more about the proprietor of the shop. Mr. Moretimer fascinated Jack and his interest had most certainly been piqued after the events that unfolded. If he could hide somewhere in the shop, he could observe the old man and get a roof over his head at the same time; a double bonus on what looked to be a second night of horrendous weather.

Number two: upon successful completion of objective number one, help himself to enough watches that he wouldn't need to worry about picking any pockets for a very long time.

The three candles in the window were lit, as they were before. Jack unlocked the door with the stolen key.

DING!

A small bell atop the doorway chimed as it opened. He pressed himself up against the wall, making himself as invisible as possible as the sound echoed around the shop, blending in with the tick-tock of clocks. The last thing he needed was to be caught before he had even started. After waiting a few moments, satisfied he had not been rumbled, Jack proceeded through the shop towards the old man's desk at the back. As he reached his target, he wondered what might be behind the long red curtains. Imagination was not something he lacked and during that moment it was on fire with all manner of wonderful ideas and notions. With white knuckles that practically burst through the skin of his hands, Jack gripped Edgar and slipped between the curtains.

The longest, oddest corridor Jack had ever seen greeted him. It zigged and zagged, not just side to side but up and down as well, like Jubilee Walk but much, much stranger. It was very dimly lit and a constant, all too familiar sound reverberated off the walls.

Tick-tock, tick-tock, tick-tock.

Despite what the noise would have Jack believe, there was not a single clock anywhere. Lining the walls were huge portrait frames, all so ancient and decrepit it beggared belief they hadn't splintered into a million shards and fallen to bits. Jack tip toed along the corridor and admired the first frame he came to. It was completely rotten, barely holding itself together. Mounted inside it, which was impressive given the condition it was in, was a painting of an old man with wrinkles so deep Jack wondered if his skin had actually been leather, all cracked and worn from years of hard graft and punishment. On his face was a beard so bushy it could have nested a family of birds and there was so much hair on his head he could have given Rapunzel a run for her money. If it wasn't for the monocle that he wore over one eye, Jack would have sworn it was a painting of a Neanderthal caveman. As he was about to move on, Jack noticed something on the portrait, right below the hairy gentleman's Adam's apple.

Branded into his skin was the Roman numeral 'I'.

At the bottom of the frame, engraved on a weathered bronze plaque which was just about readable was a name.

Solomon Solstice.

Jack continued down the corridor until he reached the second frame. In it was a portrait of another ancient looking man but this one had a finely curled, handlebar moustache and not a hair on his head. The Roman numeral 'II' was branded beneath his Adam's apple. Another name had been engraved into a slightly less weathered plaque on the frame.

Edward Eon.

This went on and on as Jack journeyed along the corridor, each portrait very much the same; an old man with a Roman numeral scarred into the skin beneath his Adam's apple and a ridiculous name. He counted twelve in total, but the final frame puzzled him.

Why would anybody mount a portrait of nothing?

Jack knew that art was all down to personal interpretation, but it was a stretch by even the greatest art critic's imagination. The canvas inside the flawlessly conditioned frame was completely blank and the shiny golden plaque had no name on it, as though it had been mounted and forgotten about.

Or not finished yet.

A cobweb covered door, carved out of oak, brought the corridor to an end. A thin sliver of light shone through the gap where it had been left ever so slightly ajar.

Jack slipped inside and a big, messy workshop with tools and spare clock parts scattered here, there, and everywhere greeted him. Broken grandfather clocks leaned against cracked walls, damaged pocket watches were strewn across the floor and shattered hour glasses rested in dunes of sand which had previously resided within them. Jack scanned the impressive mess and wondered if his parents had abandoned him because his room was as untidy as this, if they had indeed abandoned him.

In the centre of the room, hunched over a workbench, was Mr. Moretimer. He tinkered but Jack could not see with what. Desperate for a better view, he slipped across the room, as close as he dared, and hid beneath an overcoat that had been slung beside another workbench. The view was still obscured but Jack could tell from Mr. Moretimer's excited speech that he was thoroughly enjoying whatever it was that he was doing.

'And, tonight, your final piece.'

The old man heaved a very heavy looking chest onto the workbench. As he opened it, light caught something inside and the gleam blinded Jack temporarily. When he regained his vision, Jack could see Mr. Moretimer holding a stunning pocket watch, the most beautiful piece of jewellery he had ever seen.

'Simply exquisite,' marvelled Mr. Moretimer as he worshipped the timepiece. 'The timing between the tick and the tock are magnificent. A true masterpiece and the last of its kind.' With the grace of an elephant, he slammed the pocket watch onto the work bench and smashed it to pieces with a hammer.

BANG! BANG! BANG!

Jack almost jumped out of his skin. He could barely believe his peepholes; the old man had destroyed it!

Mr. Moretimer searched the remnants of the watch until he found a tiny spring. It was so small Jack had to strain his eyes to see it between Mr. Moretimer's thumb and forefinger as he held it up and admired it. As light caught it, it gleamed bright. 'There you are. All the way from the mountains of Peru.' Mr. Moretimer placed the spring aside then tided the remaining watch parts. He counted them several times and caressed them in the palm of his hand. 'Not to worry, shouldn't take longer to fix you than, oh, nine hours, twenty-two minutes and nine seconds, approximately.' The old man put the broken watch back into the chest and got back to his work. He attached a magnifying glass to his spectacles then hummed a classical piece of music as he tinkered and tapped with hammer and tongs for what felt like an age to Jack. Finally, Mr. Moretimer wiped sweat from his brow, took a step back and admired his work.

'Take a look.'

The old man hobbled aside and slid an empty crate up to the table.

'Be very careful now.'

Something slid off the table, using the crate as a stepping-stone. About the size of a young child, it staggered across the room towards a mirror, each footstep clanged so loud the noise echoed around the room. Jack peeked out from his hiding place but when he caught a glimpse of it, he turned away in terror and curled up in a ball beneath the overcoat. He contemplated running away and never returning but it made no difference. He would never unsee what his eyes had just borne witness to, and he knew curiosity would bring him back sooner or later.

Is that thing...real?

As it observed itself in the mirror, Mr. Moretimer stood proudly behind his creation; a Frankenstein's monster of Pinocchio proportions, Hanz was made entirely of human bones, metal and watch parts. A bronze mask, fashioned like an expressionless human face covered the front of what looked to be a human skull. The name 'Hanz' was inscribed in small letters down the side of it. Despite the inhuman look, the attention to detail of Mr. Moretimer's creation was magnificent. He had used only the rarest of the rarest timepieces to bring Hanz to life and had scavenged the globe for years, using specific clock and watch elements for each body part and makeshift organ.

Only the finest would do for Hanz and the old man had spared no expense or effort to ensure his creation was as lifelike as possible. Where Mr. Moretimer had gotten the bones from to construct Hanz's skeleton, Jack shuddered to think.

'After all these years you are finally complete!'

The excitement in Mr. Moretimer's voice was palpable. Hanz admired the tiny spring that had just been fitted with eagle-eyed precision and care.

'Well?'

Despite being unable to portray any emotion, Hanz had an air of glumness about him which the old man didn't seem to notice. Although unsure if he was frozen in complete awe or paralysed by fear, Jack picked up on it. He had experienced enough misery to know it when he saw it and the miniature miracle of engineering never responded to Mr. Moretimer's prompt for approval.

'Splendid!' exclaimed Mr. Moretimer, oblivious to Hanz's lack of excitement. 'One job down but what of number two?' The old man scratched his head as he struggled to recall. Hanz performed an expressionless mime which did the trick.

'Ah, yes, of course. Our clockroach problem. How could I forget?'

Jack glanced at Edgar. 'Clockroach?!' The surprise in his voice projected it much more loudly than he had intended. If Mr. Moretimer hadn't heard, then Hanz certainly had, and he clunked off in Jack's direction.

He'll never let us out of here alive, not after we've seen what he's been up to!

58

Jack was trapped. He clutched Edgar to his chest and prepared himself for the inevitable confrontation to come. Just as Hanz was about to pull the overcoat away and reveal Jack, Mr. Moretimer, who already had one foot out of the door, called Hanz away.

'Time is of the essence.'

Like an obedient dog, Hanz did as he was told and wobbled out of the room with his master. As soon as they were gone, Jack stuck his head out from beneath the overcoat. It would have been the perfect time to search the room for anything of value, but Jack's mind was on nothing but the strange old man and his even stranger sidekick. 'Forget watches, Edgar; there's something much bigger going on here.' Edgar bounced at his side as Jack followed Mr. Moretimer and Hanz back up the weaving corridor, all the portraits staring at him as he passed them by. He didn't have to worry about keeping a safe distance because the corridor weaved and wound so suddenly that he would never be seen even if he was only a few feet behind. When he reached the end of it, Jack peeked out between the curtains.

Mr. Moretimer and Hanz stood in front of his desk. The old man waved his arms around in the air, like an orchestra conductor. Jack watched on as everything around Mr. Moretimer and Hanz flickered and distorted. Objects disappeared in a flash for an instant and then immediately came back in some sort of stuttering magical illusion.

Jack gawped as the whole shop flashed and disappeared, replaced for a millisecond by a forest, then, in another flicker, returned to normal. The more Mr. Moretimer conducted, the more the shop flickered, faded, and distorted until, eventually, a heavenly flash of white light exploded from thin air and illuminated the whole room. When the light faded, the shop was left in darkness. The three candles in the window had gone out and there was no other source of light. Jack rubbed his peepholes and regained his vision. Everything was exactly as it had been before the commotion began but Mr. Moretimer and Hanz were nowhere to be seen.

Jack barged through the curtain and onto the shop floor, searching everywhere for Mr. Moretimer and Hanz. He checked the entrance, but it was exactly as it was when he had entered the shop. There was no way they had gone outside; the door hadn't moved.

Stunned by what he had just witnessed, Jack's mind was blown.

Now that, Edgar, is a magic trick.

- IX -

THE HANDS OF TIME

*J*ACK gave the huge grandfather clock in the centre of the shop a thorough investigation. After checking every other conceivable hiding place, he concluded that Mr. Moretimer and Hanz must have gone into the clock. It was certainly big enough to fit at least one person inside and Hanz wouldn't take up too much room, given his stature. It was also where Jack had seen the cockroach-like insect burrow out from and Mr. Moretimer had mentioned a clockroach problem so maybe there was a nest of the creepy crawlies inside which needed destroying.

Maybe that's why he called it a clockroach instead of a cockroach? A slip of the tongue?

Why Mr. Moretimer and Hanz had chosen to go inside the clock in such incredible fashion was beyond Jack. It wasn't like there was an audience.

Well, one that they were aware of.

He really is a showman, Edgar. We could learn a heck of a lot from him.

Jack tapped on the side of the longcase; it sounded hollow and empty. Jack put his hands on his hips, baffled. If they had gone into the clock, he had absolutely no idea where or how. There were no secret compartments or trap doors, but no matter how hard he tried, he could not get the front of it open, so could not be certain there was no one inside.

'Open says-a-me!'

Unsurprisingly, nothing happened.

Mimicking Mr. Moretimer, Jack waved his arms in the air and ran towards the clock. He leaped towards it, expecting it to magically open. 'Abracadabra!' he cried, mid-air.

THUD!

Jack collided with the clock and collapsed in a heap on the floor, rubbing his head. The first thing he laid eyes on was Edgar.

Laugh all you want but I don't see your cogs doing much ticking.

Dazed and out of ideas, Jack dragged himself to his feet.

We work this con out and we'll never go hungry again.

DING!

The doorbell caught Jack by surprise. He grabbed Edgar and looked for a hiding place. The grand piano caught his peephole as it had been left with the lid propped open, a perfect haven for him and Edgar. He scrambled inside and laid across the hammers and strings of the keys. As he lowered the lid, Jack left just enough of a gap so he could see who, or what, had entered the shop.

DING!

DING!

DING!

The door opened and closed, over and over, blown by a gale force wind outside. Thankfully, nothing made its way inside. Jack breathed a sigh of relief; he had survived two close calls in quick succession.

Maybe we should just get out of here.

As he climbed out of the piano, the hammers snapped under his weight. His foot crashed straight through them and through a wooden panel just below. He yanked his leg out of the damaged piano but, as he was about to run away from the scene of the crime, Jack noticed something in the body of the piano, hidden in the hole he had just created. He reached down into it and took it.

A small, wooden chest.

Despite looking like it weighed a tonne, it was surprisingly light. Jack wondered what might be inside.

Maybe it's the secret to his disappearing act!

There was no way he could walk out now, not when he potentially held the secret to the greatest vanishing act he had even seen right in the palm of his hand. There was a tiny keyhole, but the chest was locked.

Jack removed the piece of shrapnel from his pocket and picked the lock with it.

CLICK.

Yes!

The lock opened.

Prepare yourself, Edgar; I have a feeling that whatever is in here will change our lives forever.

With eager peepholes, Jack opened the chest. A

tattered scroll sat rolled up in the bottom of it. The dust and fusty smell told Jack it had been under lock and key for considerable time.

This is it! It has to be!

Jack laid the scroll across the Persian carpet, but it kept rolling itself back up at each end. He sat Edgar on one edge of the paper to keep it flat then rolled the scroll open from the opposite end. What Jack saw was not what he expected.

A blueprint for a sun dial?

Sick to the back teeth of watches, clocks, and time-related objects, it added insult to injury. Something was scrawled across the top of the scroll in barely legible writing:

The Hands of Time.

Jack wondered if this was the design plan of a very old, valuable sun dial that Mr. Moretimer had stashed somewhere in the shop. Maybe it was something he had planned to build a long time ago but had slipped his mind. He did seem to be quite forgetful. But why had it been hidden away inside a piano?

Folk hide what they don't want to be found.

The sun dial looked unique, like no other in existence, and there were numerous design notes written all over it in a language Jack couldn't read. It definitely wasn't Latin; he had seen that before, but it looked nothing like it. He grabbed Edgar and the scroll rolled itself back up.

We may have just found an ace for our sleeve.

After thinking about all the different possibilities, Jack was much more positive that the night hadn't been a total waste of time. Just as he was about to leave, Jack glimpsed something he hadn't noticed before; a tiny slither of paper protruded from what looked like a crack in the chest.

A secret compartment!

The shop suddenly distorted and flickered, exactly as it had when Mr. Moretimer and Hanz disappeared. Jack opened the previously unseen compartment, grabbed the newly discovered sheet of paper, and sprinted towards the shop entrance. He slammed the door behind him, but Edgar's arm got trapped between the door and the frame. In such a rush, Jack didn't notice.

RIP!

A flash of blinding light exploded from inside Mr. Moretimer's Timely Creations and lit up Jubilee Walk.

We have some serious competition, Edgar, serious competition.

Jack escaped down the street, never noticing that Edgar was one limb worse off.

The light subsided in the shop, and everything returned to normal, the three candles flickered back to life and danced in the window. Mr. Moretimer and Hanz stood in the clutter of the shop. The first thing they saw was the piano. Despite the damage, Mr. Moretimer did not seem overly upset. 'Nothing that can't be repaired. Shouldn't take longer than, oh, I'd say, four hours, thirty-nine minutes and forty-seven seconds, approximately.'

Hanz tidied the mess. This had become part of his role in the shop, cleaner and general dog's body. He enjoyed it; it was something to do, and something was always better than nothing. Mr. Moretimer forbid Hanz from ever leaving the shop. There had been the odd occasion, usually in an emergency, where he had been allowed out, but Hanz had never ventured any further afield than the iron gate at the end of Jubilee Walk and that had been under the midnight sky, away from prying eyes.

Hanz alerted the old man to the open chest, laid on the floor. Mr. Moretimer's positive demeanour evaporated. 'Now this is not good.' He closed his eyes and scratched his head, like he was recalling a memory. 'It wasn't her,' he declared, seeming somewhat relieved. Something caught his eye, on the floor, in the doorway. He shuffled towards it and picked it up. Wool protruded from the perfectly torn seam of Edgar's arm. The old man closed his eyes and scratched his head once again. 'But if she gets to him with that in his possession, the consequences will be too dire to contemplate.'

Mr. Moretimer perched himself on the piano stool.

'The eleventh hour is upon us, Hanz.'

Hanz stopped cleaning and stood to attention, like a toy soldier. He had heard the old man talk of the eleventh hour and, from what he could remember, it wasn't good.

Mr. Moretimer took a moment and admired his shop.

Time is constant.

That was the beauty of it, he had always thought. Whatever problems faced the world - poverty, war, famine - time marched on unopposed in the face of it all. Time provided hope, always allowing the potential for better days and, no matter how terrible the immediate moment might have been, there was always a light to be chased at the end of the tunnel. Mr. Moretimer did not wish to contemplate a day when this might not be the case.

Remember the past, live in the moment, and look to the future.

The words had become the old man's creed. He practiced what he preached and, right then, he became one with the moment. Time consumed him and he became completely aware of every minute detail in the shop. The ticks and tocks echoed in his ears, swinging pendulums sounded like Eagles swooping through the air as he gazed at every clock and every watch through the same eyes that a father might look upon a son. He heard every little click and movement from within the inner workings of each and every timepiece in his possession. Mr. Moretimer understood; to be completely happy and content with one's world, one had to fully appreciate every second, every moment, no matter how fleeting.

Time was beautiful. It was the greatest gift mankind had ever been blessed with.

But it was under threat.

The eleventh hour is upon us.

Mr. Moretimer snapped out of the trance to a sight that chilled him to his core. The shop door, wide open, creaking in the wind, Hanz nowhere to be seen.

Little did Jack Picklewick know, he had now set

in motion a chain of events from which there was no going back.

Not for him.

Not for anyone.

- X -

RIGHT PLACE, RIGHT TIME

*V*IOLET stumbled down a deserted, foggy street, swaying from side to side, bottle of wine in hand.

The fog was so thick and heavy it was impossible to see what was coming. Not that it would have made much difference; fog or no fog, Violet was so blind drunk it was a miracle she was still on her feet. The bottle of wine had all but gone. It had worked its magic and numbed her pain, even if only for a few hours.

It'll all be over soon, anyway.

She regressed to her childhood, which had been much happier times, giggling and dancing her way down the street until she reached a bridge. The Thames raged a good fifty feet or so below but the way the fog blanketed the river in the pale moonlight was eerie yet beautiful at the same time. Violet stepped up onto the side of the bridge. Her playful demeanour faded as she watched the water crash against the sides of the bridge and erode small chunks of stone.

My name will make the front page one way or

another.

She wrestled back and forth with her demons and clouded common sense. She had left her bedsit with the intention of never going back but, as she stared the prospect of a watery demise in the face, her certainty retreated. Violet was a woman in crisis and had been for some time. Truth be told, Threadbare giving her the sack was just the tip of a very big iceberg. As she searched for the courage to jump, the time that had led Violet to the moment flashed before her eyes.

Her much older husband, Richard, was a banker and she had lived a life of luxury in her late teens. The day Violet came home and discovered his unfaithfulness with another woman changed her world forever. Violet's friends tried to convince her to stay with Richard, for her own sake, but she refused. She told them they had no respect for themselves and were driven only by money.

She was different.

Nobody disrespected Violet Flemming.

She packed her bags and left but when she tried to take their daughter, Eve, Richard refused. In a desperate attempt to force Violet to stay, Richard told her that if she walked out, she would never see Eve again. Threats like that were like a red rag to a bull with Violet so she called Richard's bluff. Problem was, Richard wasn't bluffing and, just like Threadbare, proved to be a man of his word. No sooner had Violet stepped out of the door, Richard sold the house. When Violet returned a few days later to visit Eve, the house was empty. No furniture, no

Richard, and no Eve. Where they had gone, Violet had no idea. The circles Richard moved in spoke the language of money and Violet was not fluent. Richard bought the loyalty that she thought she had earned, and it ate her up inside. Those she regarded as friends either lied to her or played dumb but no one who had been a part of her life since she married Richard seemed to know anything about his or Eve's whereabouts. When she approached solicitors to fight her corner, it seemed their silence had already been bought or they priced their services well above her means.

Violet had no option; with only the money she had in her pocket and the clothes she had on her back, she went to the city and got a job at Alfred Threadbare's factory. She hated it but it was a means to an end. If she ever wanted to build the resources required to locate Eve and take on Richard, she needed money. The job paid a pittance and Threadbare was a notorious skinflint but in a world that afforded her little in the way of opportunity, there was no other option. What she really wanted, the career she had forsaken when she married Richard, was to be a journalist. She loved stories. More to the point, stories that were real. Fiction was fun but there was something uniquely different about real stories. Her writing was fantastic, but no one would give her a chance. Single mothers, with barely enough money to pay their rent, were not taken seriously in the world of journalism, or so it seemed.

There she was, once again. No job, no money to keep a roof over her head and still no idea where her daughter was, or if she would even remember her.

History had repeated itself and Violet had nothing.

Well, almost.

As she swayed on the edge of the bridge, Violet reached into her pocket and took out a single coin, all that remained of her finances. Threadbare's words came flooding back to her:

You shall make the time both guillotine and executioner less you pay more attention to it.

Violet shouted out into the night as she tossed the coin into the surging river.

'Make it a clean cut.'

For the first time in a long time, Violet felt like she was master of her own destiny as she leapt from the bridge. Her body light as a feather, the weight of her past and the burden of her memories lifted, she closed her eyes and prayed it would be over in a painless instant. When the impact came, it felt like she had collided with a stone wall. Her whole body ached but the pain didn't go away. She opened her eyes.

If this is heaven, we've been seriously mis-sold.

Violet felt herself being dragged upwards, her back raking against the lime-scale covered stone of the bridge.

Now I see; that was hell and I'm on my way up.

When she reached her destination, Violet was not greeted by pearly gates or the Lord almighty; she was laid on top of a very well-dressed man, her face buried in his bushy beard.

Charles Pennyworth breathed a huge sigh of relief as he wiped sweat from his brow. He had displayed incredible strength for a man his size to catch Violet by her ankles and drag her back to the land of the living.

'Whatever were you thinking?'

Pennyworth spoke the Queen's English as he regained his composure.

Violet pulled her face out of Pennyworth's beard and burped, the distinct smell of alcohol creeping up his nostrils.

'Ah, I see.'

Disorientated, Violet rolled off Pennyworth. It wouldn't be long before the shock of what she had just done set in. Pennyworth brushed dirt from his finely crafted coat. He noticed the bottle of wine on the bridge, just beside where Violet had jumped.

'Impeccable taste, I'll give you that.'

Violet did her best to pull herself to her feet but in her dithered state it was an effort. 'Non-existent ability to moderate, however,' noted Pennyworth as Violet slumped onto her backside beside him. 'An eighteen seventy-six French red is made to be enjoyed, not murdered.'

'It's all the same,' mumbled Violet, just about coherent.

'Quite the contrary,' replied Pennyworth, 'every wine has its own story.'

Violet's ears pricked up at the final word of Pennyworth's sentence.

'What would you know about stories? You're just another rich pig.'

Pennyworth was wealthy, that much was obvious from the way he dressed and spoke and, understandably, Violet had developed a dislike of anyone who looked like they belonged to the higher ranks of society. Pennyworth jumped to his feet and adjusted his well-ironed collar. 'No thanks required, by the way. Saving a damsel in distress is a regular occurrence on my evening commute so nothing out of the ordinary.' The sarcasm in Pennyworth's voice was playful rather than arrogant. Beneath the surface, Pennyworth was shaken but he masked it well. He had stayed late at work that evening and had certainly not expected to be playing saviour to a struggling seamstress.

Violet's cheeks turned a ghastly green and she threw up all over Pennyworth's shiny shoes.

'If that's as near to gratitude as I am going to get then I am happy to hear no more,' quipped Pennyworth. He had a knack of seeing the funny side in everything. No point in lingering on misery. There was certainly enough of that in the world - he knew it as well as anybody.

'Come along, let's get you home.'

Violet swiped Pennyworth's helping hand aside and slurred her words.

'I don't need your help.'

Pennyworth smiled; one characteristic he admired above all others was determination, especially in the face of unbeatable odds. Despite Violet's insistence, her mind and body were at complete loggerheads.

'What we want and what we need are sometimes

not necessarily the same.'

Violet gave in and allowed Pennyworth to assist her. Luckily, she had not stumbled far from home and when she finally mumbled her address to Pennyworth, he was relieved that he would not have to drag her far. He escorted her to her front door, which was more of a challenge than he first anticipated given that Violet had become a dead weight under the wine's influence.

'Home?'

Pennyworth wanted to be certain before he left Violet to what was guaranteed to be one hell of a headache the following morning. She slumped in a heap at the front door of her scabby, terraced bedsit.

'Until the landlord doesn't get his rent,' slurred Violet.

Pennyworth crouched down beside her and put a hand on her shoulder.

'There are two kinds of people in this world: those who write their own story and those who allow others to write it for them.'

There was a sternness in his voice, yet he spoke with compassion. 'If you remember any of this tomorrow, I do hope you will try to make the best of what appears to be a very bad situation.' Reaching into his deep pockets, Pennyworth took a handful of coins. Far too intoxicated, Violet never noticed him slip them into hers, which he had hoped would be the case. A great judge of character, Pennyworth had deduced that she would have thrown the money straight back in his face had she been aware.

'Wait,' slurred Violet. 'Who are you?'

Pennyworth whispered something then disappeared into the night. His words echoed in her head as she lost consciousness and escaped from reality in a much less finite way than she had sought earlier that evening.

Somebody in the right place at the right time.

- XI -

ALONE IN THE NIGHT

THE streets of London were nothing like Hanz hoped they would be.

Jubilee Walk was all he had to compare them to, and they were a far cry from that. Tracking Jack had not been a difficult task for Mr. Moretimer's mechanical apprentice. After he caught up, he had kept Jack within his sight, keeping just enough distance that he wouldn't be seen. Jack was nifty and navigated his way across London with skills that Sir Francis Drake would have admired but despite his youthful energy, eventually, a human heart and human muscles would grow tired.

Hanz had neither of those.

Two beady eyes peeked out from beneath the hooded cloak Hanz had garbed himself in to hide his appearance. Mr. Moretimer had kept him a secret, probably due to the negative attention it would draw. At least that's what Hanz had always thought. After all, it wouldn't be every day a person came across a living being made entirely of clock parts and bones. His eyes were human but just how Mr. Moretimer had come across them was anyone's guess. Hanz did not look human in the slightest but was as alive and kicking as Queen Victoria herself. The old man had crafted him in the image of a human, and because of that, he could think and make decisions like one.

On the few occasions he had ventured to the end of Jubilee Walk, Hanz had spent the time staring out through the bars of the wrought iron gate, wondering what was so bad about him that Mr. Moretimer felt the need to keep his existence a secret. The old man had always assured him that the reason wasn't because of what was bad about him but what was bad about others. It had made no sense to Hanz at the time but now, as he stumbled down the late-night London streets, he finally understood.

Never ending rows of weathered buildings towered overhead which, combined with the narrow streets that ran below, engulfed Hanz. The streets, spoiled by the grime which spewed out from an ever-increasing number of factories, were home to the dregs of society; humans who were either homeless and fought to the death over scraps of mouldy food or who were sick and in desperate need of medical attention. Both instances were perfect examples of how low and desperate humans could sink when kindness was in short supply. For the first time in his manufactured life, Hanz felt an emotion he had never experienced:

Fear.

Whilst Jack had grown accustomed to the streets, Hanz was an innocent, naive child, experiencing a harsh reality for the first time. If he could feel, Hanz would have felt the cold bite his mostly metal exterior as he ran down the street. If he could smell, his nostrils would have begged to be stitched up to avoid the putrid stench. The few streetlamps that were lit flickered and cast the darkest of shadows from figures that loomed on every corner. Hordes of rats pitter-pattered across the cobbles and down overflowing drains. Faceless beggars accosted him, grabbing him with boney, calloused hands. When he did not respond to their pleas for money, they shoved him aside.

A tall man strode by, so tall it was as if he walked on stilts, twice the size of a normal man.

'Get out of my way, kid!'

Frightened, Hanz stumbled into a small crowd of homeless people and bumped into a preacher who stood in the middle and screamed at him.

'Only God will save you!'

Hanz backed away but tripped and fell onto his backside. The preacher stood over him and continued his doomsday homily. 'A storm is coming, a plague like no other. You better pray for salvation with the rest of us sinners or suffer the eternal wrath of Lucifer himself!' Hanz crawled away as fast as he could whilst the preacher returned to his homeless clergy.

A pub door flew open and two drunk men barrelled out onto the cobbles, beating each other senseless. They tripped over Hanz, and their fracas continued, on the ground. Hanz dragged himself to his feet but bumped straight into an old lady. She turned around and revealed a long, hook shaped nose that stuck out from a spot covered face. She spoke from a mouth that displayed no teeth, only rotten, bleeding gums. 'You drink fox blood, do you?' The old lady cackled like a witch as Hanz took flight. Wherever Jack led him, Hanz found himself surrounded by new horrors. He craved the sanctuary of Mr. Moretimer's shop but something spurred him on.

Father has been kind. If I help him, maybe he will be kinder.

Hanz had no idea what Jack had taken that had prompted Mr. Moretimer to declare the eleventh hour - the latest possible time before an extinction level event occurred - but, if he could get it back for him, maybe he would be rewarded with that which he wanted more than anything else in the world but, for some reason, had been denied:

A voice.

With far less artistry than Jack, Hanz bundled through the rabble of society's cast-offs until he was about ten metres behind. Much to his relief, he finally emerged from the slum onto an embankment which led down towards the Thames. Jack sat there, his legs dangling over an eroded edge just above the water surface. Hanz found a hiding place behind a derelict barge and observed Jack, who tidied up the torn seam where Edgar's arm had previously been attached. If the teddy bear was to stand the test of time, it would need attention at some stage. After Jack gave up playing doctor, he sat Edgar beside him and removed the stolen scroll from his pocket. Hanz noticed that Jack had a habit of making one way conversation with Edgar, even though he never got a response. It made him feel slightly better about his own inability but, at the end of the day, it was a stuffed toy. It wasn't living and breathing.

Not like me.

Hanz watched a while longer and deduced that the scroll was his target given Jack's obvious interest in it. He was totally absorbed in reading whatever was scribed on it. Hanz had to strike hard and fast as the clanging of his metal feet on the rocky ground would surely alert his target. He needed to take Jack by surprise to give him no chance to defend himself. Picking up a heavy, jagged rock; this was his chance.

CLANG, CLANG, CLANG.

Before Jack could react, Hanz was stood over him, rock raised high in the air. He felt powerful, knowing he had the ability to take Jack's life, but he paused and reconsidered, suddenly unsure whether he had it in him to do it. Jack prepared himself for the impact of the rock smashing into his skull.

It never came.

Hanz aborted the attack. He still gripped the potential murder weapon, but cold-blooded killing was not in the magnificent abomination's nature. Jack scrambled to his feet and raised his hands, ready to defend himself. Hanz pointed towards the scroll.

See, Edgar, I knew this was worth something. Why else would he send that thing to get it back?

Jack composed himself and reverted to his happy-go-lucky showman persona. He had the upper hand, now, he felt. If Hanz was really going to kill him, he would have done it already. Like a carrot on a stick, he held the scroll out in front of Hanz.

'Maybe we can come to some sort of arrangement?'

Hanz swiped at the scroll, but Jack dodged the advance.

'Okay, clearly, you don't know how this sort of thing works,' said Jack. 'I give you my terms which you can accept or come back with a counter-offer.'

Hanz lunged for the scroll again, Jack switching it between hands.

Of course it doesn't understand. It's not even human!

'I guess if we can't agree then the only thing to do is get rid of what is causing our issue.'

Jack dangled the scroll over the Thames. Hanz's eyes almost popped out as he threw himself towards Jack to stop him.

It understands enough to know this is of value.

Jack grinned. 'This is obviously worth something to your master so it would be a shame if it went down the river.' Jack strutted along the edge of the embankment and teased Hanz, pretending to drop the scroll. 'All I want is to know how you did that disappearing act. Show me and I'll hand this right back and we can all be on our way.'

Hanz stared at Jack, no response came.

This is going nowhere.

'Okay, lesson number one; the best way to settle a dispute is by talking it through.'

If Hanz's eyes could have burned holes, Jack would have looked like a piece of Swiss cheese. His words had hit a nerve and Hanz saw red, charging him down like a bull. The pair collided and wrestled on the rocky embankment. The scroll fell from Jack's grasp in the commotion and settled dangerously close to the edge of the Thames.

Come on, Edgar, don't just sit there!

Edgar remained a spectator to the fight.

If it's about your arm I said I was sorry!

Hanz got the better of Jack and pinned him to the ground. He swung a fist down towards Jack, who wriggled free in the nick of time.

Some help you are.

Jack grabbed Edgar and the scroll and ran away as fast as he could. He looked over his shoulder and saw Hanz staggering after him.

How does it move so fast?

Jack realised he wouldn't be able to outrun the thing for long; there seemed to be no reasoning with it. Up ahead was a bridge, cloaked in darkness beneath. The shadows had been Jack's ally many times before and he prayed they would offer him refuge once again. As he sprinted beneath the bridge, Jack caught of a glimpse of something at the last possible moment and stopped just in time.

An open manhole waited right in front of him, ready to swallow any unsuspecting passers-by.

Tip toes hanging over the edge, Jack wobbled and teetered, desperate to slow his momentum. After a few precarious seconds of staring down into the smelly abyss, he regained his balance. For a fleeting moment, he contemplated climbing down into the sewer and hiding but it stank so bad he had to pinch his nose. He could probably cope with the smell but, odds were, it would be crawling with rats and, even worse, cockroaches. Thinking on his feet, Jack had a light bulb moment.

I can use this to my advantage.

Standing on the opposite side of the open manhole, he goaded Hanz, who staggered towards him with increasing speed. Just as Jack had, Hanz saw the manhole at the last possible moment but, unlike Jack, the metal Hanz was made of weighed much more than human tissue. That, combined with the speed of Hanz's approach, threw him into a state of imbalance which was impossible to recover from.

Hanz looked to Jack for help.

It was strange; even though the man-made creature had the same constant expression thanks to the mask which covered its face, Jack glimpsed sadness in it. The words he had spoken to the sleeping homeless girl as he gifted her his last morsel of bread beneath the bridge came flooding back.

We're all in this together.

Jack felt a sudden empathy with Mr. Moretimer's manufactured companion.

It just wants something; God knows I can relate to that.

Inspired by a sudden change of heart, Jack threw out a helping hand, but it was too late. Hanz lost his balance and tumbled into the sewer. It must have been a long way down as the splash of the sewage when Hanz crashed into it was barely audible.

Jack wasn't quite sure why he felt guilty. It was a machine, man-made and absent of any form of emotion but he had sensed something human in Hanz, right before the fall. Whether it was fear or sadness, or both, it unsettled Jack and he felt sorry for it. Maybe it was to Mr. Moretimer what Edgar was to him. The thought of that only intensified his guilt. Whatever the reason, there was nothing Jack could do now. Human or inhuman, nothing would have survived that fall. Doing his best to quell his guilty conscience, Jack put all his brainpower into how he could turn tragedy into opportunity.

This is our chance, Edgar. We need to strike whilst the iron is hot.

Jack fled the scene in such a rush that he failed to notice something moving in a patch of weeds which grew between the cobbles. A plant root slithered out and snaked along the ground, circling itself around the open manhole like it was stalking its prey. Then, it plunged down into the depths of the sewer.

For years, Mr. Moretimer had kept Hanz hidden away from searching eyes with bad intentions. Despite his well-meaning actions, Hanz had revealed himself and it hadn't taken long for one particular pair of eyes, with incredibly bad intentions, to track him down. If, by some miracle, Hanz was still capable of running, now was the time for him to do so.

- XII -

ALL WE HAVE IS TIME
AND CHOICE

*T*HE streets were not much friendlier in the day than they were during the night, but Jack was glad to see the sun rise.

He hadn't slept a wink with the strange cocktail of emotions that had been coursing through his veins all night. At least it had spared him the recurring nightmare. Excited at the prospect of what might be if he could somehow strike a deal with Mr. Moretimer, he was also, at the same time, racked with guilt. He didn't feel any better having had the rest of the night to come to terms with his role in Hanz's fate.

If Mr. Moretimer asked him of Hanz's whereabouts he would have to lie. There would be no way the old man would do business with him if he knew that he was shaking hands with the person who had engineered the untimely demise of his engineering miracle.

Edgar dangling beside him, and sack of belongings slung over his shoulder, Jack made his way along the street, slipping in and out of crowds of people.

'Let me do the talking, Edgar.'

He reached the wide-open wrought iron gates at the top of Jubilee Walk. Ever since Jack had first laid his peepholes on the strange street, he had done nothing but think about it, running the sight, sound, and smell of it constantly through his imagination. He had memorised every turn it took and every detail along the way. Unlike the morning he awoke in the old man's shop, Jubilee Walk was deserted; no bustling crowds, no endless line of extravagant customers outside Mr. Moretimer's Timely Creations.

Just him.

He stopped outside the shop and rehearsed his pitch. Through the window, Jack could see Mr. Moretimer sat at the grand piano, which had been repaired. The old man didn't move a muscle, like he was frozen in some sort of trance or deep meditation.

Jack took a deep breath and marched into the shop.

DING!

The chime of the doorbell snapped Mr. Moretimer back to life. He unfroze and played the piano as if he had just taken a short interval, fingers dancing across the keys to the tune of a Baroque Toccata, as well as any concert pianist. The old man played entirely from memory, his eyes closed, lost in the music. Jack was mesmerised by Mr. Moretimer's skilled hands, the left in perfect unison with the right with never a wrong note played.

Like clockwork.

Donning his showman persona, Jack whipped out a deck of cards and shuffled them as he swaggered towards Mr. Moretimer.

'Allow me to introduce myself properly. You won't believe your peepholes; you'll ooh, you'll aah, you'll be amazed by the fantastically bizarre as the world-renowned, preposterous--'

'Master Jack Picklewick.'

Mr. Moretimer spoke without opening his eyes.

Jack winked at Edgar.

Our reputation proceeds us.

'It is time you and I had a meeting of minds.'

Mr. Moretimer paused his performance with abruptness, as if he couldn't remember the rest of the piece. A long middle C echoed throughout the shop until he transitioned into a much slower paced Minuet, hoping Jack hadn't noticed his momentary memory loss. 'You've changed your tune,' said Jack. 'Couldn't get me out of here fast enough, yesterday.' Mr. Moretimer brought his performance to an end and checked the time on the pocket watch which dangled around his waist.

'It was not the time.'

Mr. Moretimer stood and cracked his back and fingers, as if his bones had seized up. 'Events have unfolded naturally, as they always should.' Jack's confidence retreated as Mr. Moretimer approached, much taller than he remembered him to be. 'However, you make the mistake of believing that you are the only one here with something to offer.'

Mr. Moretimer opened his hand and revealed Jack's treasured family photograph, resting on his wrinkled palm.

How the hell did he get his hands on that?

Jack checked his pockets just to make sure it wasn't a forgery. There was nothing there; the old man had somehow picked his pocket whilst he was sat at the piano. How he had done it was another question.

'Thief!' cried Jack.

'Common ground is the foundation of all great relationships,' replied Mr. Moretimer.

Jack snatched the photograph from Mr. Moretimer and tucked it away in his pocket, right to the very bottom, so nobody other than him could get their hands on it again.

'I do wonder,' pondered Mr. Moretimer, 'why one would keep a photograph which conjures no memory? Is that not its purpose? To take you somewhere in your mind that your body cannot?' Jack had entered the shop cocksure of himself and ready to wheel and deal with Mr. Moretimer but now he had found himself on the back foot.

How does he know all these things?

'What if somebody could help you fill in the blanks?'

With that question, Jack's thinking changed entirely. He had gone to the shop with the intention of convincing Mr. Moretimer to give up the secret to his disappearing act but the old man had thrown a spanner in the works. Above all else, he longed to know what had happened to his family and why he had no memory of anything than the miserable London streets.

'You?'

Mr. Moretimer shuffled towards the shop entrance and gazed out onto Jubilee Walk.

'Interested?'

It could have been nonsense, another illusion performed by a man obviously well versed in misdirection and showmanship. Jack had witnessed first-hand the standard of trickery the old man was capable of, but he wanted to believe that he could really help him answer the questions that had blighted him for so long. He skipped along behind Mr. Moretimer, wanting to know more.

Light shone between the tall buildings down into Jubilee Walk, much like it had the morning Jack had awoken inside Mr. Moretimer's shop. It really was something how the weather just changed on a whim the past few months. With the pace of a slug, the old man hobbled along the street, much further than Jack had been before.

It went on and on and on but there was nothing. No more shops, no doors, no windows.

Nothing.

The only thing down Jubilee Walk was number XII: Mr. Moretimer's Timely Creations.

Eventually, the street came to a dead end. Jack observed as Mr. Moretimer approached the stone wall that formed the end of Jubilee Walk. He pressed his hand against the stone and closed his eyes. Just as he had done in the shop when he and Hanz disappeared, the old man waved his free hand in the air like an orchestra conductor.

What's he doing now?

To Jack's surprise, Mr. Moretimer knocked three times on the wall and a section of it disintegrated, revealing a doorway. The old man opened it and led Jack through and up a winding stone staircase. As the climb was clearly an effort, Jack offered to help but Mr. Moretimer refused, his pride not allowing him to accept.

Jack admired his determination and resolve; he simply wouldn't let his age stop him. Granted, it took an excruciatingly long time to do so but climb the staircase, the old man did.

At the top and out of breath, Mr. Moretimer led Jack through another door. They stood atop a roof, looking down on Jubilee Walk on one side and out across London on the other. Jack could see right across the city all the way to the horizon; he had never seen it from such an impressive perspective. Mr. Moretimer pointed his fingers to nine and three o'clock and rotated in an anti-clockwise direction, like the hands on a very slow clock.

'All we have in life is time and choice. People over complicate things but it really is as simple as that.'

Jack watched on, unsure if he was simply in awe of such a perfect view of the whole city or because the sight of an old man turning like a clock on a rooftop was something he had never witnessed before. Whatever it was, the old man was a puzzle that Jack was eager to solve.

Mr. Moretimer stopped twirling and focused on Jack.

'Choose.'

He held out a wrinkled hand.

Jack gazed at it; it was covered in strange markings and symbols.

What are they?

'Knowledge is earned, not given.'

Jack was taken aback; it was as if the old man could read his thoughts. Intoxicated with fear and excitement, a cocktail that seemed to taste more familiar the past few days, Jack looked to Edgar for approval. He didn't know if he trusted the old man but his heart, rather than his head, encouraged him to take Mr. Moretimer's hand.

'Everything you see from up here is within your grasp and is yours for the taking,' informed Mr. Moretimer, 'yet what you seek is out of sight, far beyond the horizon. Take my hand, close your eyes and, when you open them, your field of vision will be vast beyond that of any mortal being. Or, if you wish, you can choose to decline my offer and your sight will forever be limited to what you see now.'

Jack looked out across the city, the all too familiar streets he had ventured up and down for the past two years in search of answers jumped out at him. None of them had led him anywhere and he was none the wiser than he had been the day he found himself there. What did he have to lose?

He closed his eyes and took the old man's hand.

For reasons he could not fathom, Jack felt something he had not felt in a very long time. Mr. Moretimer's hand was warm; it filled Jack with trust and reassurance. He couldn't remember the last time he held his father's hand, in fact, he couldn't remember the last time he held a human hand. An energy surged through him and the hairs on the back of his neck stood up.

More than anything, Jack felt safe.

Mr. Moretimer conducted with his free hand and the scenery around them flickered, faded, and flashed, exactly as had happened inside the shop.

'Master Picklewick,' said Mr. Moretimer, 'prepare to have your horizons well and truly broadened.'

- XIII -

A SECOND CHANCE

*L*IKE a whirlwind, Violet rushed down a jam-packed street, head buried in a notebook, bumping into anyone and anything.

It was morning and the sun was already up, a new day for Violet in more ways than one. Thanks to the unfortunate after-effect of last night's wine, her head pounded but, for the first time in a long time, she was thinking much more clearly. A woman on a mission, she marched towards the offices of the London Times. When she reached her destination, Violet took a deep breath, composed herself and hammered on the solid silver door knocker so hard that it was a miracle she didn't damage the door. She was nervous, a state she rarely outwardly displayed. Today was different.

There are two kinds of people in this world: those who write their own story and those who allow others to write it for them.

The words of her mystery saviour had been ringing in her head ever since she had woken up. It was odd; her recollection of the unfortunate events was photographic - despite the volume of alcohol she had drunk. It was a sign, Violet thought, that she had been gifted the perfect memory by the grace of God.

A shame he couldn't do something about the headache.

Violet hadn't been thinking straight and had been completely overcome with emotion, but her hero had spoken perfect sense; she would be damned if she let Alfred Threadbare, of all people, write the ending to her story.

The door almost ripped off its hinges as it swung open and an older lady stepped out from within the building, her spectacles sitting so far down on the end of her pointy nose they looked they like might fall off. Mrs. Lovell did a great job of looking down on Violet, despite the fact she was much shorter.

'I do not think they quite heard you on Drury Lane.'

On any other day, Violet would have taken offense to the sarcastic comment and fired right back but it was not a day for idle disagreements.

'The editor.'

Violet was straight to the point, no graces whatsoever. If there was one thing Mrs. Lovell relished it was being difficult. She would never do it unprovoked as it would not be proper etiquette for a lady but, given the chance, she loved a good stand off and Violet's directness had got her back up.

'Rather essential for a publication,' replied Mrs. Lovell.

'I need to see him right now,' demanded Violet.

'My, my; this one does not stand on ceremony.'

'This one has a name.'

'I am sure it does.'

Violet bit her tongue so hard she almost drew blood.

'But, sadly, for it, the editor does not take unsolicited meetings,' informed Mrs. Lovell.

A change of tact was needed if Violet was going to get anywhere.

You might like to be difficult, you snooty old bag, but I can play that game just as well.

'Sales of The Times are in decline. The Morning Star is mopping the cobbles with you.' Mrs. Lovell applauded Violet's assessment with deliberate, agonising slowness.

'Great pitch; insult the man with whom you wish to secure an audience.'

Mrs. Lovell turned her back on Violet and slammed the door. Just before it closed, Violet shoved her foot through the doorway and stopped it. It was much heavier than she thought it would be and the impact of it on her foot hurt but there was no way she was giving up.

'I have a story for you, ready to print, right now.'

Mrs. Lovell shoved her face in-between the small gap that was left between the door and the frame, her nose poking out. She had met her match in the heel digging stakes.

'A story of love lost, a hopeless woman saved from suicide by a mysterious gentleman, right here on the streets of London.'

Mrs Lovell was unmoved.

'And who is your source?'

'I am,' cried Violet, 'I'm the hopeless woman.'

Mrs. Lovell laughed.

'Of that I have no doubt but do not preach to the choir. Just because you put something in ink does not mean it is true.'

From behind the door, a male voice spoke.

'Actually, Mrs. Lovell, that does sound rather familiar.'

Charles Pennyworth stepped out from behind the door and onto the street, steaming hot cup of tea in hand.

'Although, I believe the mysterious gentleman was originally described by the source as a rich pig.'

Violet couldn't believe it; the man who had saved her life worked at one of the biggest newspapers in all of London and she had insulted him. She died inside but then, something happened which she did not expect.

Pennyworth smiled and extended his hand.

'Charles Pennyworth.'

'You're a journalist?' Violet shook Pennyworth's hand.

'Editor, actually, but, once upon a time, yes.'

Violet was speechless.

Editor?!

'Your story certainly intrigues but attempted suicide is hardly front-page news, these days.'

Pennyworth had developed a soft spot for Violet, but he was not going to make it easy for her. Everything he had, he had earned through hard work, and he believed others should do the same. Violet plucked up some courage and did her best to demonstrate her usual fire and passion.

'There are two kinds of people in this world: those who write their own story and those who allow others to write it for them. I believe I am the former and would be an asset to your paper.'

Pennyworth chuckled, the irony of Violet using his own words against him not lost.

'There are, indeed, Miss?'

'Flemming. Violet Flemming.'

Pennyworth smiled a genuine smile which was reflected by Violet.

'A number of construction workers have gone missing at Alfred Threadbare's new development, all of them vanished without a single trace. The police have just brushed it under the carpet. Either they don't give a hoot about a few missing working-class gents or they're on Threadbare's unofficial payroll. If you ask me, when something smells fishy with Alfred Threadbare, then it usually is. Scratch the surface enough and you'll find something buried beneath it, eventually.'

'You're giving me a job?'

Violet couldn't believe her luck. Yesterday she was on the verge of suicide and here she was, face to face with the editor of the London Times.

And he's giving me a job!

'A trial,' Pennyworth responded. 'If you can put something together that sells papers then we'll talk further.' Violet was as giddy as a schoolgirl, and she couldn't hide it.

'I won't let you down!' Violet trotted off on her way.

'A thank you would suffice!'

Pennyworth had a nice, personable manner but he hadn't become successful by being a pushover. He felt it necessary to remind Violet that she had never actually thanked him for his actions on the bridge, even though it fell on deaf ears.

Mrs. Lovell voiced her displeasure as she and Pennyworth took themselves back inside the office.

'Rude and abrupt. No place for her here.'

Pennyworth stroked his beard as he replied.

'I suppose two would be a zoo.'

Mrs. Lovell was offended but he was right; she was the older version of Violet, hard-nosed and no holds barred. He had appointed her as his personal assistant for exactly that reason. Mrs. Lovell didn't suffer fools and would always give an honest opinion. However, there were times when a little tact was called for and that was something which had escaped Mrs. Lovell over the years.

Sipping his tea as he stood in the window, Pennyworth watched Violet disappear into the crowds of people on the streets outside.

'I fell off a bridge once,' Pennyworth declared, 'making mischief with my friends and I slipped. Landed in a boat delivering the morning papers.'

'And?' Mrs. Lovell snapped back, still upset.

'You could say journalism saved me.'

'Shakespeare must be turning in his grave.'

'My point is, should those in a fortunate position not afford others the same opportunities they have had?'

Pennyworth's logic was well intentioned and

hard to argue against, but Mrs. Lovell saw Violet as a direct threat; she would not welcome her with the same open arms that her boss had.

'I know bad news when I see it.'

Mrs. Lovell sulked back to her desk and carried on with her work as Pennyworth picked up a copy of the London Times' biggest rivals, The Morning Star.

'Problem is, that seems to be what sells.'

Again, Pennyworth was on the mark. The news stories that involved death, doom and gloom were what sold papers and the last thing he wanted to do was to litter his pages with more of that. He longed for something different, something unique that would shift just as many of his papers as any horror story. He crossed his fingers and prayed that Violet Flemming maybe, just maybe, would be the one who brought it to him.

- XIV -

THE REALM OF TIME

*W*HEN he finally opened them, Jack couldn't believe his peepholes.

Where the heck am I?

One thing was certain; he was no longer on Jubilee Walk, or anywhere in London for that matter.

A forest, like nothing that existed anywhere on Earth, surrounded Jack on all sides. Edgar dangled by his side, the pair of them completely dwarfed and insignificant. Vast beyond belief, greener than the greenest plant and with monstrous tree roots that sprawled every which way, it was like something out of a Jules Verne novel. Some trees were humongous, others were tiny. Some were old, some were young.

Click, click, click, click, click.

It sounded like the forest was infested with crickets as the sound constantly echoed throughout the woodland, but Jack quickly realised it wasn't the case. From every tree dangled a single pocket watch, like a Christmas bauble. Each indicated a different time, but they all ticked along, one second at a time. The noise was never-ending and provided the only sound that could be heard. No birds, no bees. Just the hands of what seemed like a million pocket watches, all ticking along.

Tick, tick, tick, tick, tick.

The scene around Jack flickered and faded. Trees disappeared and were replaced by the familiar surroundings of Jubilee Walk. It was almost as though Jack was still somehow there but not, at the same time. The flickering stopped and Jubilee Walk disappeared, completely replaced by the forest.

This is amazing!

'Indeed, it is,' replied Mr. Moretimer as he hobbled out from behind a tree and did his best impression of a magician who had just pulled off a trick.

'Welcome to the Realm of Time!'

This is the greatest magic trick I've ever seen!

'Whilst you may regard me as a magician of sorts,' said Mr. Moretimer, reading Jack's thoughts once again, 'I can assure you that this is no illusion.'

How does he know what I'm thinking?

'I don't know what you are thinking, I know what you have thought.'

Stunned, Jack was unsure what to say or even think.

'We have travelled across the Meridian, and you are now standing in the Forest of the Living.'

He's definitely a showman; Realm of Time, the Meridian, Forest of the Living. Edgar, you need to remember all of this for our show.

'What's the Meridian?' enquired Jack.

'The divide I built between the Realm of Earth and the Realm of Time.'

Jack touched a tree. It felt real but he knew

enough about magic to know that it had to be a deception. Even so, he found himself wondering - what if it wasn't a magic trick? What if there really was more to Mr. Moretimer than met the eye and he could really help him solve the mystery of his past? Jack wanted to believe but his head wouldn't allow him to be completely seduced by the thought.

Mr. Moretimer led Jack through the forest, slowly zig zagging in and out of trees. 'Every tree you see here represents a single human life in the Realm of Earth.' Jack touched a pocket watch that hung from a branch on a very tiny tree. 'Her time has only just begun,' said Mr. Moretimer.

As the old man made his way through the forest, tree roots recoiled at his feet and formed a path for him. The instant he passed, they regrew and became the sprawling mass of foliage they had been before. Jack thought it best to keep up or risk being trapped in a jungle of roots and bushes.

'Some of these time pieces tick and tock for a considerable amount of time. Others stop sooner than expected and when they do...'

Right on cue, a huge tree shrivelled. The ground opened beneath it and swallowed it up until it existed no more. Jack leapt back, avoiding being dragged into the ground with it. The soil reformed and left no trace that the tree had ever stood there. 'So,' mused Jack, 'you're telling me that whenever a person passes away in the Realm of Earth or whatever you call it, a tree here dies?' The comment seemed to amuse Mr. Moretimer. 'Absolutely not, that would be ridiculous.' On random trees all around, leaves fell and swirled to the ground. The pocket watches that hung from them stopped and tick-tocked no more. They withered and were swallowed up by the ground, leaving the pocket watch laying on the ground.

'When a watch stops here, the time of someone in the Realm of Earth is up.'

From between the trees, a huge giant with twelve eyes stomped with the grace of a rhinoceros. On one arm it carried a larger-than-life wicker basket.

'Ah, just in time.'

The giant picked up the pocket watch and put it into the basket.

Jack hid behind Mr. Moretimer as the giant passed them by, as if it had not even noticed their presence.

'What is that thing?'

'Oh, don't worry; the Time Collectors are a very sedate, peaceful race. Well, for the most part, anyway. There was one time when...when, erm...' Mr. Moretimer scratched his head.

'When what?' asked Jack, hanging on his every word. The old man struggled to remember.

'I can't quite recall. Not to worry, I am sure it will come to me.'

The Time Collector disappeared into the forest.

'That thing looks like it could eat us alive,' said Jack.

'It could,' replied Mr. Moretimer, 'but its purpose is to collect dead pocket watches.'

Jack had never heard a timepiece described in such a way. 'You mean broken?'

Mr. Moretimer waved his arms around in the air as if he was conducting his invisible orchestra again. The scenery flickered and faded until the whole forest disappeared and was replaced by another, very different, forest.

As far as Jack's peepholes could see, the land was barren, and an eerie mist permanently hung in the air. Vast canyons could be seen off in the distance and the ground was cracked and dry, from which a seemingly infinite number of withered trees were rooted. They were not like the trees Jack had been surrounded by in the other forest; they were completely bare, spiky branches sticking out like knives at all angles, not a single green leaf in sight. Flying in and out of the trees were small creatures that were a cross between a dragon and a bat. They were in the air everywhere, scavenging for anything that looked like it might provide an adequate meal for them.

'Don't mind the Spirit Dragons,' said Mr. Moretimer, 'they only bite if provoked.'

Carved into the trunk of every tree was a name, a date, and a time. Every now and again, another leafless tree sprouted up from the ground. The place resembled a neglected graveyard and wouldn't have been out of place in a scary story. If the other forest was the Forest of the Living, then Jack was sure he stood in the Forest of the Dead. Mr. Moretimer confirmed Jack's suspicion. 'All humans end up here,' said Mr. Moretimer. 'The trees are a physical record of every soul to have ever existed in the Realm of Earth, all chronicled here where they remain for all eternity.' Through the mist, Jack could make out several Time Collectors but instead of collecting pocket watches, they hung them on the lifeless trees.

A tree sprouted directly beneath Jack. He jumped aside, just before he became a reluctant decoration. He looked at the tree and admired the name carved into it. He didn't recognise it; it could have been anyone.

'Every soul?' asked Jack.

Mr. Moretimer nodded. 'The Forest of the Dead is infinite. Like the universe itself, it expands and expands. It would take much, much longer than a human life expectancy to ever reach its ends. I wouldn't want to even approximate just how long it would take. Careful!'

Mr. Moretimer pulled Jack aside; a Time Collector almost stood on him as it took a pocket watch from its basket and hung it on the tree. 'The watch contains the legacy of the deceased. A permanent record of a person's actions all the way from birth to death.'

Jack gawped.

'This forest contains the life story of every human ever to have lived.'

Mr. Moretimer wandered off through the forest as Jack digested the unbelievable information he had been given. One theory Jack had considered was that he and his family had been in some sort of fatal accident, and he had survived. That would explain why he had no recollection of anything before being on the streets. Maybe he had banged his head so hard it had given him amnesia. Jack usually put the idea to bed as he hated the thought of it but, as he stood in the forest graveyard, he couldn't help but wonder if he was not that far from the truth.

What am I thinking? This is all just an elaborate illusion!

Besides, it would take an eternity to search the sprawling mass that was the Forest of the Dead even if it didn't turn out to be the greatest visual hoax ever performed. Jack fought off his wandering curiosity and ran off in pursuit of Mr. Moretimer, who was some way ahead in the distance.

As he adventured through the woods, ducking beneath spiky branches as he went, Jack could not help but feel that one day, illusion or not, he might find himself back here in search of the answers he so desperately needed. After what felt like an eternity wandering through the woods, Mr. Moretimer and Jack reached a clearing. They were still somewhere in the barren land and the clearing was surrounded, on all sides, by lifeless trees, as far as the eye could see, but what Jack was introduced to next really blew his mind.

A mountain.

A HUGE mountain.

If there was a word in the dictionary to describe something bigger than a mountain, what Jack gazed upon would have been given that title. He had heard stories on the streets about a mountain of epic proportions that a fellow called Andrew Waugh had discovered. Mount Everest, it was called. Jack had never seen any pictures of Everest, but he was already convinced that there was no way it could possibly be taller and grander than what stood before him.

'Mount Evercanever.'

Mr. Moretimer introduced the biblical land mass. 'Or, the Million Mile Mountain, if you prefer.' Jack's eyes followed the mountainside up and up and up, as far as they could. He could only see so far; a layer of cloud surrounded the mountain, making it impossible to see the summit. 'That really goes up a million miles?' Jack felt stupid even asking but, given what he had already seen, it would not have surprised him if the name was an accurate description. 'Such a wonderful imagination.' Mr. Moretimer laughed and ruffled Jack's hair. 'But it does conjure the appropriate sense of grandeur.' Jack glanced at Edgar.

Don't you say anything. I don't know what to believe, anymore.

The old man hobbled along towards a huge, crystal-clear lake which surrounded the Evercanever. A good distance out from the water's edge was a boat with a single oar. Mr. Moretimer never broke stride as a rickety pier formed beneath his feet, piece by piece, creating safe passage out to the boat.

The mountain was inaccessible by land. Like a Medieval castle moat, Mount Evercanever was surrounded all the way around its base.

'Come, Master Picklewick; we must first cross the Bottomless Lake.'

Mr. Moretimer invited Jack aboard the boat which he then rowed at a snail's pace out into the lake. Each pull of the oars looked like it took its toll on the old man but, still, he toiled away.

Jack wondered whether the lake was really had no bottom. He could not believe how clear the water was as he looked over the side of the boat and saw all manner of incredible, prehistoric looking creatures swimming beneath the water. Dipping his hand in, Mr. Moretimer slapped Jack's arm with the oar. 'What was that for?' complained Jack, yanking his hand up out of the water. 'The Bottomless Lake is designed to protect what is atop the Evercanever. The water is deliberately inviting but, unlike everything else you have seen thus far, this is an illusion. Beneath the surface are horrors way beyond anything in your nightmares, all designed to keep what lies ahead safe. Put your hand in if you want, be my guest, but shuffling that deck of cards will become something of a challenge if a Triple Jawed Goblin Shark takes a shine to it.' Jack sat on his hands. He didn't fancy being a one-handed magician.

The rest of the journey played out in silence with Jack taking in his new surroundings. Eventually, the boat ran ashore at the base of Mount Evercanever. Mr. Moretimer climbed out and heaved the oar aside. 'I hope you are feeling fit as a fiddle.' Mr. Moretimer smirked.

Surely, we are not climbing up that?!

'Worry not, Master Picklewick, one minute in the Realm of Earth is the equivalent of one year in the Realm of Time.'

'How long will the climb be?' asked Jack.

Mr. Moretimer checked the time on the pocket watch which dangled from his waist. 'The time in the Realm of Earth is currently eleven thirty-four and seventeen seconds ante meridiem. If we leave immediately then it should be eleven thirty-nine and forty-two seconds ante meridiem.' Jack did the maths.

'Five minutes? To get to the top of that?'

'In the Realm of Earth, yes. Here, for us, five years.'

'Five years?!'

'Approximately.'

Jack was speechless. Surely the old man was pulling his leg. In his current physical condition, in five years it would be a miracle if Mr. Moretimer was still breathing. 'Can't you just do the hand waving thing and magic us to the top?' Mr. Moretimer shook his head. 'As we discussed previously, Master Picklewick, knowledge is earned, not given.'

'I didn't ask for this,' said Jack. 'Correct, you did not. You chose it and the choice is still yours. If you feel you cannot possibly keep up with an old man, I can take you back right now and you can resume your street begging and failed magic tricks.'

How does he know all of this?!

'Or,' Mr. Moretimer continued, 'I can show you the way to a performance on the grandest stage of all.'

The old man had a way of appealing to Jack's curious nature, almost Pied Piper-like. He led him towards a stone staircase that had been carved into the mountainside and spiralled all the way around it. Half of the steps were either damaged, crumbling or missing but, as Mr. Moretimer ascended, stairs magically appeared and repaired themselves, providing them with safe passage up the mountain. The journey was long and draining, mentally more than physically. Strangely, not one of Jack's muscles ached or felt tired and not once did he ever feel hungry or thirsty. It was the endless spiral around the mountain that took its toll. The demoralisation that descended whenever Jack felt like they were near the summit, and he would look up and see nothing but more steps and clouds. The sun rose then fell, time and time again. The higher up the Evercanever they trekked, the larger the sun seemed. It never once got colder, no matter how high they got. Whenever Jack looked down, all he saw was a carpet of cloud, so he had no idea how far above ground level they were. Thunder rumbled but the storm never came. Winds blew but Jack was never once unbalanced.

Finally, a wooden sign told Jack they had reached the summit.

Mt. Evercanever Summit -
390001238574819939393858 4 feet.
Approximately.

Jack felt a sense of achievement like never before. He had conquered the Evercanever.

'Only a handful have ever been here,' said Mr. Moretimer. 'Even fewer have seen where we are going next.'

It was silent atop the summit, probably because they were so far away from anything that resembled life.

Maybe this is heaven?

'How long have we been walking?' asked Jack.

'As long as I said we would be. Five years, approximately. In the Realm of Earth, a mere five minutes.' Jack found it almost impossible to comprehend. It certainly felt like a long time, but five years was out of the question. Jack hadn't aged a bit, but the old man looked older, his beard much longer and features more weathered. 'Forgive my inability to give you a precise time,' Mr. Moretimer apologised, 'but, as time never stands still, I am unable to give you the exact timings because the number I would have stated would be inaccurate by the time I finished my sentence.' Jack couldn't have cared less; it was a long time, but the old man's logic explained why nothing was ever precise with him, unless it was in the past. All Jack could contemplate at that moment was how a mountain could grow so tall.

'It was designed that way.' Mr. Moretimer read Jack's thoughts again.

'Designed?'

Mr. Moretimer nodded. 'The Forest of the Living, the Forest of the Dead, the Bottomless Lake, Mount Evercanever. Everything within the Realm of Time, was designed and created for one specific purpose.'

'And what's that?'

'To protect what resides in the Constance, of course.'

'The Constance?'

'Enough talk, I'll show you.'

Jack skipped along behind the old man, who suddenly stopped, as if he had forgotten something.

'Be wary, Master Picklewick. This is the point of no return.' Jack clutched Edgar tight. 'Once you step foot inside the Constance and learn the secrets within, there is no going back to normality for you.'

I think that ship sailed some time ago.

Mr. Moretimer shuffled across the Evercanever summit. Jack looked towards Edgar. His faithful companion seemed to give him a look that suggested he should turn back. Undeterred, Jack advanced. From out of nowhere, a snowstorm started. A complete whiteout of the Evercanever's summit made life difficult for Mr. Moretimer and Jack, who plodded through the soft carpet of white. Jack held his hand out in front of him; the snowfall was so bad that he could no longer see. He was blind, swiping at nothing but thin air, trying to grab the old man's cloak. Panicking, Jack came over claustrophobic as the snow disoriented him, no clue which way to go. Even if the snow did stop, he had no idea where he was going. The summit of Mount Evercanever was broad and sprawling. A hand grabbed Jack and dragged him along.

'Forgive me if I lose my bearings.'

Jack heard the old man's voice but if it hadn't been for the wrinkled hand dragging him along, he would have had no idea which direction it came from. 'I would say it has been, oh, three thousand, seven hundred and thirty-four years, six months, eight days, four hours, fifty-five minutes and nine seconds since I was last up here.'

'Approximately?' joked Jack.

'You're catching on,' celebrated Mr. Moretimer.

As quickly as it had descended upon them, the snowstorm dispersed and vanished. Jack wiped snow from his eyes which blurred his vision. 'Here we are,' declared Mr. Moretimer. Jack's sight gradually returned but he found himself rubbing his peepholes in disbelief once again.

The Constance was a humongous, ancient cathedral which stood atop the summit of the mountain. Jack had seen St. Paul's in London on many an occasion and he had always been impressed by the great building, but this was something else. It combined the grandeur of St. Peter's Basilica in Vatican City with the gothic architecture of Notre Dame. Jack had heard stories of a great cathedral being built in Spain that, supposedly, would take a hundred years to complete; Gaudi's La Sagrada Familia. People spoke of it like it was a masterpiece, like no cathedral in the world, anywhere, ever.

They've clearly never seen this.

Much older than the pyramids, the Constance was weathered beyond belief, but the amazing architecture still stood tall and proud, despite the many harsh winters it had seen. The stonework contained faded intricate patterns, much like the markings on Mr. Moretimer's skin, and there were the tallest stained-glass windows that Jack had ever seen. In the entrance, a huge pendulum swooshed back and forth beneath a clock face, creaking and groaning like it needed lubricating. It hung low from where it had sagged over the years and scraped along the floor below, creating a trough. Jack counted seven seconds between swings.

'I've never seen a cathedral like it.'

'You most certainly haven't,' said Mr. Moretimer, 'because it is not a cathedral.'

'Looks like a cathedral to me.'

'The Constance is a vault. I built it with my bare hands, laid its foundations deep beneath the surface of the mountain. What you're looking at now is just a front, a distraction designed to hide its true purpose.'

'Which is?'

Mr. Moretimer ignored Jack's question and hobbled off towards the entrance. 'Mind the pendulum!' he yelled back.

You'd have to be blind to miss it.

Jack trailed behind Mr. Moretimer.

If the Constance on the outside resembled the world's greatest cathedral, then, on the inside, it resembled the world's greatest library.

'Welcome,' bellowed Mr. Moretimer, his words bouncing off every wall, 'to history.'

With peepholes that looked like they might explode, Jack scanned the vast hall in which he stood. It was lined, floor to ceiling, with book after book after book, every single one bound in a leather case. 'Every single moment in time, however insignificant and however incredible, is chronicled here.' Mr. Moretimer circled like the hands of a clock. 'Exquisite, isn't it? Each book you see represents a single day in history, all the way back to the dawn of time.' Jack chuckled to himself. There was absolutely no way that any of what the old man had said was true. It was an illusion, it had to be. There was no way that every single moment in time had been chronicled in the books. How could anybody know every single event that had occurred throughout history? More to the point, who had the time to write it all down? *The greatest storyteller, magician, and showman I've ever seen, I'll give him that.*

Mr. Moretimer searched a shelf, checking the spines of every single book.

'Ah, here we are.'

He heaved a book out from its place and dusted at least an inch of dust and cobwebs off the cover. A clockroach scuttled out which the old man promptly stomped on before Jack noticed.

'Page six thousand and seventy-three, paragraph four, line two.' Mr. Moretimer was definitive in his instruction.

'Approximately?' Jack raised a mocking eyebrow as he spoke.

'History is precise, Master Picklewick, not approximate. What has happened is in the books, literally, and should not change.'

Surely it can't be changed.

Jack flicked through the pages of the book. There were so many pages it was an effort to even open it. He turned through the pages until he reached Mr. Moretimer's specified page. Reading along in his head, Jack's eyes widened.

Jack Picklewick tried to help but it was in vain as Hanz tumbled into the sewer.

Jack slammed the book shut.

'That wasn't my fault, you sent him after me.'

'No,' replied Mr. Moretimer, 'Hanz made a

choice. He went after you of his own free will.'

'It was an accident.'

'I know, Master Picklewick, I know.'

He must have followed me and witnessed everything; it's the only rational explanation.

Deep down, Jack wanted to believe that it wasn't all just an elaborate deception and all the fantastic things he had seen in the so-called Realm of Time were real, but his head would not give in to his heart. He handed the book to Mr. Moretimer and paced up and down, wrestling with his thoughts.

'It's an incredible illusion, I'll give you that. But you saw me coming a mile off.' The old man turned his back on Jack and walked towards a doorway at the end of the huge corridor. The door led to an atrium that was pitch black. All that could be seen was a spiral staircase that descended deep into the ground below. It went deep. Really deep. The stairs spiralled down into the blackness as far as the eye could see and then even further still.

'Actually, Master Picklewick, what is coming is the only thing I cannot see.'

The old man led Jack down the spiral staircase. The stairs had been masterfully crafted, and each step contained more strange markings in vivid detail.

'These must have taken forever to make,' said Jack.

'I've had a lot of time,' responded Mr. Moretimer. They descended through the darkness until, eventually, they reached the bottom. Still pitch black, Jack shouted out.

'Hello!'

His voice echoed and bounced around multiple times. The room was huge, that much was obvious from the never-ending echo. The only other sound that could be heard was the same scratching noise Jack had heard within the walls of Mr. Moretimer's shop. Jack could just about make out Mr. Moretimer, who conducted and waved his arms in the air. Light illuminated the room from huge candelabras which sprang to life. The room itself was circular and there were twelve enormous podiums that ran all the way around the edge. Eleven statues stood atop each podium, holding up the roof, but the twelfth was empty. In between each statue were more bookshelves, floor to ceiling, overflowing with heavy, leather-bound books. Jack ran towards the podiums and investigated. The statues were of the same people Mr. Moretimer had portraits of in his shop. The Roman numerals even corresponded too.

'They look like wizards,' observed Jack.

'Not wizards,' replied Mr. Moretimer.

'Fathers.'

Mr. Moretimer guided Jack on a tour of the hall, stopping at each statue to give him a history lesson. 'Allow me to introduce you,' said Mr. Moretimer, beside statue number one, 'to Solomon Solstice; the first Father.' Jack could not help but be amazed by the sheer size and detail of each statue.

'The second one is Edward Eon.' Every statue had an equally strange name.

Mr. Moretimer toured Jack around the entire hall until he reached number twelve, where no statue stood.

'Why is this one empty?' Jack queried.

'The twelfth Father's time is not yet up so he is yet to be immortalised.' Jack gazed at Mr. Moretimer and took a wild stab in the dark.

'You're the twelfth Father?'

'The penny drops.'

'Father of what? Christmas?' Jack chuckled at his own joke but Mr. Moretimer was not impressed.

'Time.'

On one hand, Jack thought the whole thing sounded completely insane but, on the other, it made perfect sense; the watches, the clocks, the scribing on his skin, the Roman numerals branded beneath his Adam's apple. If Father Time was indeed a real person, Mr. Moretimer was about as near to how he would look as Jack could imagine. 'These eleven possessed the title before me.' Mr. Moretimer whirled around and pointed at the eleven gargantuan statues that stared down at he and Jack. 'They presided over time and ensured it remained constant from the moment the Hands were created.'

The Hands?

A thought flashed through Jack's mind.

The Hands of Time!

'On the blueprint I...' Jack considered his next word carefully, '...borrowed; is that the Hands of Time?' Like a schoolteacher delivering a lesson, Mr. Moretimer paced the hall and confirmed Jack's assumption. 'It keeps time constant, always ticking onward.' If the old man was the teacher, then Jack was the model student, full of questions and enthusiasm. 'Don't all time pieces do that?' Mr. Moretimer crouched down before Jack and stared into his eyes. 'The Hands of Time is no ordinary time piece, make no mistake about it. It can manipulate time. If it fell into the wrong hands the consequences could be disastrous.'

For the first time since meeting him, Jack whole-heartedly believed the old man. There was such conviction to his words that it was impossible not to believe that he spoke anything but the truth. Jack clutched Edgar, which did not go un-noticed by Mr. Moretimer. 'My memory is not what it once was but, if it serves me correctly, you wanted something unique? Something real?' They were Jack's exact words, and they were true; he did want something real.

A family.

My family.

If the old man really was Father Time, then surely, he could tell him what happened to his family. Jack ran towards a bookshelf and looked at the dates on the book. He clambered and climbed up the bookcase, heaving books out one by one until he found the one he wanted.

1st January 1897.

The date was significant to Jack as it was as far back as he could remember. Prior to that date, he had no recollection of anything. He had memorised it from the date on a newspaper, so he did not forget. He opened the book, but it almost took his hand off as it snapped back shut before he read a word, like it had a mind of its own. It flew back into its place on the shelf.

'You will find the answers you seek but now is not the time.'

Jack was annoyed with Mr. Moretimer. He could have quite easily just let him open the book and read about what had happened to him. 'I do not control the books. What has been written has been written and cannot be undone. When you are ready, the truth will reveal itself, as time intended it.'

Mr. Moretimer slipped into a trance again, like how Jack had found him in the shop. He snapped out of it just as quickly as he fell into it and seemed in much more of a hurry.

'We must go.'

Mr. Moretimer dragged Jack out of the Hall of Fathers, up the endless spiral staircase and back out of the Constance.

Surely, he doesn't expect us to walk back down that mountain?!

Before Jack could ask the question, a clockroach scuttled across his foot. He panicked and waved his foot around, trying to shake the insect off. 'Get it off!' screamed Jack. The creature lost its grip and fell to the ground.

'Blasted things!'

Mr. Moretimer hobbled off in pursuit of the tiny insect. Jack followed but kept his distance. He watched as the clockroach buried its way into the ground. As it did, the scenery atop the Evercanever flickered and distorted, like it had when they first arrived in the Forest of the Living. Flashes of Jubilee Walk appeared then disappeared equally as fast.

Mr. Moretimer plunged his fingers into the

tiny hole the clockroach had created and dragged the creature back out. He held it up for Jack to see. 'If you see any more of these,' said Mr. Moretimer, 'squash them.'

The old man squished the Clockroach in his hands and black liquid splurged from his fist. Jack looked through the hole and saw Jubilee Walk, clear as day, as if he was looking through a spotless window onto it. He pressed his eye to the ground, trying to see more but, as he did, Mr. Moretimer conducted with his hands and the hole stitched itself up.

'What's all that about?' asked Jack.

'No time to explain now, we have more pressing issues.' Mr. Moretimer seemed to know things that Jack didn't and, being the curious young boy that he was, it frustrated him.

'Why the rush, all of a sudden?' asked Jack.

'She has Hanz,' replied Mr. Moretimer as he conducted once again.

'Who does?'

'Mother Nature.'

This just gets crazier and crazier. But, at least, he's alive and safe; that's my conscience clear.

As the scene flickered and faded, a worried look painted the old man's face. 'I assure you, Master Picklewick, as of six minutes and thirty-two seconds ago, approximately...

...nobody is safe.'

- XV -

TIME IS OF THE ESSENCE

*J*UST like that, the familiar sights of Jubilee Walk flickered and flashed back into view and Jack was back as if he had never left.

Couldn't he have just done that to get us up that mountain?

'Knowledge is earned not given!' Mr. Moretimer shouted as he hobbled towards his shop as fast as he could.

How does he do that?!

Jack hurried behind him into Mr. Moretimer's Timely Creations. 'If she gets the Hands of Time, it will be the end of everything.' Mr. Moretimer paced the room, back and forth, ants in his pants.

Jack had always thought of Mother Nature as being a loving, caring being, if she really existed. Surely, she would not want anything bad to happen to anyone.

'Do you understand the saying, hell hath no fury like a woman scorned?' questioned Mr. Moretimer. Jack didn't have a clue what he was talking about. 'Well, you will, when you meet Lady Augustus.' Mother Nature, Lady Augustus, Father Time; Jack's mind was frazzled.

'Why would it be the end of everything?' asked Jack.

'She wants The Hands so she can rewind time and make herself young again.'

'Who wouldn't want to do that if they could do?' Jack did not share the old man's concern.

'Lesson number one, Master Picklewick: time is constant. If you forget anything I am going to teach you, make sure it is not that.' Like an obedient student, Jack nodded. 'If time gets rewound then you, nor anybody, will exist anymore!' exclaimed Mr. Moretimer.

Ah. Now I see the dilemma.

'For thousands of years, I have kept the Hands of Time hidden from her. The shop is all just a front. You've seen the weather being more erratic and extreme?'

Jack nodded.

'Well,' continued Mr. Moretimer, 'that's her frustration spilling over.'

Mr. Moretimer's explanation would have sounded completely ridiculous but after what Jack had seen with the old man it was perfectly believable. Mr. Moretimer held out his hand. 'I shall be needing back those plans.'

Jack emptied his sack of belongings and revealed the scroll on which the blueprint design for the Hands of Time was etched. Mr. Moretimer snatched it and rolled it out across the top of the grand piano but, for some reason, he shook his head.

'No, not this one, the other one you took.'

I didn't take anything else.

Jack racked his brain. He looked towards Edgar for his input. When he saw the teddy's missing arm, his memory returned. He had completely forgotten; in the rush of getting out of the shop before Mr. Moretimer and Hanz caught him.

The secret compartment!

He rummaged through his belongings again and pulled out the other scroll, rolling it out across the top of the Hands of Time blueprint.

It was another design plan.

Of Hanz.

Every little detail, every part that the old man had used to build and create Hanz was clear to see. Jack couldn't quite believe just how many parts had been used to piece him together. Mr. Moretimer stood back and allowed Jack to take it all in. At first, he didn't understand why the old man was so concerned about Lady Augustus discovering Hanz.

Then he saw it.

Right at the core of Hanz, acting as his heart: The Hands of Time.

The perfect hiding place.

Mr. Moretimer swiped the blueprint from the piano and rolled it back up. 'We must get Hanz back before she discovers what she has. If we don't, it will be the end of humanity and the world as you know it.'

'We?' said Jack.

'Our choices are entwined, Master Picklewick. Even if you could, would you really walk away after what you have learned, knowing you could have done something to stop it?'

'Somehow, I don't think my magic tricks will save the world.'

'You're the Preposterous Picklewick and so much more than that; you just don't know it yet.'

Jack had entered the shop looking for a magic trick that would propel him off the streets and onto the greatest theatre stages of England.

'When the time comes,' said Mr. Moretimer, 'you shall be performing for the entire world.'

- XVI -

A BRUSH WITH NATURE

*H*ANZ opened his eyes.

The fall down the manhole had been unpleasant to say the least but thanks to the incredible craftsmanship of Mr. Moretimer, he was still in one piece, mostly, other than tiny little pieces that had broken off. Or, maybe, the sheer volume of rats and human excrement had broken his fall. Swept away by a slurry of filth, there had been little Hanz could do to drag himself up out of it and he had found himself being dragged away through London's maze-like sewer network. If he could smell, his makeshift nostrils would have been polluted with a stench that would turn even the strongest stomach. He struggled and wrestled with the tide of slop to no avail.

CLANG!

Hanz collided with a sewer grate and found himself pinned up against it. With nowhere to go and unable to fight the flow of the sewer slop, Hanz gave up and consigned himself to swallowing London's filth.

If only I could cry for help.

There was resentment in his thoughts. Whether

or not the capability to speak would have improved his fortunes was debatable but, still, it would have given him a slither of a chance. After some time, the slurry calmed and Hanz slumped to the ground. The excess rainwater that had run down into the sewer system gradually declined, at least until the next storm. Still up to his knees in filth, Hanz waded through the water, trying to find his way back. He heard a squeaking sound and saw a rat, half trapped in a pile of rubble. His helpful nature kicked in and he went to the rescue, pulling aside stones that held the little rodent in place. The rat scampered away, followed by several others that had been trapped beneath. He wondered whether anybody would come to his rescue.

A splashing sound caught Hanz's attention; it wasn't the sound of sewer water but, rather, the sound of something steadily making its way through it. It could have been more rats or frogs.

Or maybe, it was something worse.

Is this the plague that preacher spoke of?

Hanz felt something swimming around his ankles but couldn't see through the thickness of sewage. He plunged his hand beneath the surface and groped around until he grabbed hold of something. It felt soft and squidgy and whatever it was had wrapped itself, several times, around his ankle. He yanked at it, but it held on like a vice. The more he pulled and tugged at it, the tighter it wrapped around him until it whipped Hanz off his feet and submerged him beneath the slop. Blinded by waste, Hanz could feel himself being dragged through the mess, bouncing off the hard, uneven sewer basin. Whatever had a grip on his ankle was taking him away.

After what felt like a lifetime of being tossed around in the tide of filth, Hanz was heaved out of a sewer duct and onto an embankment beside the Thames, on the edge of a forest. Rubbing sewage from his eyes, Hanz glanced at his ankle and saw his kidnapper; a plant vine, wrapped like a snake around his lower leg. He followed the trail of the vine which led right across to the forest edge. Before he had chance to free himself, Hanz was dragged again, away from the sewer duct and into the forest at breakneck speed. Tiny parts of his body broke off as he collided into hard rocks and tree stumps. His view was distorted by the amount of shrubbery, grass and foliage that slapped him in the face every time he dared to raise his head to sneak a peek at what laid ahead of him.

'You are in my world now, not his.'

The female voice, no louder than a whisper, sounded like it was right above Hanz but there was nothing there. It bounced around from tree to tree and filled the environment all around him.

It was her; he was sure of it, the one his father had spoken of on numerous occasions. If what Mr. Moretimer had told him was true, she had eyes and ears everywhere in the natural world and now she had him in her sights. Hanz closed his eyes and accepted the inevitable, praying for some sort of miracle.

When he finally opened them, he had stopped moving but his predicament had not changed. He tried to move an arm, but nothing happened.

He tried to move a leg.

Same result.

Hanz looked down and saw he was strung up between two trees. Instead of rope, he was held prisoner by tree branches which wrapped around his wrists and ankles. Hung on trees all around him were wind chimes, ringing out despite there being no breeze. The trees formed a perfect circle around him, like a woodland Stonehenge, and at the foot of each tree sat a half-melted, unlit candle.

Hanz looked towards the sky. Tree branches and leaves formed and intertwined, forming a canopy of foliage overhead, a natural prison ceiling.

Other than the wind chimes, it was silent. Even the sound of insects and wildlife was absent. Hanz wondered if he still had sewage in his ears.

Then he heard it again.

That whispering voice.

Her voice.

'All my children are loyal, my dear.'

Hanz saw her, swaying on her knees in the distance, like she was deep in some sort of meditation. She hummed to herself, in beautiful sounding tones, like a songbird. Garbed in old rags made of leaves, long straggly hair draped all the way down to her feet from a hood which hid a natural beauty the likes of which Hanz had never seen before. He could just about make out some of her features, even though she did her best to hide them beneath the hood. Her age was evident by lines that creased in her forehead and beside her vibrant green eyes. Why she wanted to hide her face, Hanz wasn't sure. In her hands, she held a round orb which resembled planet Earth. It swirled inside with miniature versions of the planet's continents.

It's her; the one he always spoke about.

Mr. Moretimer had spoken about Mother Nature, or Lady Augustus as he referred to her, many a time and described her as being "as beautiful as a dormant volcano." From out of the ground, either side of Augustus, two large tree roots grew. They twisted and turned, wrapping themselves up in knots until they took on the form of two elderly women, almost identical in appearance to Augustus. They had no legs; their lower halves rooted into the ground like trees, despite their upper halves being human in form. The one on the left whispered calmly in Augustus's ear but the other one raged, screaming and shouting as if each were trying to convince her of something.

Hanz remembered something else Mr. Moretimer had told him about her that had always stuck with him; whenever Augustus was in her human form, she appeared with her two "sisters"; visible depictions of the two sides of her personality. Nature could be calm and beautiful, but it could also be violent and destructive. Her two sisters reflected this. They counselled Augustus, who would always hear them out and then make her decision which was mirrored in the weather, based on her mood.

'Think of them as projections of her thought process, played out before your very eyes,' Mr. Moretimer had said.

Augustus raised her arm and a long, bony finger pointed towards Hanz. The sisters shrivelled back into the ground and tree roots slithered along the ground, like snakes, towards him. Lady Augustus moved with elegance, gliding along like a ballet dancer, and whenever her path was blocked by a plant or a flower, she moved around it and gently brushed by. She caressed the plant life with the tenderness a mother would show a new-born child.

When Augustus spoke, her mouth didn't move. Her voice was everywhere; she seemed to inhabit all that was natural around him. She stroked the orb in her hands and, when she finally reached Hanz, the two tree roots wrapped themselves around him, like weeds.

'I wonder whether he feels the same about you as I do my creations?'

The tree roots tightened around Hanz's throat. He was scared, despite not being able to outwardly portray the matching expression. Augustus stared at her reflection, which looked back at her from Hanz's mask. She obsessed over the creases on her face and turned away when she could bear no more.

'Where is it?'

Hanz knew exactly what was being referred to.

Little finger-like branches sprouted from the end of the root and stroked where Hanz's vocal cords should have been.

'Hardly surprising.' Augustus's voice echoed around the forest.

'The only voice that old fool listens to is his own.'

Even if Hanz had the ability to answer, he had no idea where Mr. Moretimer had hid it. Hanz had never seen the Hands of Time. He had been told by Mr. Moretimer about the mystical device that controlled the movement of time, but he had never been so lucky to see it. The old man had often told Hanz that it was better that he didn't know where it was. He wondered why; it wasn't like he would be able to tell anyone where it was.

The tree roots wrapped around Hanz's metallic face.

'Disgusting. So...'

The tree branch fingers tapped Hanz's head.

'...un-natural.'

The tree roots unwrapped themselves and reformed as the sisters, either side of Augustus.

'Let's see how loyal something manufactured can be.'

The sisters snaked themselves around Hanz.

'You will tell me where it is,' said Augustus, 'or they will take you apart, piece by piece, until you are no more.'

The sisters began unscrewing tiny parts of Hanz and tossing them into the soil.

Humans had robbed the Earth of its natural beauty and resources for years. Augustus would make things right; cure the disease that was humanity and transform the Realm of Earth back to the way it had been intended:

Beautiful.

- XVII -

BACK TO WORK

I cannot wait to see the look on his face!

Violet's thoughts ran away with her as she marched towards her former place of employment, scribing equipment at the ready.

She felt like a proper journalist, even though she wasn't being paid, and she fully intended to make the most of the opportunity that Pennyworth had afforded her. The fact that the lead she had been gifted involved Threadbare's business was just the icing on the cake.

Violet strutted through the factory doors and marched past row after row of onlooking eyes on her way to her former boss's office.

'I haven't gone soft overnight,' declared Threadbare, who barely even looked up as she barged through the door.

'Actually,' said Violet, thoroughly enjoying the moment, 'I'm here from the London Times.' A sense of pride and achievement that she hadn't felt before filled up her senses, although she knew it would be short-lived if she didn't turn something in that Pennyworth could print. Threadbare chuckled to himself. He put his pen down and left his work for a moment.

'I shall entertain your delusion, if only to provide me with some comedic relief over my evening cigar.'

Threadbare sat back in his chair and put his feet up on the desk, hands locked behind his head.

Arrogant sod, he'll change his attitude soon enough.

Violet flipped open a page on her notepad, pen at the ready.

'Workers at your development vanishing off the face of the Earth is great for me but less so for you.'

Threadbare laughed.

'Accidents occur on building sites every day. Dangerous business, you know.'

'Apparently so,' Violet quipped back. 'I'm curious as to how common it is for accidents to occur and there be absolutely no trace of a body, anywhere, after the event.'

Threadbare didn't even flinch. He already knew all about the mysterious disappearance of the construction workers and had been as shocked as anyone to hear of it. Not that he cared much, he was more frustrated that he had to replace them. Most of the stone masons and joiners who had been working at the site were either missing or had quit, believing that they were building on some sort of sacred site and the disappearances were God's way of warning them off. Only those who were so hard up for money that they would rather take their chances with the wrath of the almighty than quit their jobs had stuck around.

The investigating police officer happened

to be an acquaintance of Threadbare. He was a regular attendee at Threadbare's hellfire club, a monthly gathering of persons of quality. In other words, the very rich or very well-connected social elite of London. Threadbare wasn't a massive fan of having police at his home but providing the odd complimentary stogie and Scotch to the long arm of the law had worked in his favour on previous occasions when it came to his business affairs. His dodgy tax payments, or lack thereof, never seemed to raise any issues. He acquired the land on which his new development was being built despite there being numerous, well-founded objections to building work in that area and the disappearances that Violet was enquiring about had been brushed under the carpet with very few questions asked.

'Maybe their pathetic little lives had not worked out in the manner they had hoped so they just gave up and threw themselves in the Thames,' mocked Threadbare.

The sarcasm in his voice angered Violet but she maintained her composure.

Don't let him get one over on you, again.

'Okay,' said Violet, 'I thought I'd do you the decency of coming to you first before I actually went up there to check it out myself.'

Threadbare sat forward in his chair.

'You are actually serious, aren't you?' Threadbare didn't believe for a second that Violet had been employed by a newspaper but the look of grit in her eyes made him doubt himself.

'Deadly.' Violet smirked as she spoke. 'It's going

to be so satisfying when the one great story I've been looking for also happens to be the one that causes a hell of a lot of trouble for you.' Threadbare leapt to his feet and leaned over the desk, staring Violet dead between the eyes. He had never taken kindly to threats, especially from women. 'You never liked me as your boss so I doubt you would be enamoured with me as an enemy.' Violet backed off, happy that she had touched a nerve. 'Asking questions is my job now.' When Threadbare replied, he spoke with so much venom that Violet was worried he might turn into a cobra and strangle her. 'You are a seamstress. A lower than the dirt on the sole of my well-heeled brogue, working class seamstress. And that is all you will ever be.' Violet bit her tongue again.

Now is not the time.

'Thank you for your time, Mr. Threadbare.'

Violet marched out of the office, past the rows of her former colleagues, all clambering for a look at the disturbance in Threadbare's office. Unlike the last time she left the factory, she felt a hell of a lot better about herself. She hadn't thought for a second that Threadbare would help her. She wasn't even sure he had anything to do with it, although she secretly hoped he did so she could drag his name through the mud. Her finest hour would be his worst. All she had wanted was to show Threadbare that she was living her dream and, in the biggest irony of them all, it was a story that involved him that had given her the break.

As Violet marched across London and prepared for her trip out to the building site, she had no idea that the story she was about to stumble upon would result in her name being in the newspaper, one way or another.

A potential front page awaited.

As did the obituaries.

- XVIII -

A STORY BEGINS

*V*IOLET reached the deserted building site just as the sun went down. It was much further out from the city than she had anticipated, and it had taken several hours to get there under her own steam, but she intended to give it a very thorough investigation.

The whole site was off the beaten track and appeared to be completely shut down. She noted that the River Thames ran directly beside it and that a large area of woodland had been cut down to make way for the factory. She wondered why Threadbare wanted to build in such a remote area; maybe he planned to expand further and cut down more trees once this new factory was up and running.

Violet navigated her way around the barbed wire fence that protected the perimeter of the site. It didn't seem to be damaged and was fully intact, so she deduced that if the workmen had been abducted, the kidnapper had not broken in. They must have had access to the site in some way.

Maybe they were already on the site? Maybe it was Threadbare himself, annoyed with the slow progress of the men?

Her mind raced, dreaming up all sorts of possibilities. She reigned them in for the time being as she didn't want to get too carried away. She was playing the role of both detective and journalist, and she had a duty to remain impartial and unbiased despite her deep dislike of Threadbare. The entrance to the site was open and unguarded, no padlock or chains. Violet did not need to be asked twice and she quickly slipped through the unlocked gate. The factory that would eventually be completed, if Threadbare could convince anybody to work on it again, would be huge. The sheer amount of forestry that had been cleared for the foundations to be laid proved that. Violet made her way through the site, investigating abandoned machinery and equipment for anything she might be able to use to create a story. Most of the skills she used in her previous job did not involve searching for missing persons but there was one skill that would serve her well and come in useful in her new venture: an eye for detail.

Just ahead of her, a solid silver pocket watch protruded from the rubble covered ground. Not the usual run of the mill watch, it was impossible to miss, gleaming on the ground. Whoever it had previously belonged to must have been from good stock; an investment partner maybe, come to check on how Threadbare had spent his money.

Threadbare Investor Loses More Than Money.

Violet could visualise the headline she might use to introduce her crowning glory to the world as she approached the watch. Crouching down before it, she dug it out from the rubble, dusted it off and found her fingers covered in dirt and another substance.

Blood.

The sun set and bathed the site in darkness. Disarmed from her sight, Violet felt suddenly vulnerable. The wind picked up and clouds formed above her. Her senses heightened, every sound seemed to be louder than usual - the whisper of the wind, the ripple of the River Thames in the distance. Fight or flight in full flow, her legs took control. She ran as far as she could until the River Thames prevented her from going any further.

What if the workers hadn't been kidnapped? What if they had been murdered?

With a potential killer on the loose, Violet's appetite for giving the site a second investigation had all but evaporated. There was no way she was going back up there. Instead, she trudged along the embankment, a mixture of rock and sand, as fast as she could without tripping over. Ice cold water lapped at her toes, which were gradually numbing. Eventually, Violet came across a sewer pipe which spewed filth out onto the Thames embankment. At first, she paid little attention but felt compelled to go and check it out. She was certainly cut out to be a journalist or reporter of some kind. Anybody with half a brain would have run and never looked back but Violet's intuitive nature beckoned her towards the open sewer.

When she reached the entrance, she looked down and saw something that made her both fearful and hopeful at the same time.

All it takes is one great story.

A small piece of metal shone in the mud. She picked it up and examined it. It looked like a cog from a watch. Was it a coincidence that this looked like it belonged in a watch and the impossible to miss watch she had seen moments earlier had gone missing? A little further away from the sewer was another piece of metal, gleaming in the light.

A tiny spring.

Further ahead from that was another piece of metal, and another, and another, all looking like they had come from the inside of a watch.

A trail left behind by a killer who collects the watches of his victims.

Violet was already concocting a story as she followed it all the way up to the edge of the forest.

I haven't come all this way to let this slip through my fingers.

Ignoring her brain telling her to turn around, Violet ventured deep into the forest, following the trail. The trees were impressively tall and made it impossible for her to see anything of the outside world. Thankful for the rays of moonlight which splintered through the branches above, she turned around; there was no sign of the edge of the forest. God only knew how far she had trekked. She was committed; there was no going back.

Violet followed the trail with relative ease. It was direct, almost a perfect straight line. She navigated along it, over huge tree roots and between small valleys. If a tree or bush got in the way, the trail took the most direct route around it.

Whoever did this and wherever they were going, they were in a rush.

Violet's logic made perfect sense. After all, if somebody had just broken the first of the ten commandments, they would have been in a rush to get away. She wondered about the watch parts that were leading her way.

Maybe they broke off something? Or, maybe, somebody left them as clues, so they could be found? If they did, then they couldn't have been dead when they were taken!

Any sensible person would have turned around there and then but Violet was so sure that this was the one great story she had been searching for that she was blinded by illusions of grandeur. She was thinking more about the look on Threadbare's face when her writing caused sales of the London Times to skyrocket than she was about her own safety. It would be no good having the scoop of the century if she took it to her grave. She didn't care; the risk was worth the reward, and she would simply follow the trail back out again.

CLUNK.

The sound of metal on metal echoed around the forest.

Eyes darting in all directions, Violet searched for the source of the sound. It was all she needed to spur her on in her quest. She followed the trail further through the foliage. Eventually, a clearing appeared in the distance. It was odd, she thought, that such a clearing would randomly appear in the middle of such a huge, sprawling mass of trees. It looked like some sort of Pagan ritual site, wind chimes hanging from trees and candles, all of which were lit, dotted across the ground. Violet had read plenty of old stories about witchcraft and spells and this place certainly wouldn't have been amiss in any of those. She hid behind a particularly thick tree that provided her with enough cover should she need it.

CLUNK, CLUNK, CLUNK.

The noise was much louder, but it was dark in the centre of the clearing which impaired Violet's view. The only way she would see anything that she might be able to use for her story would be to get closer. Her heart pounded in her chest and blood pulsed through her veins faster than it ever had before as she moved out from her safe refuge and tip-toed into the darkness. Would she find herself face to face with a killer? If she did, what would she do? Would she stand any chance of getting away if she was attacked? Violet wasn't looking for any answers to the questions, she just wanted to get a look at whatever made the noise so she could write a factually accurate report. She crouched down and crawled on but winced as her hand pressed down on something sharp and metallic. She picked up the object - another watch part. As she fumbled around in the muddy forest dirt, Violet noticed that there were endless watch parts scattered all over - springs, clock hands, straps, chains, and coils. In a rare break of cloud, moonlight sprinkled between tiny gaps in the trees and a carpet of metal glistened. It was like a scrap yard for broken watches.

Why would they steal them and then destroy them?

The moonlight subsided, the break in cloud short lived. Violet's eyes adjusted to the darkness, and she was able to see a little more than before. The closer she got, the more she saw until the source of the noise was revealed in all its glory. If she hadn't been looking at it with her own eyes, she wouldn't have believed it.

There, staring right back at her, tied between two trees, was the most inhuman looking thing she had ever seen. It wriggled and struggled when it saw her. Metal watch and clock parts clanged and scratched on what looked like bone as it tried to free itself.

What the hell is this?

It looked like something out of a science fiction novel. Was this the killer? Kidnapping then murdering humans and using watch parts to build itself a body, discarding the ones it didn't want?

Why would it tie itself up?

It looked like it was being held prisoner. Maybe there was something far worse in the forest and it was building a horrific creature to carry out its evil deeds? Either way, it was a story like no other and nothing like anything Violet had expected to stumble upon. Somebody, or something, had created whatever it was; a mixture of man and machine, proof that life could be engineered and manufactured by hand. It stared at Flemming and opened its mouth, but no sound came out.

Is it trying to tell me something? Yes, it is!

She lip-read the word that the creature was trying to say.

Run.

Violet scrambled to her feet and backed away until something stopped her. A tree blocked her path. She wheeled around but what she saw took her breath away, and not for a good reason. Petrified into the tree bark was a human being.

A dead human being, terror in its now lifeless eyes.

Violet screamed as she scrambled away from the tree and ran, following the trail back out of the forest. She dared not even look over her shoulder. Even though she had made no notes that could be used in her report, it didn't matter.

There was no way she would unsee or forget the horrors she had just seen.

- XIX -

A CRAZY CLAIM

*P*ENNYWORTH'S heart jerked in his chest as Violet barged through the door of the London Times and slammed it behind her. 'What in God's name?!' Mrs. Lovell barely had time to finish her sentence as Violet shoved by her and marched straight over to Pennyworth's desk. If he hadn't already been woken at the crack of sparrows by a noisy cockerel, Pennyworth might have appreciated the shock to his system and if Violet hadn't been as excited, she might have noticed that Pennyworth clutched his chest in genuine pain.

'You won't believe what's up there!'

By the looks of her, Pennyworth couldn't decide whether Violet had been up to Threadbare's development or if she had just had another night on the wine. She was a mess; hair all over the place, the same clothes she had worn the last time he saw her, all dirty and scraggy and, to top it all off, she looked as though she hadn't slept a wink.

'Have a seat, Miss. Flemming.' Recovering from the shock of Violet's surprise entry, Pennyworth offered her a chair, but she was far too excited to sit down, marching around the office as she regaled him with her discovery. Mrs. Lovell watched Violet like a hawk.

'It's not human,' Violet repeated, over, and over.

'What's not?' Pennyworth listened with genuine interest. Was this the story that would catapult the London Times back in front of the Morning Star? By the sound of Violet's enthusiasm, he believed it might be.

'The killer,' Violet continued. 'It was right there with me!'

It?

Pennyworth felt his heart jump in his chest once again. He had sent her to snoop around the site for any sign of foul play on Threadbare's part that he could use to spin a storyline, not put her in harm's way.

'Slow down, slow down,' said Pennyworth, 'you were face to face with the kidnapper?'

'No, not kidnapper; killer! I saw it, in the forest. I'm sure of it, right there in front of me, before my very eyes.'

Pennyworth looked into Violet's bloodshot eyes. He was still trying to deduce whether she had been drinking. Her words were all over the place and she raved like a mad woman.

'Proof?' enquired Pennyworth, 'You have concrete evidence that those workers were killed?'

'Yes!' yelled Violet, 'There was a dead man, stuck, no, what's the word? Petrified, that's it! Petrified in tree bark. I saw it, right in front of me.'

Pennyworth sighed and slumped in his chair.

'I'm afraid that's not proof, Miss. Flemming.'

Violet took Pennyworth's words to be an attack on her morals. She may have been direct and to the point but one thing she wasn't was untrustworthy.

'Are you calling me a liar?'

'No,' replied Pennyworth, convinced by her snap reaction that there was some truth to what she spoke, 'but we can't just print wild assumptions. We would be receiving a writ from Mr. Threadbare's solicitor for slandering his good name.'

Violet scoffed.

Good name.

'We simply cannot afford to be sued. I need facts, backed up by hard evidence, before I can print anything of that nature. I am afraid your word won't cut it in this business.'

'Can tell she's green,' smirked Mrs. Lovell, 'I told you she's bad news. She'll have us shut down, the laughingstock of the city press.' Violet marched towards Mrs. Lovell's desk and slammed her fists down on it.

'I know what I saw.'

Mrs. Lovell pinched her nose.

'I can't decide whether it is the tripe you're spewing or if it is you, yourself, who stinks.'

Pennyworth sprung up from his desk and stood between the two women before he had a full-blown fight on his hands.

'That's enough, both of you.' Pennyworth's intervention seemed to be enough to calm the dispute, even if only for the short term. He invited Violet to take a seat at his desk once more which she finally accepted.

'I'm afraid, Miss. Flemming, that Mrs. Lovell is right.'

'I'm a smelly liar?'

'That's not what I meant,' Pennyworth backtracked. He wondered if giving Violet the opportunity had been the right decision. If she and Mrs. Lovell were to argue every time they crossed paths, he wasn't sure he could cope with it.

Not in his condition.

Pennyworth grabbed his chest again and winced.

'Are you okay?' asked Violet.

'I'm fine,' responded Pennyworth.

Although Flemming looked less than convinced, she didn't push the issue further. She was far too wrapped up with her story.

'Right,' Pennyworth regained his composure, 'let's start right at the beginning. Walk me through exactly what you did when you left this office yesterday.'

Violet began her tale and spared no detail, described from an almost photographic memory. She would definitely make a fantastic writer with her impressive visual descriptions, Pennyworth thought. Even so, he couldn't help but be sceptical of her tale. He had to be. As editor of the newspaper, he would be held accountable for anything that he published. With smaller claims and matters he could afford to twist the truth slightly but when it came to accusations of foul play, and, more specifically, anything to do with Threadbare, he had to make sure the words he printed were gospel.

Threadbare was a proud man and he and Pennyworth had clashed before. The result was Pennyworth having to pay a substantial amount of money to him as compensation for a story that had been printed in the paper which he couldn't prove. He had never liked Threadbare; the man was the total opposite of him. They disagreed over many political issues and Pennyworth would have loved to get one over on him, which was what led to him being careless before. It cost him a lot of money and he had to lay people off as a result, which was something he hated to do. If he was ever to get Threadbare over a barrel, he needed to be sure of the facts. They had to be concrete.

Petrified, even.

Pennyworth wanted to believe but he couldn't, not one hundred percent. Threadbare had deep pockets and enough money to silence even the most honest officer of the law but Violet's claim that the kidnapper was some sort of murderous robot would have stretched even the imagination of Charles Dickins.

'I'm telling you,' continued Violet, frustrated that the person she hoped would believe her apparently didn't, 'it was strung up between two trees and was made entirely of bone, watches and clock parts.'

Pennyworth had interviewed enough people in his time to know when someone was lying. Violet was a passionate, driven woman. That much was obvious. A liar, she was not.

'I believe you.'

'You do?' said Violet, relieved.

'You do?!' exclaimed Mrs. Lovell.

'Problem is,' Pennyworth stood and paced the office, deep in consideration, 'the public won't.'

Violet's newly gained optimism vanished in an instant.

'Not without proof.'

Pennyworth walked towards a cupboard in the corner of the office, opening it and rummaging through it until he found what he was looking for.

A camera, a flash, and a tripod; cutting edge technology which Pennyworth kept under lock and key. He had spent a small fortune on buying it for the business but only ever used it if he felt it was worth the risk in taking it out.

'If we need proof, then proof we shall get.' Pennyworth smiled at Violet, who returned the gesture. Not a fan of the idea, Mrs. Lovell made her feelings known.

'I've heard some balderdash in my time, but this takes the biscuit. You aren't seriously entertaining this nonsense, Sir?'

Pennyworth grabbed his coat from a stand behind his desk and walked towards the exit with Violet by his side. 'If we aren't back by nightfall, send a search party.' Pennyworth waved goodbye to Mrs. Lovell and held the door for Violet.

'After you.'

Violet led the way as she and Pennyworth rushed out onto the street, slamming the door, and leaving Mrs. Lovell behind them.

If looks could kill, Mrs. Lovell would have been in front of a judge, destined for the gallows. She had worked for Pennyworth for years and wasn't about to be pushed aside by an amateur upstart like Violet. She looked out of the window and watched Pennyworth and Violet turn the corner at the end of the street. Once they were out of sight, she removed a telephone directory and flicked through the pages, running her index finger down the page until she found the name she was looking for. She circled it with a pen, so she didn't lose sight of it then picked up the telephone and turned the dial until it rang. An operator connected the call for her and someone on the other end answered, annoyed that they had been disturbed.

'I have some information you may find useful.'

The voice on the other end of the phone didn't sound interested.

'Fine,' said Mrs. Lovell, 'but I thought you might like to know about the actions of a rather nosey young lady called Violet Flemming.'

The voice perked up, interested.

'There will be a cost attached but we can discuss that in person.'

Silence for a moment.

The voice responded and Mrs. Lovell smiled.

'Perfect. I will be there in an hour.'

Mrs. Lovell hung up, a sneaky smile on her face. The phone directory remained open and circled in ink was a single name:

Threadbare, A.

- XX -

THE BOOK

'*A*AAAGGGHHH!!!'

Jack clutched Edgar and screamed as another clockroach scuttled out from a glowing hole in the wall of Mr. Moretimer's shop. The old man conducted with his hands until the hole stitched itself up and disappeared.

'Don't just stand there!' Mr. Moretimer exclaimed.

Jack froze with fear, forcing Mr. Moretimer to take matters into his own hands. The old man stomped on the insect, black goo splurging onto Jack's shoe which he wiped off in disgust. 'You are going to have to come to terms with this phobia. We shall be seeing a lot more of those things before our work is done.' The mysterious holes and the clockroaches were appearing more frequently but Jack did not want to tell the old man about his nightmares. It was bad enough having them for company every night without having to think about them during the day.

'Where are they coming from?' Jack asked. No sooner had he finished his sentence than another two holes appeared, one in the floor and one in mid-air. Clockroach after clockroach poured through which sent Mr. Moretimer into a frenzy, dancing around the shop, waving his arms around, stitching the holes and stomping on the insects at the same time. It was like he was performing some sort of new dance style that hadn't quite caught on yet. Jack was neither use nor ornament as he closed his eyes and tried his best to block out the thought of the creepy crawlies.

Mr. Moretimer slumped onto the piano stool after he squashed the final clockroach. He huffed and puffed, sweat pouring from his wrinkled brow.

He's aged since we first met.

Time didn't look as though it was on Mr. Moretimer's side and Jack was right, he had visibly aged in the few days since Jack first laid his peepholes on him.

'What you see are tears in the Meridian,' said Mr. Moretimer, slowly regaining his breath. 'Those clockroaches are eating through it.'

Jack thought about it for a moment. 'Surely a few insects don't matter if Mother Na--'

'Don't call her Mother!'

Mr. Moretimer cut Jack off before he could finish his sentence. 'Mother makes her sound older in her mind and she's angry enough as it is. Witch would be more fitting than Mother, but I very much doubt she would take too kindly to that either.'

'Okay,' Jack rethought his choice of words, 'surely a few insects don't matter if Lady Augustus rewinds time?'

Mr. Moretimer paced the shop floor, up and

down, over, and over.

'The Meridian has served its purpose well. It has kept Augustus contained here in the Realm of Earth where she can do no damage to anything in the Realm of Time. However, it has also kept other things out of the Realm of Earth.'

The old man approached a dusty shelf, high up in the farthest corner of the shop and took a thick, leather-bound book from atop it.

THUD!

Mr. Moretimer dropped it onto the floor at Jack's feet, a mushroom cloud of dust rose into the air. Jack bent over to pick it up but almost put his back out.

Wow, that's heavy.

'There is a big difference between one who is misguided and one who is pure evil. Lady Augustus is an immediate threat, make no bones about it, but there are things in this universe that are far, far worse, and ill-intended than her. The Meridian provides a shield for the Realm of Earth from such an evil. It has stood the test of time for thousands upon thousands of years but, like all walls, it needs maintenance, once in a while.'

Jack hung on Mr. Moretimer's every word, like an engrossed child listening to a master storyteller. 'In my twilight, I appear to have become a tad forgetful and have neglected it.'

'And now cracks are appearing?' asked Jack.

'Precisely.'

'So, those...' Jack shuddered, '...clockroach things will just keep coming?'

Mr. Moretimer nodded.

'Inside Mount Evercanever, buried down in the deepest depths, is the life-force of the darkest darkness. Somebody so vile, so terrifying, I dare not even think his name. I trapped him there millennia ago and have managed to keep him contained but his will, his thoughts, his blood has manifested itself within the clockroaches and buries its way out in pursuit of what it desires most in the universe.'

'The Hands of Time?' asked Jack.

Mr. Moretimer shook his head.

'He has another agenda.'

The old man pointed towards the book.

'Read.'

Jack brushed dust and cobwebs from the book cover. There was no title on the cover where one would usually be. In fact, there wasn't one anywhere. It was ridiculously thick and would undoubtedly take some time to read but Jack's eyes shone with anticipation, nonetheless. 'The answers you seek, and so much more beyond those, reside in those pages.' Mr. Moretimer's words were music to Jack's ears but when he tried to open the book, the cover would not budge, like it was glued shut. He pulled and tugged but the cover did not move an inch. He felt like King Arthur trying to pull Excalibur from the stone. Surely it would budge, eventually.

It didn't.

'Consider it a gesture of good faith, the third movement of a symphony before the big finale. When the time is right for you to learn from the information it protects then you will learn but, until then, we have other business to attend to.' The carrot had been dangled in front of Jack and then pulled away equally as swiftly. 'You could open that for me, you're just being difficult.'

'I cannot,' replied Mr. Moretimer, 'What is written inside is for your eyes only. Be patient; the time will come.'

'It won't if Augustus gets her way,' moaned Jack.

Mr. Moretimer snatched the book away from Jack and put it back onto the shelf.

'All the more reason to make sure she doesn't.'

Jack slumped onto the floor, put his head in his hands and cried. The answers he craved were within his grasp, but he couldn't have them. He considered for a moment that the old man might be using him for his own ends. It wasn't out of the realm of possibility. He had only met him a few days ago. What loyalty did he have to him?

Another hole appeared and another clockroach ran from it. Mr. Moretimer dealt with it as before.

'I cannot allow this to continue. The leak must be plugged at the source immediately.'

The old man sat down beside Jack and took his hand, reassuring him. For the first time in a long time, he felt like he had a connection with somebody other than his teddy bear. At least Edgar was consistently uninspiring and not full of grand promises and bravado. At the current moment in time, Jack wasn't sure which he preferred.

'You promise I'll have answers? This isn't all tomfoolery?'

'Although I cannot approximate when it might be, when it is time for you to know, you will know.'

'Promise?'

'Never a truer word has left these lips.'

Jack trusted the old man even though he wasn't exactly sure why. At first, he thought it was the uniqueness of the shop that had pulled him back to Mr. Moretimer but, the more he was around him, the more he felt like there was a familiarity there, an unexplainable yet well-established connection. He hadn't had a father figure for so long and Mr. Moretimer had taken him under his wing and off the streets, showing an interest in him when others would not. Despite his initial doubts, Jack knew that what the old man had shown him in the Realm of Time was real.

You can feel what's real.

Whatever the reason, Jack trusted that the answers to his questions resided in the leather-bound book that sat atop the dusty shelf in the corner of the shop.

'Now,' said Mr. Moretimer, 'if you would be so kind as to help an old man to his feet, we have work to do.'

Jack complied and took one last glance at the book before he focussed his attention on the task the old man was about to set for him.

'Bring Hanz home.'

Jack was flabbergasted. 'You're sending me, a boy of twelve, to rescue the thing that tried to kill me from the thing that's trying to destroy humanity?'

'Consider it an audition.' Mr. Moretimer's

response did not fill Jack with confidence. 'You're the Preposterous Picklewick, are you not?'

Picklewick got to his feet and wiped his teary eyes.

'The world-renowned,' Jack replied.

'Sleight of hand, pick pocketing and misdirection are all skills that I would imagine will equip you well for such an errand.'

The potential confrontation with an almighty God like Mother Nature didn't sit well with Jack, despite Mr. Moretimer's faith in him.

'What will you be doing whilst I'm risking life and limb?' asked Jack.

The old man contemplated his answer.

'Pest control.'

- XXI -

THE RESCUE BEGINS

*J*ACK stood at the edge of the forest beside the building site. It had been a trek and it still wasn't over.

When he had complained to Mr. Moretimer about how far he would have to walk to locate Hanz the old man just reminded him he had spent five years scaling Mount Evercanever. In comparison, it was a light jaunt. As insane as it was, there was no comeback and Jack swiftly retracted his grievance.

Thanks to his extraordinary gifts, Mr. Moretimer knew exactly where Augustus was keeping Hanz prisoner which made Jack's task somewhat more straightforward.

'If it has already happened,' the old man declared, 'then I know everything about it. If it is in the process of happening, I can approximate an outcome but if it hasn't happened yet then your guess is as good as mine. My job is to ensure time ticks on. I am the steward of time, not a prophet.'

On his way over to the forest Jack had contemplated whether being "the steward of time" was a gift or a curse. There had been many fantastic human achievements throughout history but also a lot of things that might be better being struck from the record. Mr. Moretimer had given Jack little information other than telling him that Hanz was somewhere in the forest, stating that he just needed to "follow his instincts" and do "whatever feels right at the time."

More unhelpful, cryptic mumbo jumbo.

Despite not doubting that Mr. Moretimer had his best intentions at heart, Jack had hoped for some more useful advice than what he had received. Given that there was the very real possibility he would be face to face with an ultra-powerful, resentful force of nature hellbent on the destruction of the human race, Jack believed he had every right to question that his "instincts" would stand up to anything she might throw at him.

Maybe it won't even come to that.

Jack quietly hoped that he would simply find Hanz, shake hands with him, put their previous differences aside and then casually wander back to the shop but, deep down, he had a feeling that wouldn't be the case. A violent crack of thunder shook him to the bone. The sky clouded and rain poured from the heavens. Usually, he wouldn't have batted an eyelid. Getting soaked on the street was a given for Jack but, now he knew about Augustus, the weather had taken on a whole new meaning.

She's in there.

Thunder cracked and Jack jumped out of his skin once again. He ran into the forest, hoping that the trees would provide some protection from the rain.

Out of the frying pan and into the fire, more like.

The forest was dark and sprawling but, after spending some time in the Forest of the Dead, Jack did not feel overly intimidated by it. That he now knew there was a book in Mr. Moretimer's shop which would answer all his questions and allow him to piece his past together, he had all the motivation he needed to get the job done. The trees sheltered him from the full extent of the rain, but it must have been heavy as it still managed to break through in places.

Where to start?

Jack knew he might be in the forest for a very long time, judging by the size of it.

'Hanz is damaged, so look for anything un-natural,' had been Mr. Moretimer's words of advice.

Jack wandered the edge of the forest; it ran all the way down to the River Thames. He scanned the ground for anything that might give him a clue where to start. Just next to the building site, he noticed an open sewer duct that spewed filth out onto a muddy bank which then trickled down and polluted the Thames.

He fell down a manhole so must have come out of there!

Jack sprinted towards the sewer and, sure enough, in the slop covered ground, gleamed the same tiny spring that Mr. Moretimer affixed to Hanz the first time he ever laid his peepholes on him. As he picked it up, he noticed the spring sat beside a set of footprints. They didn't look like Hanz's footprints. His would have been much smaller and less normal in appearance. In fact, there were two sets of footprints.

Had the old man lied to him? He had told Jack that Hanz had been taken by Augustus alone. Jack checked again to be sure. There were multiple sets of footprints, for sure. He could tell by the different size and shape, possibly a male and a female.

Maybe he just forgot.

By his own admission, Mr. Moretimer had been more forgetful of late, but another possibility crossed Jack's mind.

Maybe something else has happened but it hadn't happened when the old man told me.

This prospect concerned Jack more than the first. What if it was the name who the old man dared not even think? What if enough of the clockroaches had gotten through the Meridian and there was something worse than an angry Mother Nature lying in wait for him?

Either way, Jack wasn't turning back. He looked at Edgar, ever faithful at his side.

Whatever happens, this is certainly more interesting than our usual day.

The teddy bear did not look as keen as Jack as he made his way into the forest, tracking the footprints and various pieces of broken metal as he went. He came across a tiny stream in which floated tiny, fiddly watch parts. Jack wondered whether it would upset Mr. Moretimer, knowing how much of a fuss he had made over the ever so tiny spring, that Hanz appeared to be falling to bits.

It felt like he had walked further than he did up

the Evercanever when Jack finally reached a clearing; a perfect circular opening in the middle of the forest, lined by trees on all sides, each with wind chimes hanging from their branches and candles at their base.

Exactly how the old man described.

The moment was bittersweet for Jack.

On one hand, there was no sign of Lady Augustus but, on the other, there was no sign of Hanz, either.

Am I too late? Has she already found the Hands of Time?

Jack hoped he was wrong but, regardless, Hanz was gone which gave him an entirely new problem to solve. He wandered into the middle of the clearing but, as he did, he noticed something out of the corner of his eye. In each of the trees that formed the clearing, something appeared to be stuck in the middle of the trunk.

That can't be. They look like...

Jack screamed at the top of his lungs. In each of the trees was a lifeless body, petrified within the trunk. Dead eyes stared back at him, unable to warn him of the danger he might find himself faced with. He ran and prayed that he would not find himself added to Lady Augustus's collection of condemned environmental killers.

- XXII -

HANZ'S ESCAPE

*A*BOUT an hour before Jack arrived on the scene, Violet led Pennyworth deep into the overgrown woods.

Despite being able to simply follow her own footprints and the trail of watch parts, she remembered the way perfectly from memory. Pennyworth's physical skills were put to the test as he scrambled over tree roots and scraped through bushes. 'Come on, keep up,' Violet called back to him as he un-tangled his trousers from a tree branch. Pennyworth lugged the camera, tripod, and flash with him, doing his utmost to protect it from getting damaged. When Violet had said they were going off the beaten track, he didn't think it would be as beaten as it had turned out to be.

'I am doing the donkey work, don't forget.'

Violet rolled her eyes and grabbed the tripod from him.

'Better?'

'Careful with that, it's worth a pretty penny!'

Pennyworth tried to grab it, but Violet had none of it.

'Save your chivalry for if it's actually needed.'

166

Violet marched off at breakneck pace. A searing heat suddenly spread through Pennyworth's chest, so extreme it dropped him to one knee. He clutched his ribs, directly over his heart, but as quickly as the pain came on, it disappeared. Thankfully, Violet hadn't noticed as she was too busy bulldozing her way through the forest. It was not the time to burden her with his heart problem. Pennyworth did not want her sympathy; getting the London Times back to its rightful position as the premier newspaper in the capital was his top priority and it appeared that Violet had struck gold. His dodgy ticker could wait a while longer.

'Stop.'

Violet reached the clearing and stopped in her tracks. Pennyworth caught up with her, huffing and puffing.

'You sure you're okay?'

'It would seem I spent all my energy rescuing some lunatic who jumped off a bridge.'

Violet cracked a rare smile, Pennyworth's tactic for changing the subject successful.

The wind chimes that hung from the trees were perfectly still and silent.

'It was strung up between two trees, right in the middle.'

'And the dead body?'

Violet glanced around and pointed towards a tree. 'That one.'

Pennyworth struggled to see anything from where they were stood. 'We need a crystal-clear photograph that nobody can argue with,' he informed her. Violet surveyed the area. Watch parts were still scattered across the ground, and nothing seemed to be any different than it was from her first visit. She prayed it was the case. Bumping into the killer unrestrained was not a prospect she relished. As they crept further into the clearing, a slight breeze rattled the wind chimes but neither Violet nor Pennyworth noticed; they were far too focussed on what might lay ahead. Pennyworth glanced at the trees around them.

'Looks like our killer likes to keep souvenirs.'

The mystery of the missing workers was solved as there wasn't just the one body, as Violet now saw. In each tree surrounding the clearing was one of the missing factory workers, embedded within the bark. Violet turned away, unable to maintain eye contact with any of the lifeless bodies.

'You think Threadbare knows?' she asked.

'Do you care if he does?' responded Pennyworth. 'People will speculate and draw their own conclusion.'

Violet felt a sense of satisfaction knowing that Threadbare would, at least, be made to squirm once this news was in the public domain. Whether he knew about it or not, one thing was for certain, given the nature and current condition of the deceased, there was no way they had met their demise at the hands of anything human.

Just then, Pennyworth saw it, the killer of which Violet had spoken.

'Heavens above.'

Any doubts Pennyworth had soon evaporated

as he gazed upon the magnificent creature. There it was, as real as anything else he had ever seen. He couldn't take his eyes off it. Now she saw it again, neither could Violet. Despite it clearly not being human, it was truly a marvel to behold. Whoever, or whatever, had made it had accomplished a masterful piece of engineering.

'Whatever this thing has done, if it doesn't capture public imagination, I don't know what will,' remarked Pennyworth, in complete awe.

Despite impressing his observers, Hanz was in a bad way, still strung up between the trees but missing bits and pieces from various places. His inability to answer any of Augustus's questions about the whereabouts of the Hands of Time had led to them being separated from his body.

Even if Hanz could speak, he had no knowledge of what she sought. The Hands of Time was as much folklore and myth to him as it was to her which was why she thoroughly checked every timepiece she came across, ensuring it wasn't the device she sought. When she was satisfied it wasn't, she discarded it and tossed it aside. Realising she was getting nowhere with Hanz, Augustus had given up and considered a different approach. If Mr. Moretimer genuinely valued his astonishing achievement of engineering then, surely, he would come to its rescue. That is when she would strike. What she hadn't counted on was the intervention of Violet and Pennyworth. Violet tip toed closer towards Hanz. She felt braver this time around but wasn't sure whether it was because she had the back up of Pennyworth or if it was because Hanz looked like he was unconscious. 'Careful,' whispered Pennyworth, 'I've saved you once already.'

Up close, Violet couldn't help but be even more impressed by Hanz. She hadn't been able to see before, but in such proximity, the level of detail and craftsmanship was impressive.

Beautiful, even.

You don't look like a killer to me.

Pennyworth attached the camera to the tripod, ready to snap a photograph that would surely become front page news not only in London but across the country and even the globe. He held up the flash and pressed his eye up to the viewfinder but stopped short of taking the picture.

'You should do this.'

Pennyworth stepped away from the camera and invited Violet to do the honours.

'It's your story.'

Violet hadn't been used to any form of generosity from an employer before and she appreciated the gesture, much more than Pennyworth realised. She stepped behind the camera and looked through the viewfinder, her finger pressing down on the shutter button.

At that very moment, Hanz awoke and writhed around, thrusting violently in his organic shackles. Pennyworth recoiled in horror and Violet's finger slipped off the shutter button, momentarily shaken. As soon as Hanz saw Violet, he settled, relieved it wasn't Augustus back for a second round of unwelcome tinkering. He recognised her from before. Violet returned the stare and looked deep into his eyes, trying to read and get the measure of him. She felt pity; the over-riding feeling she got from Hanz's vacant, emotionless eyes was one of sorrow. Violet stepped away from the camera and walked towards him.

'Steady on,' warned Pennyworth, 'that thing killed all those men.'

The more Violet looked at Hanz, the more she considered an alternative.

What if it didn't kill them? What if it was something else?

'If this is our killer, why would it be tied up like this?'

'Maybe somebody got here before we did and saved the police a job?' responded Pennyworth. Violet surveyed the area. The forest seemed a lot darker than it did a few moments ago and droplets of rain fell from above. 'Either way, we've got our story. Killer or not, people will believe this thing is capable of such atrocities.' After spending so many years in journalism, Pennyworth had realised that the general public were much like a courtroom jury. The most experienced lawyer armed with the most convincing evidence would have had a hard time defending something that looked like Hanz. Impressive or not, he was different and in the eyes of society different was rarely well received. It wasn't Pennyworth's job to worry about that, anyway. All he had to do was present the facts and let the reader decide.

Bravery much increased, Violet reached out and touched Hanz's face. He did not flinch and seemed to welcome a human touch.

'I really don't think this thing is responsible.'

She noticed a name inscribed down the side of the mask.

Hanz.

Pennyworth pulled Violet back behind the camera and urged her to take the photograph.

'It does not matter one hoot what we think. We just report the facts that multiple men have been killed and embalmed in tree trunks and that this thing was in the vicinity. Let the reader be judge, jury and executioner.'

Hanz wriggled again.

It isn't trying to hurt us; it's trying to free itself.

Violet picked up a sharp rock and hacked at the vines which held Hanz prisoner.

'Have you lost your mind?' Pennyworth asked.

Thunder roared and cracked each time Violet struck until Hanz clattered onto the ground, free from the clutches of nature. Not wasting any time, he scrambled to his feet and wobbled away out of the clearing and into the forest.

'It's getting away and we still don't have a photograph,' yelled Pennyworth. Violet thought for a moment; Hanz was a story in himself, and people would be intrigued as to what he was, killer or not, although she had convinced herself that the former wasn't the case. They would both be dead if he was. She yanked the camera from the tripod and sprinted after Hanz.

'Be careful with that!' cried Pennyworth. Rain droplets poured from the treetops above and pooled into puddles on the already muddy ground. 'If you'd listened to me, we would have what we need already and would be on our way back to the city.'

In Pennyworth's haste to keep up with Violet, he dropped a roll of camera film from his pocket.

Hanz ran as though he was running for his life and if Violet had seen the large vines which snaked across the ground at breakneck pace behind them, she would have known that was exactly what he was doing.

When he reached the edge of the forest, Hanz had no idea how long he had been running for. A field, populated with tall golden crops, much taller than he was, greeted him. He welcomed the sight of something other than trees.

It felt good to be out in the open, even though the rain still poured down from above. Hanz wondered for a moment if he might rust but that was the least of his worries. He couldn't be sure just how big the field was or how far the rows and rows of crops went on for, his view obscured by the height of them. They reminded him of the narrow London streets, which didn't sit well with him given his experience of them so far. London and, more specifically, home, was on the other side of the forest but, as far as he was concerned, home might as well have been on the other side of the world.

A rustling noise startled Hanz and he ran into the field, brushing aside corn and barley as he went until it opened into a huge crop circle. Nothing grew there, as if it had been cleared for something.

On the opposite side of the circle, from out of

the crops, strutted the Von Kargers. None of the three brothers said a word, just strolled towards the centre of the empty circle. In one hand, Artemis held a leather briefcase which he placed down atop the ground. On the palm of his other hand, sat a clockroach. Hanz watched on from the distance, curious as to why he would be in possession of such a thing. He knew the Von Kargers were antique dealers, but they were also mercenaries of sorts, selling their unique skills to the highest bidder, regardless of which side of wrong or right they sat. Their presence unnerved Hanz. Were they working for Augustus? Or somebody else?

The clockroach scurried from Artemis's hand, across his chest, down his other arm and settled on top of the briefcase. Two fangs shot out of its mouth and bit down into the leather before it buried its way inside. Artemis looked Hanz dead in the eyes and smiled an unsettling smile. He tipped his bowler hat to Hanz then led Boris and Chlodwig back into the crops. The briefcase popped open, and a ray of light burst from inside it, shining all the way up to the heavens above. Hanz felt compelled to take a closer look but, as he took a wobbly step towards it, a clown climbed out from the briefcase!

At first, Hanz thought it was an illusion. He had seen enough of his father's tricks to know that everything was not always as it seemed. The clown juggled three balls and cycled on a unicycle, doing laps around the crop circle. It had deep black eyes, a stark contrast to the white make-up that covered its face. Hanz watched, mesmerised by the oddity's act, until something else appeared.

A strongman heaved a huge atlas stone out of the briefcase then climbed out and lifted it high above his head. For certain, it was no illusion. What was happening was very real indeed.

One by one, all manner of circus acts climbed out of the suitcase.

More clowns pranced around and poked each other.

Fire breathers blasted flames from their mouths into the atmosphere, singeing the crops on the edges of the circle.

Sword swallowers shoved sharp steel down their throats and into their bellies.

Contortionists walked on their hands; legs tangled around their necks like some sort of human pretzel.

Trapeze acts set up a frame and swung from side to side, high above the field.

A bearded lady stroked facial hair that Mr. Moretimer himself would have been proud of.

Animals - lions, tigers, elephants, monkeys, and exotic birds, uncaged and free to roam the field appeared from within the briefcase, a real sight to behold. Despite their unique differences, everything that popped out of the briefcase had one thing in common: Jet black eyes.

Finally, in an explosion of light accompanied by fireworks which lit up the dark, clouded sky, a full big top tent erupted from within the briefcase and popped itself up, completely filling the crop circle. A blood red carpet rolled out and stopped perfectly at

Hanz's feet, showing him the way to the entrance. A Ringmaster, garbed in a bright red jacket and top hat danced out of the tent and cracked a whip at Hanz's feet.

'Roll up, roll up; the greatest freak show on Earth is in town!'

Freak show?

It looked like a circus to Hanz but, the closer the Ringmaster got, the more he understood the choice of words.

The Ringmaster's face was heavily scarred, as if he had been burned in a fire, disfigured all down one side. Like everything else that had appeared from the briefcase, his eyes were black as the night. Not a pretty sight but, then again, neither was Hanz. The Ringmaster put an arm around him.

'Step right up and see the fantastical freaks within. The world may have cast them out but here they are welcomed, no! Celebrated, with open arms.'

Hanz knew what it was like to be different.

He was different.

The Ringmaster's words were music to Hanz's mechanical ears. He allowed himself to be seduced inside, his escape from Augustus put on hold in the strangest of ways. It looked like a circus, but it was like no other anywhere in the Realm of Earth and, although it was free to enter, the cost to exit was much, much higher.

- XXIII -

A BRIEF HISTORY
OF TIME

*F*ifteen.

Mr. Moretimer repaired another tear in the Meridian. Problem was, no sooner had he worked his magic than another two appeared.

By the sands of the hourglass, I'm far too old for this!

As he traversed the rocky summit of Mount Evercanever, Mr. Moretimer looked like a man carrying the weight of the world on his shoulders. When he finally reached The Constance, he stopped and took a moment to appreciate his amazing feat of architecture. Each Father Time before him had kept time in their own way but The Constance was his creation. It had stood the test of time and served its purpose, but the tide was turning and Mr. Moretimer felt it in his bones. He wandered through the vast halls, taking everything in and savouring the moment, as if he somehow knew it might be the final time that he would make the journey. He had been the longest serving Father Time since the Order of Fortellers had created the role. It had been his privilege and honour to have served for as long as he had but it hadn't been without sacrifice. Hiding from Augustus had meant going into self-imposed isolation but there had always been the possibility that, one day, she might find him. For that reason, Mr. Moretimer vowed never to fall in love. Love was a fantastic emotion, the most powerful and enduring of all emotions, in fact, but it would make him vulnerable. Only having to worry about himself meant there was nothing she could ever use to leverage against him. Not taking a wife meant he was unable to ever be a real father and that was the one thing he had always struggled to come to terms with. As his loneliness dragged on, Mr. Moretimer could stand it no longer and took matters into his own hands. He knew he would never have a real son so he created something that he hoped would stand in as an alternative:

Hanz.

The one thing he deprived his creation of was a voice. If it could talk then it could be used against him to give up his location. From the moment he was created, Mr. Moretimer kept Hanz close by, always at his side and always within his reach so no harm could come to him. Despite the physical company Hanz provided and the care that Mr. Moretimer afforded him, there had only ever been one thing in his life that he truly loved. It had always been there, an ever-faithful soul mate that stood by him through the long years of isolation and never once wavered.

Time.

It was all he had ever had, and he felt entirely at one with it. But, as the years passed, it had wearied him and taken its toll. His time was almost up.

The eleventh hour is nigh.

As he passed by wall after wall of books, Mr. Moretimer reflected on the events he had presided over. Monumental moments when humanity changed and progressed; the signing of the US Declaration of Independence, the beauty and creativeness inspired by the Renaissance period and the abolishment of slavery. He felt an immense sense of pride that these events happened on his watch but there had also been terrible times which highlighted just how low humanity could sink if it went unchallenged. In the mind of Mr. Moretimer, there was one glaring issue with history and it was one that he could do nothing about.

Some things do not age well.

It was all a matter of perspective, and each passing generation had its own ideas about wrong and right as they became increasingly advanced. The birth of one great era meant the death of another; one person's hero was another's villain and so on. Regardless of how each generation might look upon the past, whether it judged it as good or bad, Mr. Moretimer believed history served a great purpose:

To remind humanity.

The Constance had been built for that exact reason; to protect history and ensure it was remembered as it had happened. If the Realm of Time was destroyed, it would all be lost and if humanity could not be reminded of its greatest failures, then there would always exist the possibility that it might repeat them. Mr. Moretimer was the first Father to document all of time for such a purpose. His stroll down memory lane took him through the Hall of Fathers. He admired the statue of every one of his predecessors, shrines that the Order of Foretellers had carved for him so that when the time came, he could tell the tale of the great legacy of Father Time to his chosen successor. Solomon Solstice, the first Father Time, stood tall and proud. Mr. Moretimer felt insignificant beside him. He was the only Father to be handpicked by the Order of Foretellers. He had overseen the dawn of time, when the solar system and the planets were formed, and had laid the foundations for all who succeeded him to build on.

I wish I could have seen it; oh, how incredible it must have been!

Mr. Moretimer knew it was possible. He had resisted the urge to rewind the Hands of Time himself so he could see the beginning of all things but, whenever he felt tempted, he always remembered the words that had been ingrained into him by his predecessor:

Time is constant.

As he wandered past each statue, Mr. Moretimer reflected on each of their achievements. Some reigned longer than others and some had been more successful than others. A Father's time was over when he felt he could no longer keep pace with it. Mr. Moretimer had never doubted himself, always optimistic about his own ability but the world was changing and advancing at an incredible pace with which he could no longer keep up. He had never, ever forgotten anything, but he found his memory failing him regularly. Given the number of things he had to remember, that was a major problem.

It was time for some new blood.

When he reached the eleventh podium, Mr. Moretimer sat down before it. He pondered the day the eleventh Father, Christopher Chronos, had passed on his powers and handed over responsibility for the Hands of Time. Despite his flaky memory, he remembered the moment vividly. At a time when it was a miracle to see it, he was initiated on the day of his twelfth birthday. Chronos's words had stuck with him throughout his stewardship:

"You have only two jobs. The first; keep time ticking on. It must remain constant. Humans will make the same mistakes over and over, but it is not your job to interfere, no matter how much you may want to. It is no coincidence that a sundial is circular; time has no end. It is infinite but will repeat itself. Just as the shadow of the sun crosses the same markers each day and just as the sand in an hourglass recycles itself when turned over, civilisations will rise and then fall, again and again. You must keep faith that humanity will recover and be better than it was the time before. Never, ever interfere."

It was also in that moment that Mr. Moretimer first saw the Hands of Time. When Chronos handed the device over to him, time became his responsibility.

Chronos's words proved to be true. Time and time again, Mr. Moretimer witnessed civilisations come to fruition, prosper, and then crash down through arrogance and ignorance. The Greeks did it, the Egyptians did it and the Romans did it. Mr.

Moretimer hated watching them fail and so vowed to help humanity. Alongside the two jobs Chronos had outlined, he took it upon himself to help humans break the endless cycle and the Constance was born. Even so, it was inevitable that change would occur but, from then on, each time humanity destroyed itself, when it rose from the ashes it learned from its mistakes and advanced itself just a little bit further.

But now, on Mr. Moretimer's watch, humanity faced certain doom from which it would never recover. If Augustus took possession of the Hands of Time, he would go down in history as the Father who failed to keep time the way it was meant to be.

Constant.

Mr. Moretimer gazed towards the currently empty twelfth podium.

My podium.

When his time was up, he too would be immortalised in stone, a permanent reminder of the history he helped write.

He would have preferred to be on the right side of it.

Just before he made his way out of the room, through a door that resided between the twelfth and the first podium, Mr. Moretimer pondered the future. When his reign as Father Time was over, he would need to bestow the honour on his successor. He had already made his choice. The decision had been made years ago, when he was instructed to find the "Thirteenth" by the Order of Foretellers.

Just like any device which told the time, there were only twelve numbers on the Hands of Time so thirteen was something that had not been considered when the great device was created. The Order of Foretellers told a prophecy of the end of time where an evil would descend on the universe and only the one known as the Thirteenth would be able to stop it. This incarnation of Father Time would be the one to bring the universe out of darkness and into the light of a new dawn.

Mr. Moretimer searched far and wide for the Thirteenth; he went to the ends of the Realm of Earth until he finally found what he was looking for - a baby boy, born exactly the way the Order of Foretellers had described. After a series of unfortunate events befell the boy, Mr. Moretimer intervened and brought him before the Order of Foretellers to seek their blessing. However, once the baby was confirmed to become the Thirteenth, his life was in immediate danger. Formally identified, he was known to the darkness, which would stop at nothing to destroy him and end the prophecy. Mr. Moretimer had no choice but to hide him away until it was time. When it was, the Thirteenth would have to choose to become the next steward of time. Mr. Moretimer believed in choice and consequence and that an individual should be responsible for their own destiny. If the Thirteenth chose not to take up the honour of becoming a Father, then it was not meant to be and the prophecy a fallacy.

Mr. Moretimer recounted the remainder of Chronos's words:

"The second job is just as important as the first: keep the darkness at bay. For good to exist so must evil

otherwise how can a good deed be judged? Darkness falls every evening but then the dawn comes and gives way to light. That is just enough to maintain the balance of the universe. If more of it were to enter the Realm of Earth, it would consume it. Keep it at bay until the coming of the Thirteenth."

Mr. Moretimer had become so fixated on hiding from Augustus that he had neglected the second responsibility. Augustus was an imminent threat to humanity, and she needed to be dealt with, but he knew she was not the darkness of which the Order of Foretellers spoke. Cracks and tears were appearing frequently in the Meridian and the darkness was seeping into the Realm of Earth in the form of clockroaches.

He stepped through the thirteenth door and into an atrium blanketed in total darkness. Flame lit torches mounted on the walls exploded into fireballs, seemingly brought to life by the presence of Mr. Moretimer. They highlighted a stone staircase that wound down, even deeper into the heart of Mount Evercanever, so deep it was impossible to see just how far into the mountain it went. On his descent, Mr. Moretimer passed through three solid stone doors, as thick as they were wide. As he reached each one, he heaved back huge iron bolts, so stiff it was as if they hadn't been moved for centuries. With a few orchestral flicks of his wrists, he commanded the doors to open and they promptly obliged. On the opposite side of each door, there were no keyholes, bolts, or locks; whatever Mr. Moretimer was headed down towards was meant to stay there.

When he finally reached the bottom, the staircase led into a huge cavern in the heart of the mountain. Mammoth sized stalactites hung from the roof, developed over thousands and thousands of years, and the stone steps were replaced with precarious looking rope bridges that zig-zagged from one side of the cave to another. About fifty or so feet below, a lake of molten rock filled the entire cave. It hissed, swirled, and spat as Mr. Moretimer braved the bridges, making his way towards its surface.

As close to the lake as he could get without being burned alive, Mr. Moretimer conducted and the molten rock parted, revealing scorched, rocky ground beneath it. Like Moses crossing the Red Sea, Mr. Moretimer shuffled between the partition of lava. At the centre was a small metal grate, chained by twelve humongous padlocks, which covered a mine shaft. Any ordinary metal would have melted under the searing heat of the lava, but this had been forged by the Order of Foretellers themselves. He knew he had to go down the shaft to find the source of the clockroach leak but the thought of what he might face terrified him to his core. He was no match for it. In his younger days, he had battled it once and had managed to keep it at bay but now, in his twilight, he would not stand a chance.

Mr. Moretimer conducted and, one by one, the padlocks unlocked. The grate seemed to take an age to open. It raised up and crashed onto the scorched ground with a thunderous echo which shook the cavern. The stench that crept out from the shaft polluted Mr. Moretimer's nostrils and he turned away in disgust. Carved repeatedly, all over the back of the metal grate, engraved in all directions, in different shapes and sizes, was one word.

Makutu.

Mr. Moretimer pushed the name from his mind. He dared not even think it. To carve a word into metal fashioned by the Order of Foretellers was no small feat. It could withstand the heat of molten lava so no way could it have been done with any ordinary blade or knife. The old man shuddered at the thought of the fingernails which had no doubt been responsible as he stepped down into the shaft and onto a wooden platform. Rotten beyond belief, it creaked and groaned, a miracle that it didn't splinter beneath his weight. He grabbed a rope attached to a pulley and ran it through his hands. The descent down the mine shaft was rickety and perilous. Pieces of the wooden platform snapped away and shattered without any notice. Each time a piece broke, he grabbed the rope and clung to it, just hoping he didn't awaken what resided in the depths below. A clockroach scuttled up the pulley rope and across his hand. He grabbed it and squashed it, black liquid seeping out. The creatures were eating away at the rotting wood of the platform.

I better get moving.

Unlike before, during his reflection in the Constance, Mr. Moretimer wanted to be in and out of the mine as quickly as he could.

When he reached the bottom, it was scorching hot, like he had descended into the depths of hell itself. Mr. Moretimer grabbed a wooden torch that was attached to the wall beside the lowered platform. He conducted his hands and the torch combusted into fire. The flames were a damp flicker, however, and never reached their potential. Only the dimmest of light was afforded, as if the darkness he found himself surrounded by somehow fought it off and held it back. The ground moved beneath Mr. Moretimer's feet and he immediately knew what it was.

Clockroaches.

Lots of clockroaches.

Absolutely everywhere, crawling and scuttling all over each other, were thousands, if not millions, of the pests. They completely carpeted the ground, leaving not an inch of it uncovered.

CRUNCH!

With each step, Mr. Moretimer crushed the creatures beneath his boot. He wouldn't lose any sleep over it but the sickening sound itself turned his stomach. The mine shaft was a series of tunnels dug through the mountain and propped up by unstable wooden beams which creaked under the sheer weight of the earth above. They had once been strong and rigid, but time had taken its toll and they looked as though they might give way at any moment.

Mr. Moretimer held up the torch which ever so slightly lit the way ahead. He had a choice of three tunnels; one was packed full of clockroaches, all over the ground and ceiling. The other two were insect-free. He knew which one he would rather not venture down but, unluckily for him, that was the path he had to take.

The tunnels were like mazes, and it would be quite easy for somebody to get lost in them for years. They had been designed and built that way by Solomon Solstice, under the instructions of the Order of Foretellers. Much like the Ancient Greek labyrinth in which the Minotaur had resided, the mine acted as a prison. What Solstice had banished within it was never meant to find its way out. On the one occasion it had, Mr. Moretimer had acted and forced it back within, keeping it at bay as he had been charged.

CRUNCH! CRUNCH! CRUNCH!

Mr. Moretimer tracked the clockroach trail but the light from the torch faded and left him consumed in total darkness, the never-ending scuttle of the clockroaches his only clue that he was anywhere at all. He conducted his hands and the torch re-lit and flickered intermittently, trying to fight its way back to life but it kept fading, always suppressed.

It is still down here, of that there is no doubt.

The light stabilised just enough so that Mr. Moretimer could see through tightly squinted eyes. As he ventured further through the tunnel, something on the walls caught his attention. There were certain places the clockroaches skirted around and avoided. At first, he thought he was looking at Egyptian style hieroglyphics, but it wasn't the case. Just like on the back of the mine shaft grate, engraved into cave walls and the many wooden pillars and planks which kept the tunnels from collapsing, was the word again.

Makutu.

Mr. Moretimer looked away. If he let it get into his head, it would break into his thoughts. If it broke into his thoughts, it would creep into his brain and if it crept into his brain, it would seep into his entire body and consume him. Eventually, Mr. Moretimer managed to shake the thought and continued down the tunnel. To his surprise, the further he went, the lighter it got. If there was natural light, then that meant he must be closing in on the source of the clockroach leak. He hurried, as fast as he could, until he reached the end of the tunnel and, when he did, he stopped and stared in horror at the sight that greeted him.

A skyscraper of a clockroach nest.

The tunnel opened into a ginormous cave which the nest filled, towering all the way up to the roof and spreading across the walls. Clockroaches spewed out of it, like lava pouring from a volcano. To make matters worse, the light had indeed been coming from there and, when he saw the source of it, it confirmed Mr. Moretimer's worst fear. Hundreds of tears, all different sizes, some as small as pennies and others much bigger, all around the cave; in the walls, in the ground and even in thin air. His eyes flitted between each one of them, affording him a glimpse of the Realm of Earth on the other side. Rain drops even poured through the bigger tears into the Realm of Time. Clockroach after clockroach buried its way through the tears, becoming larger with each invading insect. The darkness had found a weak point and was laying siege to it.

The Meridian was under attack.

This is too far gone. By the time I repair one, another ten will have appeared!

The clockroaches paid Mr. Moretimer no attention whatsoever as they continued their mission, chomping and chewing their way through the Meridian and creating more tears. They were not interested in him. They were doing the bidding of something else which had only one target.

It truly is relentless.

Mr. Moretimer found himself thinking the word again and did his best to push it from his mind.

Makutu.

Lord of Darkness.

There was nothing Mr. Moretimer could do to repair the tears, not on his own. The task had become too big for him. All he could do was pray that the prophecy was true; the Thirteenth would bring the universe out of the darkness when it inevitably escaped into the Realm of Earth.

It's all my fault. I could have prevented this, prophecy, or no prophecy.

Mr. Moretimer's thoughts changed in an instant.

Something had happened.

It played out right before his eyes.

Jack and Hanz were in serious, serious trouble.

- XXIV -

JACK'S PURSUIT

*J*ACK surveyed the clearing and weighed up the possibilities. He decided there were only two:

Augustus had destroyed Hanz or, by some miracle, Hanz had escaped.

What do you think, Edgar?

Jack looked towards the bear for advice and, as usual, Edgar stared back at him, vacantly.

If she had the Hands of Time, surely time would be rewinding?

Given the heavy rain and constant cracks of thunder, Jack deduced that the second was the more likely scenario and Mother Nature was making her displeasure known to the world. However, the forest was huge and Hanz could have been anywhere. Jack would have to search the entire thing; he knew he couldn't go back to the old man alone. The fate of the entire world was in his hands!

No pressure.

As Jack pressed onwards, he felt something push up into the sole of his shoe. He glanced down and saw an object laid discarded on the ground, a clue as to Hanz's whereabouts, maybe.

Jack picked it up.

A roll of camera film.

Who would be taking photographs out here in the middle of nowhere?

He had only ever seen a few cameras in his time on the streets and they always belonged to journalists. Unless a person was rich, a camera was not a household luxury. It made him think about his family photograph; his parents must have been financially well-off. If the mansion in the background wasn't proof enough, the fact they even had a family photograph backed up the theory. Only those with money would have been able to afford a private shoot.

Jack dragged his thoughts back to the situation at hand, it was not the time to be daydreaming. He fiddled with the roll of camera film. It was cutting edge technology and he felt privileged to have it in his hands. He had heard people talk about something called Kodak film. Up until recently, camera images had always been captured on glass plate negatives. Film was a revolutionary creation.

Whoever was here is a professional.

Had they helped Hanz escape? Whatever had happened, Jack was no wiser. The film could have been there for days or weeks, even.

Well, Edgar, this will get us some marigolds if this all goes pear shaped.

Jack tucked the camera film into his pocket and searched the clearing. He noticed the wind chimes, dangling from tree branches, each one swaying and chiming in the breeze. For a moment, he was back in the Forest of the Living, only with the wind chimes replacing the pocket watches.

A humming, singing sound filled the air. Jack searched all around for the source, glancing here, there, and everywhere. Trees swayed violently from side to side and the wind chimes sounded in unison. **She's here, somewhere.**

Not wanting to hang around to find out, Jack ran deeper into the forest. If he was going to find Hanz, he needed to do it quickly. He ran and ran, as fast as his legs could physically go until he could see the clearing no more. He wasn't quite sure how far he had gone but the forest was almost pitch dark and he found himself stumbling over things, tripping, and tumbling on his way through the foliage.

SPLASH!

Jack fell, head-first into a muddy puddle. As he wiped mud from his eyes and water from his ears, he heard a unique sound.

A pipe organ dancing its way through a song. The sound was unmistakable.

A circus organ!

He followed the noise, which got louder as he went.

If I ever go in another forest again, it will be too soon.

The streets seemed a far more safe and normal option to Jack, even despite the dirt, famine and disease that plagued the cobbles. The Forest of the Living was the more appealing of the three but still, Jack got the impression he had only seen a snapshot of it and there would be many more surprises deeper within it that the old man had failed to mention.

The sound of the pipe organ was almost deafening as Jack got closer to its location. At the very edge of the forest was a corn field, with crops so high Jack could not see over them. All he could see was something protruding in the distance, sticking out above the corn. Convinced he was on to something, Jack ventured through the crops until he was greeted by a strange sight.

A big top circus tent.

In the middle of a corn field?

Jack wasn't so sure why it appeared odd. Nothing seemed so far-fetched anymore or out of the realms of possibility. It did occur to him that the old man might have had a hand in it or, at the least, know what it was doing there in the first place.

A Ringmaster strutted out from the entrance towards him, his face heavily scarred down one side and eyes completely black.

'Roll up, roll up! Admission is always free for the Circus of the Night.'

The old codger has definitely got something to do with this.

Jack glanced at Edgar, dirtier than ever thanks to the trip through the forest. The teddy bear's expressionless face somehow seemed to warn against a trip to the circus.

Captain Nemo would've never set sail if he had you as his first mate.

Jack hurried through the entrance of the big top tent. In his mind, it was a win-win situation. There was always the possibility that Hanz had also stumbled upon the circus, so it made sense to check it out. But, even if he hadn't, the quickest way to anywhere was in a straight line so going through the tent would be much faster than navigating all the way around it. Plus, it gave him an excuse to check out the circus and be a child again, even if only for a moment.

As Jack vanished into the Circus of the Night, tree roots and vines slithered through the crops and surrounded the tent, ready to pounce. The Ringmaster, completely unafraid, stood his ground.

'Keep out of this, Witch; your petty vendetta wilts in insignificance to the will of Makutu.'

The Ringmaster's voice was different. It was deep and animal-like, monstrous even, like he had been possessed by something. The roots and vines hissed and cursed but did not retreat. The Ringmaster opened his mouth, so wide that he no longer looked human, and let out a blood-curdling roar. The ground cracked like an earthquake had shaken it, opening it up and leaving a gaping abyss which ended the advance of nature. The Ringmaster smirked as he marched into the tent, the tree roots retreating into the forest.

Huge cumulonimbus clouds formed in the sky, directly above. There may have been other mystical forces at work in the Realm of Earth, but Lady Augustus had her own agenda, and she wasn't going to let anybody, or anything, get in her way, no matter how evil or terrifying it may be.

- XXV -

CIRCUS OF HORRORS

*H*ANZ wobbled through the backstage area of the circus and recalled his trip down the London streets.

The freakish appearances of the circus acts were like something out of a nightmare, but he felt comfortable with them. They didn't stare at him or turn away in fear, as his father had suggested others would.

They admired him.

The individuals he had bumped into in the city had frightened him and pushed him aside but in the Circus of the Night the outcasts of society welcomed him with open arms.

A hulk of a woman approached. Hanz knew the difference between a man and a woman; she certainly had all the features that distinguished one from the other, but she was incredibly muscular. Her biceps bulged so much that her clothes barely fit her, huge veins popped out of every muscle, like an inflated road map. She looked like she had the ability to crush a man alive.

Or possibly, even eat.

The woman towered over Hanz, who was

completely dwarfed by her physical presence. He guessed she must have easily been over seven feet tall; an impressive feat for a man, let alone a woman. Yet, he was not afraid.

The woman crouched down before him and spoke with a heavy Eastern European accent in the softest tone he had ever heard.

'You are incredible.'

She studied his features with jet black eyes.

'Do you mind?'

Hanz shook his head, and the woman ran a finger down his metal face.

'A thing of beauty,' the woman announced, 'a rare treasure.'

Although Mr. Moretimer had often told Hanz how special he was, it was the first time in his life that he felt it. The woman smiled. 'My name is Roxanna, strongest woman on the planet.' Hanz admired the crowd of other so-called freaks who gathered around him, each of them gazing upon him with warm smiles and awe-filled eyes. 'Strange, isn't it? The first time you feel it. In here, you are accepted for who you are,' Roxanna lamented, 'Unlike out there.'

Fingers reached out and touched Hanz, every freak in attendance wanting to feel his presence like some sort of Messiah. He enjoyed the attention.

A small child covered head to toe in hair slid out from the crowd and held out a hand. Hanz shook it and noticed the long claws which protruded from his fingers. He also had fangs for teeth, which gave him a speech impediment. 'My name is Vladimir. A privilege to meet you.'

Privilege?

If Hanz could have replied, he would have. Instead, he looked away, ashamed by his inability to speak and return the friendly gesture. Roxanna put a reassuring hand on his shoulder. 'Here, you have a voice, even if you cannot project it yourself.' The kind words of the big, scary looking woman comforted Hanz. He felt at home. After all, the freaks were all just like him.

Abnormal.

'Hanz!' A familiar voice broke the trance which Hanz found himself slipping into.

It's him.

Jack rushed towards him.

Hanz's peaceful calmness gave way to anger.

'We need to go, right now. You aren't safe here.'

If you hadn't stolen from father, I wouldn't even be here.

'Come on, the old man sent me to bring you home.'

The mention of Mr. Moretimer suddenly brought mixed emotions, something that had never happened before. On one hand, Hanz was reminded of his comfortable but lonely life in the shop. But, on the other, it stirred up feelings of resentment. He had been hidden away from the world for so long, a world that his father had constantly told him would reject him.

He lied to me. These people love me. Why would he do that?

Hanz was torn. He stood between Jack - the way back to the life he had always known - and

Roxanna - the new life he had just discovered.

'Jack Picklewick!' Roxanna exclaimed, almost as if she was familiar with him.

Jack was taken aback. He was certain he had never crossed paths with the woman before. With a face that would haunt even the hardest person in their nightmares, she wasn't the forgettable type.

Our reputation really does proceed us, Edgar.

The circus freaks immediately lost interest in Hanz and surrounded Jack. Instead of the loving family that accepted Hanz as one of their own, they circled Jack like hungry sharks stalking their prey. The black of their eyes grew deeper as they closed in around him.

'Do I know you?' asked Jack.

'I know you,' Roxanna replied, grinning like a starved wolf would look at a long-awaited meal.

Hanz watched on, disappointed that he was no longer the focus of attention.

He's doing it again, causing problems for me.

Roxanna's voice changed. When she spoke, it sounded the same as the Ringmaster's voice, like she had been possessed.

'I know you very well indeed.'

Clockroaches spilled out from Roxanna's mouth and descended on Jack, who screamed and tripped over, landing on his backside. His nightmare seemed to follow him everywhere. As soon as Hanz saw the insects, he realised it was all an illusion, a trap set up by the Von Kargers on behalf of the one who his father had told him never to even think about.

Makutu.

FLASH.

A puff of smoke rose into the air and accompanied the flash of light. Roxanna, Vladimir, and all the other circus freaks clawed at their eyes, the light burning them. The clockroaches scurried away in search of darkness.

Jack glanced across the backstage area and saw two people; a woman hid behind a camera and a man stood behind her, holding a flash above her head.

'Got it!' exclaimed Flemming.

Where have I seen her before?

Jack racked his brain until it came flooding back to him.

I stole her pen!

Happy they had what they had gone for, Flemming and Pennyworth ran for the exit. Jack turned towards Hanz, who had made a run for it himself in the opposite direction. He scrambled to his feet and pursued Hanz, dodging through the crowd of circus freaks who still scratched and clawed at their eyes.

'Wait!' yelled Jack.

His cry fell on deaf ears as Hanz escaped through a pair of huge red curtains which hung down from the top of the tent all the way to the floor. Jack brushed through them and found himself in a small room full of sword swallowers, all practicing their act with long shiny blades shoved all the way down their throats. Hanz was nowhere to be seen. On the opposite side of the room was another set of curtains. There was nowhere else Hanz could possibly have gone, not from what Jack could see anyway. As he was about to resume his pursuit, the sword swallowers all turned their attention towards him, drawing a variety of equally sharp and strangely shaped swords and pointing them at him. Their eyes turned black and one of them spoke, in the exact same monstrous voice as the Ringmaster and Roxanna.

'It's about time you and I were formally introduced. Maybe you should consider sticking around.'

The sword swallower hurled his weapon with inhuman speed and strength straight at Jack. It shredded his collar and pinned him against the curtain. Like an advancing army, the sword swallowers descended on him, blades raised high in the air. Jack struggled and his shirt collar ripped away, freeing him. He didn't hang around; he had no interest whatsoever in finding out who was so desperate to meet him. He sprinted straight at the crowd of advancing sword swallowers and slid between their legs, ducking, and dodging the razor-sharp blades that were swung and heaved in his direction. Thankful he still had his head attached to his shoulders, he dashed through the second set of curtains.

I've never seen any of these people in my life, how do they know who I am?!

With no time to catch his breath, Jack found himself in another room but, this time, he caught a glimpse of Hanz escaping through another set of curtains on the far side. A group of firebreathers all turned towards him in unison, holding flaming torches. Just like in the previous room, one of them spoke.

'You certainly are the hottest commodity around.'

Multiple infernos raged towards Jack as the firebreathers unleashed their talent on him. The heat was unbearable as the flames licked his face and singed his hair. Seizing his opportunity as the firebreathers reloaded, Jack ran as fast as he could, again ducking and diving beneath and between their legs. Another blast of fire launched in his direction just as he skidded through the curtain, narrowly avoiding being burnt to a crisp.

Could this possibly get any worse?

The room Jack now found himself in was dark. It took a few moments for his eyes to adjust. When he regained his sight, he was filled with relief.

Hanz!

Mr. Moretimer's manufactured apprentice stood just ahead of him. Having had quite enough of the circus for one day, Jack approached him.

'Come on, let's get out of here.'

Hanz never moved, entirely fixated on the darkness ahead. Jack's eyes had adjusted somewhat but he couldn't see whatever it was that Hanz seemed unable to turn away from. Out of the corner of his eye, Jack caught a glimpse of a wooden sign. Five words were painted on it.

Do
Not
Feed
The...

Before Jack read the final word, a snarling roar broke the silence in the room. Jack could only imagine where exactly in the room it had come from, and it felt even more terrifying without his sense of sight. He grabbed Hanz who jumped into defence mode and knocked his hand away.

'Two heads are better than one,' whispered Jack, not wanting to attract whatever beast was lurking ahead in the darkness. Hanz considered his options; maybe a temporary alliance might not be a bad idea, at least until he got back home. Augustus was one thing, but Makutu was something entirely different altogether if what his father had told him was true. Before he had chance to fully make up his mind, the circus freaks, led by Roxanna, spilled through the curtain behind them. A firebreather spat a fountain of flames into the air which illuminated the room. It wasn't a good sight; a huge lion, foaming at the mouth, blocked the only other way out of the room. The flames subsided and left the room in darkness again.

'You cannot run from your destiny,' Roxanna barked in the monstrous voice.

'You're a dead man walking.'

The baying crowd of bloodthirsty freaks prepared to pounce. Jack had no option; he took Hanz by the hand and pulled him along through the darkness, hoping the lion was as blind as they were. The room illuminated once again as the firebreather exhaled a never-ending geyser of flames. He must have had the lungs of an opera singer to keep the room alight for as long as he did. The lion roared, stalking Jack and Hanz who were trapped between the approaching mob and the hungry King of the jungle. Jack noticed something on a wooden crate just beside them.

A lion tamers whip.

He grabbed it and whipped it at the feet of the lion, keeping it at bay. Hanz waved his arms around, like he had some sort of genius plan. Jack handed him the whip, but he snuck away behind the crate, leaving Jack on his own.

'Hey!' shouted Jack as Hanz used his small physical size to his advantage and disappeared entirely from view.

He's just double crossed us, Edgar!

Roxanna and the freaks were within fingertips reach and the lion, eyes as black as night itself, roared and snarled. Either way, Jack was finished. Just then, he felt something brush against the back of his head.

The whip!

He looked up and saw Hanz on top of a galley which hung overhead and ran all the way across the top of the tent, the whip dangling down. The lion pounced, just as Roxanna swung her huge, shovel-like hand at Jack. In the nick of time, he jumped up and heaved himself out of harm's way, climbing up the rope all the way up to the galley where Hanz held out a helping hand.

Disaster struck.

As Jack took Hanz's hand and dragged himself up to safety, Edgar fell from his grasp.

The teddy bear tumbled through the air into the crowd of circus freaks. Jack screamed in horror.

Edgar had been his only real friend, the only one who listened to him in his time on the streets. He couldn't leave him behind, not a cat in hells chance. Inconsolable and not thinking straight, he let go of Hanz, fully prepared to put himself in danger to save his companion. For a moment, Jack felt weightless, like time stood still.

Why am I not going anywhere?

He looked up and saw Hanz clinging onto him with a vice-like grip.

'Let me go! He's my best friend.'

The more Jack struggled, the tighter Hanz held him. It was suicide and surely Jack would see that once he calmed down and saw sense. Eventually, Jack gave up the struggle. Deep down, he knew Hanz was right. They had to get back to the old man; humanity depended on it, Edgar or no Edgar. Jack took one final look as Roxanna picked his ever-faithful companion up from the floor and grinned.

'Sooner or later, your past will catch up with you,' she snarled.

The comment lingered with Jack as Hanz tugged his sleeve and hurried him away along the galley. It ran all the way into another room which was filled from top to bottom with circus luggage and prop boxes. They descended a ladder at the end of the aerial walkway and dropped down into the room. There was only one way into this room and Jack was certain it ran back into the lion's lair, given the position of it in relation to the galley above.

'Quick,' instructed Jack, 'move these boxes, there has to be another way out!'

Although he didn't like being bossed around by him, Hanz knew they had to work together. They tossed suitcases and clothes chests aside but there was no way out to be found. Jack heard footsteps and voices. He tossed a few more suitcases aside and something caught his peepholes, right at the back in the corner of the room. A box but not like the others. It had huge swirly lettering across the front of it, all in capital letters.

THE GREAT HOUDINI'S MAGIC BOX.

'In here,' yelled Jack. Hanz clunked towards him, and the pair shut themselves inside the box as Roxanna and the circus freaks burst through the curtain. 'I know you're in here,' teased Roxanna, 'come out, come out wherever you are.' Roxanna launched boxes aside, one by one, gradually clearing the whole room.

Inside the magic box, Jack and Hanz were squashed up against each other.

'If this is just a standard vanishing act, there should be some sort of false door in here,' said Jack, bashing the sides of the box in search of anything that might give way, a false or trap door. The noise garnered the attention of Roxanna, who was now marching towards it.

'Our destinies are entwined, Jack Picklewick,' she roared in the monstrous voice. As she grabbed the lock on the outside of the box and ripped it clean off, Jack closed his eyes, pulled Hanz close towards him and muttered the only words he could muster that might help.

'Abracadabra!'

Roxanna ripped the door from the box and launched it across the room.

Jack opened his peepholes. He could barely believe it himself; they were stood outside the tent, beside a mountain of wooden crates, animal cages and storage boxes.

'And that is why they call me the Preposterous Picklewick!' he exclaimed, preferring to convince Hanz he had performed some real magic and that he hadn't activated the false door at the back of the box. Hanz was stunned; maybe Jack did have magical powers. Regardless, the scene that greeted them was something out of a horror story.

A behemoth of a black cloud swirled directly above the circus tent and huge tree roots covered it like varicose veins.

'Come on,' cried Jack as he yanked Hanz's arm, 'we need to get back to the shop right now.'

Hanz stared at the circus tent. He had been temporarily misled into believing he had found others like him. Although he knew it had been an elaborate deception designed to lure Jack inside, he felt a great sadness within. He had enjoyed the feeling of knowing he was not the only one who was different and wondered, as he and Jack made their escape through the overgrown crop field, if he would ever experience the feeling again.

Sensing Hanz was no longer inside, the tree roots recoiled from around the tent and resumed their pursuit, slithering after him through the corn.

Back inside the circus tent, the briefcase which had spawned the whole illusion laid open in the centre of the arena. Just as it had when it had appeared, only this time in reverse, everything was sucked back inside it; animals, sword swallowers, fire breathers, Roxanna, and the Ringmaster, who roared at the top of his lungs as he was whipped into a tornado-like whirl of blackness. All were pulled from existence until all that remained was the small, leather briefcase which flipped itself shut.

Everything was as it was before, only the cornfield surrounding an empty crop circle.

From out of the corn, the Von Kargers strutted towards the briefcase, smoking cigarettes, and rolling their moustaches between their fingertips. Artemis picked up the briefcase and clicked the locks shut. A clockroach burrowed out from within it and crawled up onto Artemis's hand, squealing and chirping as it did so. Artemis laughed then spoke to the insect.

'The terms of our arrangement specified that we would provide you with an opportunity and I would be so bold to say that we provided such an opportunity.'

'We most certainly did,' Boris agreed, as he always did.

'Is he saying we are not good for our word?' exclaimed Chlodwig.

As the clockroach scuttled around on Artemis's palm, he noticed something else on the ground that hadn't been there before. He swaggered across to it and adjusted his bowler hat.

'Well, brothers,' said Artemis, 'it seems our extremely well-paid errand is not quite dead in the water just yet.'

Sinister smiles crossed the faces of Boris and Chlodwig as Artemis picked his new discovery up from the ground.

Edgar.

The clockroach crawled from Artemis's hand, burrowed its way through the seam of Jack's lost companion and nestled itself inside.

- XXVI -

HEART TO HEART

*J*ACK brushed corn from his face as he hurried through the never-ending field. He hadn't looked back once but thanks to the clanging and clunking that accompanied Hanz wherever he went, he knew he was still with him.

Eventually, the sprawling field of crops ended, and the unlikely pair reached a wall, made from hundreds of small stones and rocks. A stile had been built in a gap in the wall to allow travellers easy access to the other side.

Why break the habit of a lifetime?

Compared to scaling a London building, it would be a piece of cake. Jack ignored the stile and climbed up the wall. Hanz grabbed his leg and pointed towards the stile.

'This is much more fun. Come on, try it for yourself.'

Jack scrambled up to the top of the wall and offered a helping hand to Hanz, who made no effort to reach out. He seemed reluctant which was hardly a surprise given his past experience with Jack. He was a thief by nature; how trustworthy he was, Hanz was not entirely sure.

'I did try to stop you falling down the sewer and it was you who attacked me, remember?' Jack recounted their first encounter. Hanz was angry at the time but, upon reflection, he did remember Jack reaching out, just as he was now. Maybe he was genuine, after all.

'I say we let bygones be bygones and be friends.'

Friends?

Hanz had never had a friend before. It would be nice to have somebody other than his father. With new-found enthusiasm, Hanz took Jack's hand and clambered up and over the wall. On the opposite side was a grass bank which ran down towards a stream. They wandered down towards it, Hanz leading the way this time and Jack trotting along behind him. He instinctively knew his way back to Mr. Moretimer's Timely Creations, as if the old man had somehow pre-programmed it into him, for if the very scenario that was occurring ever happened.

'Allow me to introduce myself properly, I am the--'

Before Jack could finish his sentence, Hanz whirled around and put a finger up to his lips. He had heard Jack's stage pitch before. Jack rethought his approach.

'I'm Jack; pleased to meet you. Thank you for helping me back there with the lion.'

Jack took Hanz's hand and shook it; Hanz watched as his hand was raised then lowered repeatedly, unfamiliar with the traditional human greeting.

'This is what friends do. It's called a handshake.'

211

It was a nice moment, a brief interlude from the madness that had precluded it. However, unbeknown to either of them, the snaking tree roots and vines slithered and crept up, over and between the drystone wall atop the grass bank, sneaking up on them. They seemed to take their time, as if they were assessing the situation, listening to the conversation as it unfolded.

As the unlikely duo followed the stream, Jack assessed the damage to Hanz; Augustus had really done a job on him. He looked noticeably different since the first time he laid his peepholes on him with parts missing in random places; his chest, legs and head all had pieces removed.

She must have been torturing him for information.

Thankfully, the Hands of Time was still exactly where Mr. Moretimer had put it. If Augustus had known she could have stripped him apart, piece by piece, until she got her hands on it. Luckily for Hanz, she was oblivious.

'I'm sure he will be able to fix you,' said Jack, offering Hanz some encouraging words. Whether or not he was able to feel pain, it couldn't have been pleasant for Hanz, being dismantled before his very eyes. Jack's thoughts turned back to the Hands of Time.

I wonder if it works the same way as a human heart.

Curiosity getting the better of him, he couldn't resist asking.

'Does it keep you alive?

Hanz shrugged his shoulders, unsure what

Jack was referring to. The tree roots and vines crept closer but far enough behind to remain un-noticed.

'You know, the Hands of Time; it's your heart, isn't it?'

The tree roots halted their advance, soaking up the information.

Hanz had no idea what Jack was talking about, but cogs started to turn inside his head. It dawned on Jack that the old man may have deliberately not told Hanz the true location of the Hands of Time for his own safety. Sometimes ignorance was bliss.

He doesn't even realise it's there.

'Come on,' said Jack, shoving Hanz aside and tiptoeing down into the stream, 'let's at least have a little fun along the way.' Jack picked up a stone and threw it. Hanz watched in amazement as it skimmed across the surface of the water. 'You try it,' said Jack, picking up a stone and passing it to him. 'Flat ones go the furthest.' Hanz looked at the stone and then back at Jack, unsure what to do.

'Watch.'

Jack skimmed another one along the stream. 'It's easy, just try!' Hanz launched the stone. To Jack's amazement, it skimmed again and again, bouncing off the water all the way down the stream, as far as the eye could see. 'Wow! You're a natural!' Jack hopped across various rocks that protruded from the stream, getting his feet wet in the process. Hanz, pleased with his rock skimming effort and gaining confidence followed on. 'See,' shouted Jack, over his shoulder, 'this is much more fun.'

Without warning and with lightning speed,

the tree roots and vines swam like eels through the stream and slithered around Hanz's ankles.

SPLASH!

Jack turned around just in time to see Hanz crash into the water and be whipped away through the stream at the speed of knots.

'Hanz!'

Jack sprinted after him, but a spider's web of foliage grew and knitted itself together from beneath the water, forming around Jack. Vines recoiled, creating a small gap in the web and Lady Augustus glided in. Stroking her orb, she practically floated towards him with elegance befitting of a Queen. Jack puffed out his chest, doing his absolute best to hide the fear he felt inside. She was less physically imposing than Roxanna had been which made it somewhat easier. Face to face with her, Jack stared into the striking green eyes which sparkled beneath the hood which partially cloaked her face.

'Thank you, darling.'

Unsure what to do, Jack froze. Augustus had the full fury of nature at her disposal and could quite easily just blow him off the face of the Earth with a brutal gust of wind.

'Do not fear, your mechanical friend will go down in history as the saviour of the planet.'

Jack mustered up the courage to respond.

'Mr. Moretimer will stop you, he's just as powerful as you.'

Augustus cackled.

'That old fool is on borrowed time.'

Augustus slipped away, back into the forest. The

spider-web foliage recoiled and followed her, leaving Jack slumped on his backside, wet in the stream. He had failed Mr. Moretimer's task and Hanz was gone, once again. Only this time, Augustus knew exactly where to look.

- XXVII -

IT IS TIME

FINALLY.
Jack huffed and puffed his way down Jubilee Walk. After the events he had been privy to, he wondered whether Jules Verne's books were autobiographical accounts of real occurrences. He remembered referring to Mr. Moretimer's shop as 'The Nautilus' but never in a million years had he expected it to take him and Edgar on the journey it had done.

Oh, Edgar.
Jack felt like he had lost a limb, but it wasn't the time for mourning. He refocussed and entered the shop. A picture of calmness, Mr. Moretimer sat at the piano and played, already knowing exactly what fate had befallen Hanz. Jack tip-toed towards him. His sheepishness could be forgiven; it wasn't every day somebody gifted the fate of humankind to the person intent on destroying it.

'I didn't know she was listening.'

The old man stopped playing and closed the lid of the piano. Jack prepared for the telling-off of a lifetime.

'It is in the history books now and cannot be

undone.'

It wasn't the response Jack had expected but he was relieved, nonetheless. Mr. Moretimer got up from the piano and approached the shelf where the big, thick book with no title resided.

'Things have taken a darker turn much sooner than even I expected they might,' said Mr. Moretimer.

What could possibly be much darker than the end of humanity?

'Augustus will be the end of humanity. What I speak of will be the end of all things.' The old man took the book and dropped it at Jack's feet.

THUD!

A thick cloud of dust rose up Jack's nose again, as it had before, making him sneeze.

'It is time.'

'Right now?' said Jack, 'in the middle of all this?'

The old man's timing was questionable given the circumstances but, then again, nothing that Mr. Moretimer had said, done or shown Jack had followed any rules of convention so, in that sense, it was nothing out of the ordinary.

'To make better decisions in the present, one must fully understand the past.'

Jack knelt on the ground before the book and took a deep breath as he prepared to finally confront the truth.

Here goes.

Jack grabbed the cover and pulled it.

It wouldn't open.

He leapt up onto the book and yanked the

cover with all his strength until his face turned blue and his knuckles white.

It was no use. It just wouldn't budge.

'Soon,' said Mr. Moretimer.

Jack gave up and slumped onto his backside. Was Mr. Moretimer teasing him? 'You just said it is time?'

'It is.'

The scene flickered and distorted.

'For this.'

The old man conducted his hands, transporting them both across the Meridian into the Realm of Time. He recognised the location, instantly.

The Forest of the Dead.

The old man was nowhere to be seen but his voice boomed and echoed all around.

'To fully comprehend your past, your journey must begin here.'

Jack reached into his pocket and clutched his family photograph. He knew exactly what he was going to look for but, as he ran from tree to tree, checking the names scribed into them, he quickly realised they were organised by date, not alphabetically. He checked the various trees sporadically placed around him. Each one of them had the same date inscribed into it:

1/1/1897.

As far back as Jack could remember.

Deep down, he had always thought that something bad had happened to his parents. As he checked each tree, he found himself wondering if he even wanted to know the truth anymore. Would it even make him feel any better? Would his life improve because of knowing or was ignorance really bliss in disguise?

Then, he saw it, out of the corner of his eye. Jack stopped running and all his worst fears were confirmed in a split second.

Picklewick.

His family name carved into a tree trunk.

A pocket watch hung above it indicating the time of death.

There was more writing, probably the date of death, but it was obscured by stray branches. Jack tip toed towards the tree, dragging his heels, unsure whether to take a closer look or not. His eyes filled with tears. He had prepared himself for the possibility that his family were no longer living but, face to face with the reality, grief took hold. He wiped his eyes then brushed the spiky stray branches aside, preparing himself for the inevitable truth.

It couldn't be.

What? How is that even...?

Jack gasped for breath, panic taking hold as he desperately tried to comprehend what he was looking at. It was not a date, as he had expected.

It was another name.

His name.

Jack Picklewick.

- XXVIII -

A STORY DEVELOPS

'*W*HERE exactly are we going?'

Violet grilled Pennyworth as she trundled after him through the London streets.

'Charles Pennyworth's school of journalism lesson number one,' Pennyworth began. 'A picture paints a thousand words but when it is accompanied by cold, hard facts it becomes gospel.'

Since seeing the developed photograph at the office, Pennyworth had only one place in mind that he thought might be able to help fully flesh out Violet's soon to be journalistic masterpiece. It had been several years ago, when he first became the editor at the London Times, that he had first heard of it. Thanks to his early success, he found himself with more money than he had ever had in his pocket and regularly hob-knobbing with the social elite. Nothing screamed success more than a well-crafted timepiece and Pennyworth decided it was time he rewarded himself for his hard work and endeavour. He had heard rumours of a shop somewhere in London that might be able to assist him in his search. Three identical brothers from somewhere in Eastern Europe had first told him about it at a social gathering of high society he had attended.

Mr. Moretimer's Timely Creations, or something along those lines, it was called.

The bowler hat wearing antique dealers had frequented it many times before in various attempts to sell their wares to the shop proprietor. He remembered the conversation well, given the odd, slightly comical mannerisms of the brothers. Their names escaped him, thanks to being so distracted by their completely identical appearance.

However, on his way to the emporium, Pennyworth had a heart attack and found his way into a hospital bed instead. A strange occurrence for a man of his age, he believed it was a sign from above, warning him against over self-indulgence. Doing a full about turn, Pennyworth gave the money he was prepared to spend on the watch to the hospital that treated him and nursed him back to health. In return for his charity, the hospital named a ward after him, something that had never sat well with him. He worked in an industry renowned for putting things in the limelight, but it was never something Pennyworth himself had actively sought. He refused the gesture time and time again but, eventually, caved in after Mrs. Lovell convinced him it would be good public relations for the paper.

Since Violet had arrived on the scene, Pennyworth's heart had been acting up again and he wondered whether the palpitations were the almighty warning him against pursuing the ever-developing story that he was heavily involved in. He was far too invested and, after what he had seen, it wasn't something he could let lie. That aside, he genuinely wanted to help Violet. The more time he spent with her the more she reminded him of himself with her well-intentioned determination.

He respected her.

Admired her, even.

They stopped beside a narrow alleyway. A large, wrought iron gate gave Violet the impression that this was not a street that welcomed visitors.

'An elaborate way of saying keep out.'

'Supposedly,' said Pennyworth, 'this place is only frequented by a clientele who know of its existence.' The gate creaked and groaned as he pushed it open. Violet noticed the street sign above it.

Jubilee Walk.

'Exactly as I remember it,' reflected Pennyworth, who showed Violet the photograph again, of which Hanz was the focal point. It was a fantastic shot, the level of detail in which it depicted Hanz was impressive.

'That thing is made entirely of watch parts, the likes of which I have never seen.'

'And that brought us here because?' questioned Violet.

'Once upon a time, I sought a watch dealer who could source the rarest of the rare timepieces. According to those in the know, he had a shop on this very street. When I came to seek him out, circumstances conspired against me, and this was as far as I got.'

Violet glanced back up at the street sign. A Jubilee was an anniversary, a celebration of time. It was either incredibly ironic or incredibly convenient.

'And you think this man has something to do with that thing?'

Pennyworth tucked the photograph away and invited Violet through the gate.

'We shall find out soon enough. Worst case scenario I might finally buy the watch I wanted.'

Pennyworth pulled the gate closed behind them and they wandered down the narrow winding path. Feeling his heart pound in his chest, he prayed history wouldn't repeat itself. The path wound on and on for what seemed like an eternity until it, eventually, they reached their destination.

Twelve Jubilee Walk.

There it was, just ahead of them. It was exactly as Pennyworth had had it described to him, in the middle of nowhere down a never-ending, dead-end street. He found it hard to believe that such a shop existed in London and had always passed it off as Chinese whispers. One person's version of a story could easily alter from the person who passed it onto them until it was unrecognisable from the original but there it was, right before his very eyes.

Small, quaint, discrete.

'On any other day, this would have seemed unusual,' noted Violet, who glanced up towards the creaking sign above the shop door.

'Mr. Moretimer's Timely Creations,' said Pennyworth. 'This is the place.'

Violet pressed her face up against the glass and gazed inside. There were a ridiculous number of watches, clocks, timepieces, all kinds of weird and wonderful. Three candles resided in the window display, none of them lit.

Pennyworth turned the doorknob and the door swung open; a small bell chimed inside but the shop was in total darkness.

'After you,' said Pennyworth, 'it's your story.'

No sooner had Violet got one foot through the door than everything distorted and flickered around her. She rubbed her eyes, wondering if a fly had got through the defences of her eye lashes but the more she rubbed, the more everything seemed to distort. It was as if she had stumbled into some sort of illusion and was somewhere that wasn't really there, like a mirage. She looked back at Pennyworth to double check it wasn't exhaustion from the last few days of excitement that was causing her mind to play tricks on her.

'Are you seeing this, too?'

Pennyworth nodded.

'Maybe we should get out of here.'

Pennyworth ran outside the shop. Violet followed and stopped him, pulling him towards the window.

'Look.'

Through the window, something formed in the centre of the shop. It had the figure of a person, but it flickered and faded just like everything else. The figure solidified and everything was normal once again, the three candles in the window display sparked up.

'It's him!' exclaimed Pennyworth.

There he stood, in all his glory in the centre of

the shop; the one Pennyworth had only heard of in stories and tall tales.

Mr. Moretimer.

- XXIX -

THE PAST CATCHES UP

'*I*'M...dead?!'

Jack touched the tree to make sure it was real. As he did, it flickered and distorted. The forest disappeared tree by tree until Mr. Moretimer's shop reappeared around Jack and left him knelt before the book, exactly as he had been before. Speechless, Jack turned and faced Mr. Moretimer.

'A ghost of the past is what you are,' said the old man, as solemn as he had ever been.

The colour washed from Jack's cheeks, and he turned deathly pale. As shocking as the revelation was to him, some things made sense; the reason why nobody ever paid him or his magic tricks any attention, the reason why he had never, not even once, been caught picking pockets.

'But...how? When? Why?'

Jack could not comprehend the revelation. 'How am I even here if I'm dead?' He started to hyper-ventilate but Mr. Moretimer put a hand on his shoulder which seemed to provide some minor comfort and allow him to regain control of his breathing. Mr. Moretimer pointed towards the book.

'Learn.'

Another voice sounded from the shop entrance.

'Mr. Moretimer?'

Two people stood in the doorway.

'My name is Violet Flemming, and this is Charles Pennyworth.'

Violet reeled the introduction off like a pro.

'We are journalists with the London Times and require a moment of your time.'

Still trying to come to terms with the bone-shaking revelation, Jack had a thought; if he really was a ghost, then they wouldn't be able to see him, surely? The familiar pair looked normal enough, they certainly didn't look like they had the ability to manipulate time or nature or anything that might lead him to question reality or their intentions. Trembling, he crept towards them, terrified that he might not get the outcome he wanted. He planted his feet right in front of them. Neither Violet nor Pennyworth flinched or paid him any mind at all.

They're too focussed on the old man; I need to get their attention.

With a shaking hand, Jack tugged Violet's sleeve. She glanced down in his direction and brushed her arm, as if a cold draught had just ruffled her clothes.

She's looking right through me!

He froze, completely stunned, as Violet and Pennyworth brushed by him as if he wasn't there. Mr. Moretimer heaved out two extremely dusty antique chairs from the clutter and invited them to sit down. Pennyworth removed a handkerchief from his pocket and wiped the chair down.

'There's more history in the dust on that chair than your entire family tree, let alone the mahogany inscribed by the early Peruvian scholars. Maybe you should dust yourself down before you place your posterior on such marvellous craftsmanship,' the old man lectured, his emotions heightened due to the rapidly deteriorating situation with Augustus and the clockroaches.

'I do apologise, I meant no offense,' said Pennyworth, putting the handkerchief away and sliding onto the chair, careful not to get his freshly pressed clothes dirty again.

'And you?' Mr. Moretimer looked at Violet, who stood behind the other chair and refused the offer.

'Suit yourself. I would have thought you would be thankful of a sit down after all you've been through.'

Had she heard the old man correctly? How did he know what she had been through? Firmly on the back foot, Violet chose to keep her mouth closed and not say anything. She didn't know why but she felt a strange, almost unconditional respect for the old man, a little like a young girl would afford her grandfather. Mr. Moretimer's comment washed over Pennyworth who was keen to get straight down to business, holding up the photograph of Hanz. 'We wondered if you might know anything about this, given your knowledge and expertise of rare timepieces?' asked Pennyworth.

Mr. Moretimer took the photograph and gave it a thorough scan. It was real; an image of his creation, caught perfectly on film.

'Totally tantilising tick-tockery! Absolutely magnificent. I can only imagine the time and level of detail that went into the creation of such a thing.' Mr. Moretimer handed the photograph back to Pennyworth. 'But I am afraid I can be of little help. In my old age, I am contemplating retiring, and my memory is not what it once was.'

'So, you've never seen that thing in the photograph before?' asked Violet.

'I am sure I would remember such totally tantilising tick-tockery.'

As convincing as his performance was, Violet could spot a liar a mile off. It was a gift her former husband had enabled her to develop. She studied the markings on the old man's skin. 'That thing is covered with the same,' Violet blurted out. Mr. Moretimer glanced down at the back of his hands. They could certainly tell a story but one which would take an age to finish. The old man studied Violet hard then responded.

'Every individual has their own scars to bear but no two people have exactly the same,' said Mr. Moretimer. He continued; eyes fixated on Violet's. 'Some of us wear them on our sleeves and outwardly display them to the world whereas others choose to mask them beneath the surface. Isn't that right, Miss. Flemming?'

Violet stared into Mr. Moretimer's eyes; it was like he was looking through a window into her soul and could read her, somehow. She was so drawn in, she forgot what she had even said in the first place.

The last thing the paper needed was another complaint and Pennyworth got the impression that Mr. Moretimer was not in the mood. 'It's okay, Sir, you've been a real help.'

'Fantastic,' said Mr. Moretimer, 'then I believe it is time you were on your way.'

'Thank you for your time.' Pennyworth held out a hand, which Mr. Moretimer shook as he escorted them to the door.

'Any time.'

As Pennyworth and Violet wandered away down Jubilee Walk, Mr. Moretimer shut the shop door and put up his 'closed' sign.

'I know a liar when I see one,' said Violet. 'You saw how he just appeared out of thin air; add that to everything else we've seen and there is something BIG going on here.'

Pennyworth, despite his reservations about pushing the old man too far, was inclined to agree. 'I've seen enough to be able to justify us running with this.'

Violet smiled, ear to ear as the pair rushed off to write the story of the century.

Inside the shop, Mr. Moretimer shuffled across to Jack, who knelt crying before the closed book.

'I don't understand,' said Jack, 'why can you see me? And Hanz? And Augustus?'

'Humans only see the world through the three dimensions of space; length, width, and depth, and the one dimension of time. There are many other dimensions that exist but cannot be seen by human eyes. You are trapped in the Neither Here nor There;

a metaphysical place between the living world and the afterlife.'

Jack had heard of limbo. A place for lost souls or those who passed away with original sin; the unbaptized, but he never actually believed in it. The Neither Here nor There sounded very much like it, though.

'Why can't I remember anything before I was homeless?'

Mr. Moretimer sat beside Jack and invited him to open the book. 'All the answers to your questions reside in these pages.'

Jack wondered if there was time to read it all, it really was thick.

I'm trapped in limbo, all I have is time.

'Given the speed at which events are currently unfolding,' said Mr. Moretimer, 'I suggest you read quickly.'

WHAM!

With a mind of its own, the book flicked open and landed on a blank page. 'There's nothing there,' said Jack. 'Look closer,' said Mr. Moretimer, 'this is your story and is for your eyes only.' Jack buried his head in the book and then, like magic, words appeared, one by one, on the page.

The first of January 1887, at exactly one PM in the afternoon, Eliza Picklewick gave birth to a thirteen-pound baby boy. The midwife and the surgeon had convinced themselves that Eliza's husband, Howard, would be bringing the boy up alone since the complications of birthing such a large baby were well known. Yet, Howard sat by her side and never flinched. By some miracle, Eliza survived to hold her new-born son. The midwife told the new parents that she had never birthed such a large baby and known the mother live to tell the tale, but it all seemed like water off a duck's back, as if the couple knew everything would be alright.

Howard and Eliza Picklewick had a secret.

A dark secret.

They were members of an ancient cult known as The Horizon, a secret society of scholars who had dabbled in black magic and other mystical practices for millennia. They weren't bad people, far from it. Each member had an interest in magic and how it could, potentially, aid the development of humanity. They believed that the dark arts were infinitely more powerful than any other form of magic and if they could be harnessed and channelled through the mind of someone true of heart, they could be used for good. Interfering with such forces presented serious dangers but The Horizon believed the reward was worth the risk. They dedicated their lives to this pursuit, forgoing all other past-times and social practices.

As soon as the baby was fit and well enough to leave the house, Howard and Eliza took him to be initiated into The Horizon. Instead of baptizing babies into the Christian faith, Horizon members had their own rituals, and the baby was committed into the cult in their traditional manner. Named Jack, the boy ensured another generation of black magic practitioners would be around to continue the work of the current one.

Unbeknown to them, The Horizon was messing with powers they could not comprehend, and a force way beyond their control had crept into the most malleable mind of the whole order; the youngest - Jack Picklewick. The boy was plagued by vivid nightmares as the dark magic infiltrated his mind, unable to defend itself. Howard and Eliza tried everything they could to rid Jack of what they referred to as 'the darkness' but it was to no avail. One day, a strange, hooded man appeared on Howard and Eliza's doorstep; he looked like a wizard and had strange time related markings all over his skin. He introduced himself as Mr. Maxamus Moretimer.

Mr. Moretimer claimed he could help Jack and seemed to know things that had only ever been spoken about at top secret Horizon meetings. Not knowing what else to do and fearing the worst for their son, Howard and Eliza agreed to let Mr. Moretimer take Jack. He promised he would return with him in three days, two hours, five minutes, and twenty-two seconds, approximately, fully cured of the nightmares. Mr. Moretimer was true to his word, and he returned at approximately the time he said he would, but he carried with him mixed news; he regaled Howard and Eliza with a prophecy about the "Thirteenth", a boy born into the world who had the potential to save it from an evil that had been contained for centuries. He claimed that Jack was the Thirteenth and that the Horizon had, unwittingly, placed his life in immediate danger thanks to their meddling in the dark arts.

The evil he referred to was an all-powerful being known as Makutu. Everything that was evil in the world, Makutu could control and manipulate to his own ends. Now that he had been confirmed as the Thirteenth, Makutu would stop at nothing to destroy Jack Picklewick and end the prophecy. Howard and Eliza were, of course, horrified that they had put their son in harm's way, but Mr. Moretimer offered them a solution; he would take the boy and hide him away, far from the reach of Makutu, completely safe until the time was right for the boy to fulfil the prophecy. Reluctantly, they agreed. They sent Jack away, a teddy bear was the only thing Mr. Moretimer would allow to go with him, a gift from Howard and Eliza that they hoped would keep him safe whilst ever he slept. He promised them that when the boy was old enough to understand, he would tell him the truth in the hope he might seek them out and they could be reunited as a family once again.

Mr. Moretimer took Jack Picklewick as far away from The Horizon as he could, but he feared there would always be a part of Makutu in the boy and that, one day, he would have to reconcile with that. Mr. Moretimer placed Jack with a well-off family who lived just outside of London in the countryside and instructed them never to tell him of the circumstances in which he came to them. They believed they were adopting an orphan boy whose parents had been victim of a tragic accident. They raised him as their own and all throughout Jack's childhood, Mr. Moretimer watched over him, a guardian angel, from afar. But Jack was not stupid; he never felt like he was truly part of the family and he started to rebel. To make matters worse, the darkness of Makutu resurfaced within Jack and he began having nightmares again. These only made him want to rebel more, the darkness taking over. When Jack's foster family let it slip, one day, that they were not his real parents, Jack exploded, anger pouring out of him which destroyed half of the mansion in which he lived.

Mr. Moretimer saw only one way to truly protect Jack from the darkness, but it was the most extreme of actions and one which he hoped the boy would forgive him for.

End Jack's life to end the nightmares.

Whilst to human ears, this would sound insane, the plan was quite ingenious. Jack Picklewick had unfinished business. He longed to know who his real parents were and that was the root of all his anger. Mr. Moretimer had knowledge of the world that no other possessed and he knew that anybody who died with unfinished business would pass into the Neither Here nor There rather than the afterlife. They would remain there until they finally found peace. At that point, they would pass on to the afterlife. Of course, Mr. Moretimer did not want the boy to pass on into the afterlife and he had a plan to ensure it didn't happen. When somebody passed into the Neither Here nor There, they lost all recollection of their life prior to that moment. It was part of the reconciliation process; a person had to search their soul for what they truly needed to make peace with. But Mr. Moretimer would give Jack an unfair advantage - he would ensure that when Jack woke in the Neither Here nor There, he would have two things: his teddy bear, given to him by his real parents, and a photograph of him with his foster family. He hoped this would stimulate enough of a memory to spark Jack's curiosity. Of course, this was all a ruse - Mr. Moretimer knew Jack would never locate his real parents, not on his own, anyway, as they were thousands of miles away and not even in England anymore. It was all designed to protect Jack from Makutu until the time came for him to battle the darkness and fulfil the prophecy.

Happy with the plan, the moment finally came for Mr. Moretimer to take Jack Picklewick's life. On the eve of Jack's tenth birthday, Mr. Moretimer went to the Realm of Time and stopped the pocket watch which hung from Jack Picklewick's tree.

For two years, Jack wandered the streets of London as a ghost of the past, trapped in the Neither Here nor There, blissfully unaware of his own circumstances. But now the time had come that Mr. Moretimer had been waiting for; the time for Jack Picklewick to make a choice that would affect the future of all things, including himself.

The book slammed shut of its own accord.

Gobsmacked, Jack turned towards Mr. Moretimer.

'I saved you,' said the old man, hoping Jack would share his point of view.

The words Jack had just read replayed through his mind, over and over. The nightmare hadn't stopped. Not a night went by when he wasn't haunted by the same vivid dream, the darkness reaching out and closing in around him.

'The time has come for you to choose,' said Mr. Moretimer.

The last thing on Jack's mind was choosing

anything.

'Become the thirteenth Father Time,' said Mr. Moretimer.

'Or?' Jack snapped back.

This was the part Mr. Moretimer had been dreading. Jack had to choose to become Father Time and there had always been the possibility that he may not. Mr. Moretimer had done his best to ensure that the choice was as attractive as possible and the alternative was, well, less so.

'Or,' responded Mr. Moretimer, 'you stay in the Neither Here nor There until you find that which your heart desires most.'

My family.

My real family.

'I choose me. My family. Not the Thirteenth or whatever it is, that's what you want, your choice.' Tears streamed down Jack's cheeks as he shouted at Mr. Moretimer.

'Master Picklewick, I am afraid you do not understand,' said Mr. Moretimer. 'Once you are at peace, your business is finished.'

'So?' Jack shot back.

'Limbo is not a permanent state. Being a ghost of the past is but a temporary thing and there is only one other place you can go once your time in the Neither Here nor There is complete.'

Jack thought about it for a moment, doing his best not to allow his anger to cloud his judgement.

The afterlife.

The reality of Jack's situation sunk in. The old man had expertly manufactured a predicament which presented him with only one option, unless he wanted to be condemned to the afterlife well before his time.

'Not exactly a choice, is it?'

'Your emotion blinds you,' said Mr. Moretimer.

'You fail to see the opportunity I have provided.'

Opportunity? Is he kidding?

'Become the Thirteenth and you will preside over time, living not just one lifetime but as many as you wish.'

Black veins pulsed in his neck and on the back of his hands as Jack heaved the book aside, as far as he could with it being such a heavy thing.

'I understand your anger, Master Picklewick, I really do,' said Mr. Moretimer, 'but, at the risk of sounding unsympathetic, whatever you choose, choose quickly.'

In floods of tears, Jack stormed out of the shop and ran down Jubilee Walk, out onto the London streets. Despite them being the same as they had always been, Jack could not look at them the same way knowing what he had learned. He had been deluded and conned, his own life taken from him. He cried and cried, and it upset him even more knowing that nobody would see his tears. He glanced towards his empty hand where Edgar usually hung. His friendship with the lost teddy bear was the only thing that had been real.

How pathetic is that? A twelve-year-old best friends with a teddy bear?

He reached into his pocket and pulled out the photograph of his "family".

JACK PICKLEWICK AND THE HANDS OF TIME

It was all a lie.

Jack tore up the photograph and tossed it onto the street. He thought back to the time before he first set foot in Mr. Moretimer's Timely Creations. What had, at first, started out as a magical adventure had turned into a very real horror story. If Jack had very little when he first met the old man, he had even less having got the answers he had so desperately craved.

He had nothing.

Except a choice.

He sobbed and sobbed, but suddenly, the black veins quelled as Jack's thoughts changed. Maybe, just maybe, he could play the situation to his advantage. He knew, deep down, there was no choice, it was a no-brainer unless he wanted to rot in the afterlife. He sprinted back to the shop, as fast as he could and confronted Mr. Moretimer.

'If I agree to become the Thirteenth, would I be able to find my real family but avoid the knock-on effect of winding up in the afterlife?'

Mr. Moretimer smiled.

'The penny drops once more.'

Jack's mind raced.

'However,' warned Mr. Moretimer, 'it comes with certain responsibilities.'

'Such as?' asked Jack.

'Protect the Hands of Time and keep the darkness at bay.'

'I wouldn't exactly have a hard act to follow, would I?'

The comment stung Mr. Moretimer but it was

nothing compared to the hurt he had caused Jack.

'Master Picklewick, you do realise that I had to get you away from them. Had I not, the darkness you were surrounded by day in and out would have destroyed you there and then and humanity would have been condemned. You would never have known your family anyway.'

'You told me you know everything that has happened but cannot know the future so how can you say that?'

Mr. Moretimer had no response. Those were his words, bang to rights.

'When you come face to face with the Lord of Darkness, whenever that may be, you will understand why I did what I did.'

Despite only knowing the old man for a matter of days, he was the closest thing to a father that Jack could remember. He wanted to believe that Mr. Moretimer's actions were genuinely in his best interests. He wandered towards the book and picked it up, clutching it to his chest. There was so much pain in the pages but so much more Jack wanted to know. He opened it again and flicked towards the back. The pages were blank, as before, but no words appeared, no matter how hard he looked.

'It's your story,' said Mr. Moretimer, 'the ending has yet to be written.'

Jack put the book back on the shelf. There was no more time to waste; Jack needed to make his choice.

'Thirteen is considered unlucky for some,' said Mr. Moretimer.

Jack dried his eyes and puffed out his chest, his decision made.

'None of them are the Preposterous Picklewick.'

Mr. Moretimer smiled.

'I'll take that as a yes.'

- XXX -

AUGUSTUS PREPARES

*I*N the woods, Hanz found himself strung up between the trees, again. After Augustus had dragged him back away from Jack, he thought she would waste no time in helping herself to the Hands of Time from within his chest but, to his surprise, she hadn't laid a finger on him. Instead, she sat in silence and gazed into her orb, chanting what sounded like nonsense to him. She was preparing, searching for the perfect moment to rewind time to. Her orb showed her the Realm of Earth in all its glory, and she was scanning it for the time it was in its most unspoilt, natural beauty. The appearance of the Realm of Earth was reflected in Augustus's physical appearance so only the most absolute, perfect moment would do.

Hanz had given up struggling some time ago. The more he struggled, the more the tree roots tightened around his limbs. The only thing he could hope for was that his father and Jack would come to his rescue. The revelation that the Hands of Time was hidden within his innermost workings had surprised Hanz, but his father had always referred to him as "special".

Now he knew why.

Maybe it was also why Mr. Moretimer never let him go any further than the end of Jubilee Walk. He felt bad that he had ever doubted his father's intentions when all he was doing was looking out for him.

Augustus snapped out of her trance. She floated towards Hanz and snaked herself around him. The way she behaved like a weed unnerved him, but it was hardly a surprise; most natural plant life sprung from the ground upwards and wound itself around anything it could. She looked at her reflection in the shiny metal of Hanz and pulled the skin on her face until her wrinkles disappeared.

'How ironic,' said Augustus, 'that the most un-natural of creatures holds the key to the rebirth of the natural world.'

Augustus ran her fingers over Hanz, extremely carefully.

'There is good news for you, darling,' said Augustus. 'If it was to break, it would throw the universe into chaos, so I will be very, very gentle.' She snapped off part of Hanz's hand.

'The bad news is, for that very reason, I will be taking my time.'

Hanz closed his eyes as Augustus began dismantling him, only this time she wasn't doing so to get information. She knew the object of her desire was within her grasp.

This time, she wouldn't stop.

- XXXI -

A DREAM COME TRUE...
ALMOST

'DONE.'

Violet tossed her first ever piece of journalism onto Pennyworth's desk.

'Fast can mean rushed,' Pennyworth remarked.

'I prefer efficient,' responded Violet.

It certainly was. She had turned the story around with lightning speed and, although rushed it might have seemed, she had written and edited over and over until she was completely satisfied with it. As Pennyworth read it, Violet studied his face, doing her best to read any sort of tell but, the seasoned professional that he was, he gave absolutely nothing away. Mrs. Lovell scowled from over in the corner as she went about her work. After giving it multiple reads, Pennyworth stood and offered his hand.

'Welcome to the London Times, Miss. Flemming.'

Violet's face lit up, a direct contrast to that of Mrs. Lovell's.

'This,' continued Pennyworth, 'is going to shift some serious papers.'

Violet was over the moon; it was like a weight

had shifted from her shoulders. At last, she had the recognition she always felt she deserved, and she had just been given her dream job as a journalist. Her elation was short lived, however, as the door to the office swung open and Alfred Threadbare marched in. If Violet hadn't been taken so much by surprise, she may have noticed Mrs. Lovell cracking the most discrete of smirks. Threadbare stomped across the office until he was face to face with Violet and Pennyworth.

'Funny,' said Pennyworth, 'I don't recollect inviting you in?'

'How queer,' replied Threadbare, 'I don't recollect inviting you onto my property, either.'

A sudden wave of fear washed over Violet. Threadbare had been a constant thorn in her side and she thought she had finally rid herself of his spectre yet here he was. As far as she was concerned, his presence was never a good thing. He had something up his sleeve, something he could use to ruin her dream; she could tell by the smarmy way he swaggered across the office.

'Honourable chap that I am, I thought I would do what you seem incapable of doing and speak to you face to face.' The cynicism in Threadbare's tone grated on Violet.

'I came to speak to you!' she shot back but Threadbare completely disregarded her and spoke to Pennyworth, as if Violet was not even there.

'Come along, Charles,' said Threadbare, in the most patronising tone he could muster. 'You send a woman to do a man's job and expect me to take it seriously?'

'I gave you the opportunity to have your say and told you I was going up there!' Violet yelled, reminding Threadbare of their last exchange.

'Precisely my point,' responded Threadbare. 'You told me.' He glanced across at Pennyworth. 'I never gave your dog permission.'

Violet swung her hand towards Threadbare's cheek but, just before she made contact, Pennyworth grabbed her wrist and stopped the blow from landing. 'He'll have you arrested for assault.'

Threadbare smirked at Violet. 'Woof, woof, obey your master.'

Pennyworth did his best to lower the tension in the room.

'Mr. Threadbare, to what pleasure do I owe this unscheduled visit?'

'I have it on good authority that you are to run a story which would drag my good name through the mud.'

Mrs. Lovell kept her head down as Threadbare spoke.

'Talk of dead bodies and murders and all manner of crazy, untrue allegations. The police have conducted thorough enquiries and have found no evidence of any such thing, let alone foul and dastardly play. As such, if a story were to be printed that suggested anything to the contrary, it would leave me with no alternative other than to sue for slander.'

Pennyworth wasn't about to let Threadbare get one over of him again.

'Despite how this may burst your already over-inflated ego, Miss. Flemming has produced an incredibly well researched piece that is backed up by photographic evidence and, as the responsible publication we are, does not include anything that is not fact.'

Threadbare continued in his pompous manner, his turn to strike back in the verbal fencing match.

'Whilst I might question the credibility of the writer, I have no doubt that your paper would not print anything but the truth, my honourable friend.' He could not have sounded any more cynical if he had tried, knowing full well of Pennyworth's previous brush with the courts. 'However, there is the small matter of how you gathered said facts.'

Pennyworth knew exactly where Threadbare was going.

'Trespassing is a prosecutable offense, should the proprietor of the land choose to pursue it.'

Technically, they had trespassed on Threadbare's land. Pennyworth's eyes had been bigger than his belly and he had chosen to overlook it in pursuit of the story. However, Threadbare would have to prove that they had been on his land. 'If you have any evidence to back up such ridiculous claims then now would be a good time to show it as we will be running this story on the frontpage tomorrow.' Pennyworth stood his ground with Threadbare, which comforted Violet. She was not used to seeing people resist his bullying.

Threadbare strutted towards the door and Pennyworth smiled; he had called Threadbare's bluff.

Instead of leaving, however, Threadbare wheeled around on his well-heeled shoes.

'The prosecution calls its first witness.'

Mrs. Lovell got up from her desk and positioned herself beside him.

'If the editor's assistant were to testify that he had instructed one of his journalists to trespass on private property, it would be, in the sporting world, game, set and match.'

Threadbare basked in victory.

Mrs. Lovell avoided eye contact with Pennyworth, who was more upset than angry as he spoke. 'After all these years, how could you?'

'I've always had your best interests at heart,' said Mrs. Lovell, glaring at Violet. 'I tried to warn you she was bad news, but you wouldn't listen.'

'This story is being run whether you like it or not,' responded Pennyworth.

'In that case,' said Threadbare, 'I'll see you in court.'

Threadbare marched out of the office with Mrs. Lovell leaving Pennyworth and Violet to contemplate the situation.

'The paper can't afford another legal battle, not with somebody of his financial reach.' Violet thought long and hard. 'What if we get Mr. Moretimer on the record? If we can convince him to talk, maybe he will give us enough to make the story entirely about him and Hanz. That way, we don't have to even mention the dead workers, we just leave Threadbare out of it.'

Pennyworth wanted to drag Threadbare's name

through the mud, but Violet's idea did seem like a much cheaper and stressful alternative. After much thought, his pride got the better of him.

'No; let him do his worst.'

Violet was taken aback. This was a side of Pennyworth she hadn't yet seen.

'He thinks he owns this city and can do what he wants, well, by the time the public have read the story they'll be so amazed and intrigued that they'll not give two hoots about anything he has to say.'

For once, Violet was the voice of reason.

'It doesn't matter what the public thinks, it's what the courts will think. He has police on his payroll already and he's like a dog with a bone when he has his back up. He won't let this drop until he completely ruins me.'

Pennyworth slumped at his desk and put his head in his hands.

'Please,' said Violet, 'you saved me from him before, let me return the favour.'

Pennyworth wanted to run the story as it was. His feelings towards Violet had not biased him in any way; it was a fantastic, well written piece of journalism. The story focussed on the discovery of a living creature, made entirely of watch parts, but contained just enough back story to cast Threadbare in a bad light. Reluctantly, he put his pride to one side.

'Go speak to Moretimer, see what you can do. But, if he won't give us anything then this,' Pennyworth held up Violet's story, 'is going on the front page. I'll deal with the consequences.'

Violet was torn; the moment she had always dreamed of was all but guaranteed but if it came at the expense of the person who saved her life, she wasn't so sure she wanted it. Pennyworth couldn't run a story claiming there was a magical being living in a secret shop who had created a living creature from watch parts as they couldn't prove that he had unless he himself admitted it. A guaranteed lawsuit awaited if he ran the story involving Threadbare.

There was no alternative. Violet had to get something from Mr. Moretimer.

Whatever the cost.

- XXXII -

VIOLET'S DILEMMA

$\mathcal{I}$N Mr. Moretimer's Timely Creations, the old man briefed Jack on his grand plan for stopping Augustus.

'She's far too strong in the Realm of Earth so we need to face her where we will have the advantage.'

'The Realm of Time?' guessed Jack.

'Precisely!'

'I thought you built the Meridian to keep her out of there?'

'Make no mistake about it, Master Picklewick, there is a huge risk attached to letting her loose in the Realm of Time but her influence there can be matched by mine.'

Jack pondered how the old man was planning to stop Augustus.

Surely, he won't destroy her; if rewinding time means humanity will be snuffed from existence, then destroying the natural world will result in the same thing?

Then again, as Jack well knew, the old man had taken the most extreme of actions before, all in the name of protection and preservation.

'Our goal is to retrieve the Hands of Time

and that is all,' Mr. Moretimer chimed in, exactly as Jack's train of thought had ended. 'I am well aware that the universe cannot exist without her, and she is also aware that the universe cannot exist without me. It is not about the complete destruction of time or nature, that would be counter-productive to her goal. Whatever the outcome, time will still exist, but you and every other human being may not.'

Jack thought for a moment. 'If I'm a ghost of the past then, technically, I'm not human.'

'If she rewinds time to a point before your birth, which she certainly will, then you will not exist at all, in any form.'

The good news keeps on coming.

The shop door swung open and Violet stormed in. She had tried the nice, considerate approach before; this time, she intended to apply some pressure.

'I am afraid now is not a good time,' said Mr. Moretimer, jumping straight back into character of the friendly, absent-minded shopkeeper. Violet marched along the carpeted walkway and through the shop clutter then tossed her story on top of the grand piano.

'Tomorrow's front page.'

Mr. Moretimer picked it up and perused it to keep up appearances; he already knew what it said but he did wonder what she was going to do with it. Unless she was bluffing, her intentions were now clear and the last thing he wanted was a photograph of Hanz on the front page of a newspaper. Just as it had led Violet and Pennyworth to him, it would bring an unfathomable amount of attention in his direction. He had maintained his cover as Father Time in the shop for years without so much as a whisper but a frontpage news story had potential to expose the real reason behind the existence of the shop. It wouldn't be him dealing with unwanted publicity if everything went to plan but he owed it to Jack to ensure that his reign as Father Time began with as few distractions as possible, given what Mr. Moretimer knew he would be up against once his time began.

Violet studied Mr. Moretimer's face, just as she studied Pennyworth's when he read the story for the first time. The pair of them had great poker faces but the fact Mr. Moretimer was even taking the time to read the story suggested she had his attention. However, what she didn't know was that Mr. Moretimer, of course, already knew all that had happened. If Threadbare's ultimatum had given her food for thought, the old man served up a full, five course dinner.

'Miss. Flemming,' said Mr. Moretimer, 'I am going to offer you some information.'

Violet smiled.

Got him.

'I can give you the last known location, approximate to, oh, I'd say, zero point three milliseconds ago, of your daughter.'

The silence was deafening.

How does he know about Eve?

'But in return,' Mr. Moretimer continued, 'you must give me your word that this story of yours and the photographs you possess will never see the light of day. The consequences would be catastrophic far beyond anything you could possibly comprehend if the public were exposed to them.' Mr. Moretimer knew Violet was true of heart. Her word would be enough for him if she agreed.

He's bluffing; he's just done some digging on me. Very deep digging but digging all the same.

'Nice try,' Violet laughed it off, 'but no cigar.'

'Allow me to convince you that I speak the truth.' Mr. Moretimer proceeded to outline, in vivid detail, every tiny detail of Violet's actions since Threadbare sacked her. Stunned, she didn't know whether to be in awe of the man or afraid.

How the hell does he know all of this?

'Let me put it another way, Miss. Flemming; if there was even the slightest chance that I could tell you where your daughter is, no matter how statistically improbable or unbelievable it was, would it not be worth your silence?'

Lost for words, Violet did not respond.

Mr. Moretimer took out a pen and wrote something on the back of Violet's story. It was an address. Violet looked over his shoulder, but the writing vanished as soon as the ink had dried. Mr. Moretimer handed it to her.

'Take the time to consider my offer. No need to come back to tell me; once you make your peace, I will know and that address will either reappear or vanish forever, depending on what you choose.'

Still speechless, Violet wandered out of the shop and onto Jubilee Walk. She looked back towards the shop and wondered how such a small, insignificant looking place had just turned her world upside down. She looked at the back of her story where the old man had written and ran her finger across it, willing the words to reappear so she could have the best of both worlds. Alas, the ink had disappeared, and Violet was left with a dilemma; what she desired most in the world, professionally, or what she desired most in the world, personally. The paper went to print at midnight, so time was not on her side.

Her time to choose was now.

- XXXIII -

REWINDING TIME

$\mathcal{H}$ANZ was barely recognisable; his head and torso all that remained.

Augustus had taken him apart, piece by piece. She had been deceived by Mr. Moretimer before and wasn't taking any chances. His various parts scattered on the ground all around him, Hanz knew his time was short. Although not in any pain, the advantage of being manufactured rather than human, it hadn't been enjoyable, watching himself being dismantled. The parts were beautiful. His father had gone to great lengths to ensure only the most rare and fantastic of chronology parts were used in his construction. He couldn't remember being built; he had only become conscious the moment the Hands of Time was placed inside his chest, a mechanical alternative to a human heart. There had been times when Hanz had watched as Mr. Moretimer added or serviced certain parts and it had always taken far longer than it had taken Augustus to do the reverse.

Augustus reached her bony fingers towards Hanz's chest and tinkered away. Her face lit up. It was the first time Hanz had seen her smile, the object of her desires, finally, in her possession after centuries of searching for it.

There it was in all its glory.

The Hands of Time.

Hanz looked down at the device which resided in his chest; about a foot long, the Hands of Time was a pillar sundial with the dial mounting the top of the glass pillar. Inside the glass, a crystal cylinder resided which was split into three smaller sections.

The top section controlled the past. It rotated, incredibly slowly, so much so that the movement was barely visible, and was covered in the same sort of markings that were inscribed on Mr. Moretimer's skin.

The middle section controlled the present and it rotated steadily, just as the hands on a watch tick by. As it turned, markings appeared, inscribed as time went on, history in the making as it happened.

The bottom section controlled the future and it spun at an incredible speed, sometimes rotating clockwise and sometimes rotating anti-clockwise, out of control almost. A strange dark smoke surrounded this section.

Hanz had expected it to look regal, like something befitting of a King or Queen given the importance of it but it looked more like some sort of astrology device than it did a timepiece. It was ancient, which shouldn't have come as a major surprise given that it had been crafted millenia ago, at the dawn of time. Despite looking like something an archaeologist would dig up in a desert, it was truly a marvel.

Augustus's fingers danced over the Hands of

Time with the same love and care she showed her own creations. Despite her feelings towards Mr. Moretimer, she respected time. It served a purpose, just like she did. A shame the two had been at odds for so long.

Augustus pressed her ear against the device. There were three distinct ticking sounds as the different sections all danced at their own speed but, together, it created a noise which was music to her ears. Her sisters grew from the ground and marvelled at it, for once not arguing with one another. The Hands of Time had united Augustus and she was at peace, calm and tranquil. Clouds disappeared and revealed a glorious blue sky.

'Avalon,' a voice not unfamiliar to Augustus spoke from behind her.

She knew who it was.

He was the only one who ever called her by her first name.

'I believe you have something that belongs to me.'

Mr. Moretimer stood in the distance, Jack peeked out from behind him.

Augustus wheeled around; the peace she had found disturbed. The sky re-clouded and her sisters resumed their quarrel.

'It's too late for you, Maxamus, your time is up.'

With a flick of her wrist, Augustus disconnected the Hands of Time from Hanz. If he could have seen the look on Mr. Moretimer's face in that moment, all doubts about whether his father genuinely cared about him or not would have evaporated into the ether with him. Pain carved itself into Mr. Moretimer's wrinkled face as all signs of life left Hanz's body. After she sucked as much air into her lungs as she could, Augustus exhaled; a gale-force wind howled from her lips, ripping what remained of Hanz apart. With one, all-powerful gust, Augustus destroyed years of Mr. Moretimer's work, scattering every piece of Hanz's spectacular, individual parts to the four corners of the Realm of Earth. A tiny golden spring fell to the floor, the only physical evidence that Hanz had ever existed at all. Clutching the Hands of Time to her chest, Augustus shrivelled into the ground with her sisters.

Mr. Moretimer hobbled towards the golden spring and picked it up, a tear dripping down his cheek. Jack understood how he must have felt; it was the same way he had felt about Edgar. There were obvious differences between himself and the old man but, when he thought about it, maybe they weren't so different after all. Mr. Moretimer had spent years in the shop with a voiceless companion just as he had spent years on the streets with the same. It was easy to become attached to the only thing that could be called company. As difficult as it was for him, Mr. Moretimer put on a brave face and tucked the golden spring away into his robe.

'Now is not the time for mourning.'

Jack wondered where Augustus had gone but he knew Mr. Moretimer already knew where. 'Come,' he put a hand on Jack's shoulder. 'We can use the Meridian.' Jack considered complaining, given that the old man had made him trek all the way up to the top of Mount Evercanever without any assistance from the mystical divide.

'Desperate times call for desperate measures, Master Picklewick,' said the old man, 'but I am sure I don't need to tell you that.'

The scene flickered and faded.

When it reappeared, they were on the London streets in an industrial area, beside the River Thames. Despite it being late in the evening, the factories were a hive of activity. Fires raged from furnaces, illuminating the otherwise pitch-black street with a spooky reddish-orange smoke.

Augustus had already sprouted up from beneath the cobbles, tree roots securing her into the ground and spreading further beneath the street, tearing it up and climbing over the surrounding buildings, shattering windows, and strangling streetlamps. She glared at the factory workers, who seemed so tired from work that they didn't even notice her presence. She swayed and rocked from side to side, running her fingers through her long, thick hair.

'I've watched as humans have polluted and destroyed my beautiful creation. It only seems fair that I witness the reversal.' Jack found the first part of her comment hard to disagree with; the city streets were littered with grime, dirt, and disease; the sky was painted a constant shade of grey thanks to the never-ending black smog being pumped out from the increasing multitude of factories that sprang up across the city. There was more sewage and human excrement floating down the Thames than there were boats, and it wasn't even worth thinking about the stench.

London was a mess, of that there was no doubt, and it had all been a by-product of human innovation. Factories meant money and money equated to power so those who were actively polluting the natural world only cared about one kind of green and it wasn't the one Augustus had a passion for.

'Time is constant,' yelled Mr. Moretimer. 'You've known that since The Order of Foretellers gave you your position. What you are doing is wrong, an abuse of your power.'

'Wrong and right is just a matter of perspective,' replied Augustus. 'You're just too stuck in your ways to see it.'

Content that she had the solution to her problem, Augustus slipped her hood from her head and fully revealed her wrinkled face. In mere moments, she would be ashamed of her appearance no more. Placing her fingertips over the dial atop the Hands of Time, she turned it in an anti-clockwise direction once. The bottom section increased in speed, the changes in its direction of rotation became even more random, volatile, and unpredictable.

'Look!' cried Mr. Moretimer. 'The future is now even more uncertain, that's why it spins as it does.'

Augustus turned the dial again and the middle section came to a halt. The London Jack knew froze. The bustling factories came to a complete standstill, and everything fell silent - no more clanging of hammer and tongs, no more bad language from the workers, no more roaring furnace fires.

No sound at all.

Augustus turned the dial a third time and the middle section rotated anti-clockwise.

'That's the present being rewound. We need to act now! Remember what I told you, we all must be connected in some way for me to take us across the Meridian.'

Faster and faster, Augustus turned the device. A bolt of light burst out from the Hands of Time which spun like a tornado. Things were sucked into the device; buildings, people, canal boats, trains and other random objects all whizzed past Jack and Mr. Moretimer, turning into dust as they were sucked into the Hands of Time, as if they had never existed at all.

'It's a time reversal,' shouted Mr. Moretimer over the incredible noise which accompanied the feat.

'As the Hands turn back beyond each moment in time, everything that was created after that moment ceases to exist!'

More buildings were ripped from their foundations and the nearby factory workers clung on to anything for dear life with each rotation of the sun dial.

Thick smoke from the furnaces was sucked in black spirals into the device, along with the fire that caused it. The power of the Hands of Time was incredible and became too much for Augustus. Dropping it onto the ground, she held her breath as it clattered against the hard cobbles and bounced down the street.

'It won't break,' said Mr. Moretimer, 'it is made from an indestructible form of crystal which becomes harder as time passes.' The device rolled to a stop in the middle of the streets, not even a scratch on it.

'Go, now!' instructed Mr. Moretimer. Jack sprinted towards the device, ducking, and dodging all manner of flying debris as it was sucked in by the tornado-like time reversal. Mr. Moretimer hobbled towards Augustus to face her for what he hoped would be the final time. Augustus shrivelled back beneath the cobbles and regrew, bursting out of the cobbles next to the Hands. Jack threw himself at the device, straining his fingers towards it. Augustus's sisters sprouted from the ground and battered him away. He crashed into a wall but was immediately whipped off his feet and dragged towards the device, caught up in the time reversal. He clawed at the cobbles, desperate to get hold of something to hold on to.

'It is rewinding towards your birth,' yelled Mr. Moretimer as he marched on towards Augustus. 'You'll be sucked from existence if we don't get across the Meridian!'

Jack was whipped around in the air like a bed sheet on a washing line, flung back and forth by the force of the reversal, gradually being dragged closer towards it.

Reunited with the Hands of Time, Augustus caught a glimpse of her reflection in the crystal. She smiled as her wrinkles faded and her skin regained its youthful glow. Seizing the opportunity, Mr.

Moretimer powered through the chaos on weary legs, but Augustus saw him from the corner of her eye. Her fingers transformed into small plant roots, growing rapidly towards him, and wrapping around his throat. Her grip was so strong, Mr. Moretimer could barely breathe as Augustus held him in the air, giving him a front row seat to the dismantling of time.

Fading from existence, Jack's legs disintegrated to dust and swirled into the Hands of Time, like the genie being sucked back into the magic lamp.

With all his might and remaining energy, Mr. Moretimer shouted to his disappearing successor.

'Grab hold of her!'

Like his life depended on it, Jack screamed as he fought against the pull of the time reversal and grabbed Augustus's arm.

'It's too late, you've wasted your time,' said Augustus, revelling in the moment.

'There's no such thing as wasted time,' quipped Mr. Moretimer as the scene around them flickered and faded.

Jack prayed Mr. Moretimer's plan would work; he didn't think he could hold on much longer as more of his body faded into dust. Realising what was happening, Augustus let go of Mr. Moretimer but he grabbed her wrist and held on. Her sisters sprouted from the ground and clawed at him, doing their best to separate the great wizard from the great witch.

An explosion of white light blinded Augustus and her sisters retreated. The scene faded completely and reformed elsewhere.

Jack, Mr. Moretimer and Augustus all crashed onto the floor, the Hands of Time falling from Augustus's grip and bouncing along the snow-covered ground atop Mount Evercanever, in the shadow of the Constance.

Augustus panicked; like soldiers going absent without leave, her sisters shrivelled into the ground, knowing full well she was now on an even playing field with Mr. Moretimer.

All three of them searched for the Hands of Time which rolled with increasing speed towards the edge of the summit.

'I'll keep her busy,' said Mr. Moretimer, 'you get the Hands.'

Jack gathered all the courage he could muster and sprinted after the device. Augustus rotated her wrists over and over until two tornadoes formed and tore across the ground in pursuit of Jack. Turning her attention towards Mr. Moretimer, she whipped up all manner of extreme weather conditions, launching them in his direction; hail stones the size of large rocks and lightning bolts zapping from her fingertips.

'Okay, Avalon,' said Mr. Moretimer, rolling up his sleeves, 'one last dance, for old time's sake.'

Mr. Moretimer dodged the weaponised weather with ease, as if he was seeing things happen in slow motion. Truth was, that was exactly what he was doing. It was like the old man had discovered a new lease of life the way he casually avoided everything Augustus threw at him. Mr. Moretimer would never manipulate time in the Realm of Earth, it had to be constant or there would be chaos but in the Realm of Time he could do whatever he wanted. He could slow time down, never reversing it, or watch it unfold at whatever speed he chose. The more the old man avoided Augustus's onslaught, the more frustrated she became. The stray hail stones crashed into the Constance causing bits of it to break off and collapse. The tornadoes tore up the snow and licked at Jack's heels but Mr. Moretimer conducted his hands and slowed their advance down.

'Hurry,' cried Mr. Moretimer, 'I can't keep this up forever.'

Jack ran as fast as he possibly could and leapt towards the Hands of Time, scooping it up just before it tumbled off the edge of the Evercanever.

Yes!

Cutting Jack's celebration short, a monstrous roar filled the air, so deafening Jack had to cover his ears. The mountain shook with the force of an earthquake, knocking Mr. Moretimer and Augustus off their feet and ending their metaphysical battle.

'It's him,' cried Mr. Moretimer, 'he's trying to get out of the mountain!'

Jack felt his hands throb; his veins on the back of them turning black.

'Run, Master Picklewick,' cried Mr. Moretimer. 'Run and do not look back.'

- XXXIV -

THE DARKNESS
CLOSES IN

*T*HE nightmare came flooding back. The demonic figure that had plagued Jack's sleep for so long filled his head once again as he felt a sharp, shooting pain running through his veins, all the way up his neck.

Makutu, Makutu, Makutu.

The word repeated, over and over, in the strange language.

'Don't let him get into your head!' cried Mr. Moretimer.

Jack did his best to push the thought from his mind, his heart thumping so hard in his chest that he thought it might burst. The monstrous roar sounded, and the mountain shook so violently that the ground cracked, chasing Jack as it split open an epic abyss into which snow avalanched.

Augustus resumed her supernatural onslaught against Mr. Moretimer, who threw out both arms; one hand slowing the speed of Augustus's weaponised weather and the other delaying the rate at which the gaping divide in the summit advanced towards Jack.

Run.

The word reverberated around the inside of Jack's skull, reminding his legs not to stop, and pushing the strange word from his mind. He had no idea where he was running to and soon found himself in the middle of a snowstorm. Brutal harsh wind whipped what would normally have been velvet soft snowflakes against his skin but, in the conditions, they felt like ice daggers, slashing his face. Another roar and the ground opened beneath him, lava erupting and exploding from within, sending Jack flying. As he crashed face first into the snow, the Hands of Time dislodged from his possession and rolled towards the abyss.

No!

Chasing after it, Jack skidded through the snow, but it was too late.

The Hands of Time tumbled into the fire spitting abyss, clattering, and bouncing off jagged rocks all the way down into the heart of the Evercanever until it eventually came to rest on a ledge in the clockroach populated cavern below.

Still slipping and sliding, Jack's momentum took him over the edge and into the huge divide in the ground. Clawing at anything and everything to end his descent, he grabbed hold of a rock and hung on, his legs dangling into the void. From the depths below, steam and fire hissed and spat at him, the searing heat scorching the bottom of his feet.

Overwhelmed as he stared into the mouth of hell, Jack cried.

All I wanted was the secret to a magic trick.

The demonic figure flashed in his mind again, sharp clawed hands reaching towards him. Something grabbed him by the scruff of his neck and yanked him up out of the void and onto the snowy plain above. Jack closed his eyes and prepared to meet the Lord of Darkness.

This is it. I'm on my way to a fate worse than death.

Daring to open his eyes, Jack recognised the thick robe which dangled down into the snow, the markings on it a dead giveaway.

Mr. Moretimer!

Out of breath, Mr. Moretimer slumped beside Jack. 'I thought I had contained him, but it seems he has grown stronger. I cannot beat him, and you are not ready. You will be but not yet.'

Jack cut the figure of an ashamed schoolboy who knew he had made a grave mistake.

'It's gone.'

'Lost,' said Mr. Moretimer, 'but not gone. Our quest has become much more complex but is not over yet.'

How the old man remained positive in the face of any sort of adversity amazed Jack.

'You see, Master Picklewick, when you look back through history, there were plenty of times when all seemed lost, yet it wasn't. It is only said and done when one gives up.'

Mr. Moretimer frowned as he noticed the black veins running down Jack's neck once more.

'I thought sending you to the Neither Here nor There would free you of him, but I was wrong. A small part of him is somewhere within you but you must never allow yourself to succumb to his will. He is all that is vile, disgusting, and wrong in the universe and will stop at nothing until all that exists is cloaked in darkness.'

'Makutu? Is that his name?' asked Jack.

'Do not even think it.'

'He's the one I am supposed to destroy? The darkness from the prophecy?'

'Yes, but you are not the Thirteenth yet. Not until I formally hand over responsibility which I cannot do until we have dealt with Augustus. And you have so much left to learn, oh, by the sands of the hourglass, this is an almighty mess!'

Jack thought for a moment. If the Lord of Darkness's sole ambition was the destruction of the universe, then surely Mr. Moretimer's and Augustus's interests were aligned. What good would rewinding time be if the universe was cloaked in darkness? Her creations needed light to live and would wither and die, nature destroyed along with everything else.

'We could use Augustus's help. Two heads are better than one.'

As if he had just sat on something sharp, Mr. Moretimer leapt up into the air. It was the quickest Jack had seen him move. 'Absolutely not!'

'Why not?' asked Jack. 'She's trying to save the Realm of Earth, isn't she?'

'Yes.'

'And surely the darkness poses a much bigger threat to that than humans?'

'Well, I suppose.'

'Then what are we waiting for?'

Mr. Moretimer knew Jack was right but couldn't bring himself to accept that the person who he had been at loggerheads with for so long might be the best chance of stopping something far, far worse.

'Or you just go back in time and put him back in his place.'

Mr. Moretimer looked as though Jack had lost his mind.

'Time is constant; don't ever forget that. I may have manipulated it a little here, but it was always moving forwards. Even if I did choose to do it, time travel is not as simple as that, anyway.'

So, it is possible.

Jack had been dying to ask the question. Being the Thirteenth sounded much more fun if time travel was a genuine possibility.

'It is possible but, as I have repeatedly told you, time is constant, so should never be done.'

Jack smiled to himself, hoping Mr. Moretimer didn't see it, storing the thought for later.

'A truce with Augustus it is, then,' said Jack.

The old man begrudgingly agreed. 'Since it is your idea, I will let you do the talking. But be wary, she can be the loveliest, calm, and collected individual one minute and, well, you have seen her other side with your own eyes. I hope you have a plan to quell her.'

'You are getting forgetful,' said Jack, grinning like a Cheshire cat.

'You're talking to the Preposterous Picklewick.'

Street magic was all showmanship and Jack was

extremely adept at that. The actual magic was the ability of the magician to engage the audience with enough clever words and fanfare that they never saw how the trick was pulled off. If either of them was to sell the idea to Augustus, Jack was just as qualified as the old man. Problem was, it would be the first time his audience would be paying attention to him.

'This shall be a performance for the entire world,' said Mr. Moretimer.

'Then things have worked out exactly the way you said they would,' Jack replied.

'Approximately,' corrected Mr. Moretimer.

Jack knew his performance had to be flawless.

If it wasn't, the fate of the universe would be left hanging in the balance.

- XXXV -

AN UNLIKELY ALLIANCE

CROUCHING high atop the Constance, the highest ground they could find, Jack and Mr. Moretimer stared down at the snow covered plain below. The huge crack in the summit had grown and clockroaches spewed out of it. Just the thought of the little insects sent a shiver down Jack's spine. 'The Lord of Darkness is a giant clockroach?' asked Jack.

'No,' replied Mr. Moretimer, 'the darkness is an omnipresent, invisible force which occupies anything it can manipulate. Whenever there have been evil deeds in history, such as Henry the Eighth beheading his wives because they didn't birth him a son, that is it's will, influencing the individual to do bad things. The Lord of Darkness occupies minds that allow dark thoughts to enter. A clockroach is not a social insect, it has no hierarchy, no King or Queen. He will have easily bent them to his will and set them upon the Meridian as they are loyal to nothing else.' Jack considered the mind-boggling thought that he would, at some point in the future, be facing an enemy with many potential faces.

'When you are ready, you must face him and destroy him,' said Mr. Moretimer.

'How will I know if I am ready?'

'Do you feel ready?'

'No.'

'Then you are not. But, one day, when it is time, you will.'

Mr. Moretimer's words offered Jack no consolation. He felt worse not knowing when, or even if, he would feel ready to take on a force so powerful. He looked away from the clockroaches; they just reminded him of the nightmares, which had become reality now he knew what they were.

Where had Augustus gone? He couldn't see her anywhere.

Surely the old man knew. The last thing he said he wanted was her roaming free in the Realm of Time, unleashing her fury. Right on cue, Mr. Moretimer provided the answer to Jack's question.

'She is here,' he said, glancing down towards the entrance of the Constance, 'destroying that which I have worked so hard to conserve.'

Jack led the way, scrambling down the rock face. Mr. Moretimer followed, pleased that his apprentice had chosen to take the lead. This was exactly what was needed. Jack was still the student but would eventually become the master. He had a lot to learn but also had to make his own decisions and be confident in them, regardless of the outcome. Mr. Moretimer had learnt over his many years that indecision was far worse than a bad decision. He just hoped that the current moment wasn't one of those where the exception became the rule.

At the bottom, the huge pendulum swung,

hypnotically, in the entrance to the building.

'Wait here,' instructed Jack, 'it's you she has the grudge against, not me.' For reasons he could not quite fathom, Jack's words filled Mr. Moretimer with confidence. Maybe the prophecy was true after all. Like a caged animal desperate to be free, the roar of Makutu sounded again and the Constance shook, stone gargoyles breaking and tumbling to the ground, smashing to pieces.

'Go,' exclaimed Mr. Moretimer as more pieces of the Constance crashed down around him, 'there is no time to lose.'

In the main hall of the Constance, a strong gale blew. Books swirled through the air and were scattered across the floor. Jack felt at home, much more so than his previous visit, as he marched through the main hall, still amazed at the sheer volume of texts which resided within the archives.

How will I ever remember all of this?

Tree roots had spread everywhere, all throughout the hall, climbing up the archives and whipping books off the shelves. Some of them even looked like they were reading the books before they tossed them aside.

There was Augustus; right at the end of the corridor, flitting through books and tossing them off the shelves, one by one.

'Put those back! There's more history in those pages than your entire family tree!'

Jack surprised himself just how much he sounded like Mr. Moretimer, his influence rubbing off on him. Augustus turned her attention towards him, eyes raging with fire. Her sisters sprung up from the ground, arguing with each other and trying their best to win her ear.

'Where is it?' demanded Augustus, her words full of anger as she advanced on Jack. Terrified, he stood his ground.

'Lost.'

Augustus grew taller like a tree, as her anger built.

'But I know where it is.'

Jack's performance began.

'I also know why you want to rewind time so badly and I completely understand. We have made a mess of your planet, believe me, I know. I've lived on those stinking streets for the past two years, suffocating in foul fumes and sleeping in the grimmest grime.'

Augustus glared at Jack, unmoved.

'Maxamus sent you to do his dirty work, I see. I admire your bravery, coming here to face me, but if you are trying to change my mind then your efforts are in vain. The Realm of Earth was once so special in its youth; green lands, striking blue skies and crystal-clear waters. The Earth was beautiful. I was beautiful.'

'You are beautiful,' responded Jack, grabbing Augustus's attention.

'There is beauty in age,' continued Jack, 'some of the most beautiful sights I have seen have been the oldest. Sure, some places are in a mess but the things you just described still exist. You say Mr. Moretimer is stubborn, yet you are no different; you focus on everything that is wrong with the Earth rather than what's right about it. It's like when you look up at the sky at night; the thing you see more than anything is darkness but there are many stars there, shining bright, even though they seem so small and outnumbered.'

For a moment, Jack thought Augustus was going to strike him down with a lightning bolt or strangle him with her roots, but she softened, shrinking back down to her usual size, and facing him.

'You think I am beautiful?' asked Augustus.

'Yes,' answered Jack. He had realised some time ago that both the old man and Augustus were ego maniacs, so in love with their own work that a little bit of flattery would disarm them, at least for a moment or two.

'Not all humans are bad and there are many who love the natural world you created. When I become Father Time, I promise you I will also become a steward of the Earth and do all that I can to guide humanity and keep your creation as beautiful as I see it right now.'

Augustus pondered Jack's words.

'You are different.'

'I am the Thirteenth.'

Even if she wasn't entirely convinced, Augustus was listening.

'Would you rather take a chance with me, something different, or let the darkness which is about to break through the Meridian destroy everything you love entirely? The prophecy told by the Order of Fortellers states that I will be the one to bring the world out of darkness and into the light. Imagine how beautiful your creation will look, bathed in glorious light with no fear of darkness or misdeeds to pollute it.'

Augustus fell into a trance, visualising what might be. She knew that if the darkness got into the Realm of Earth, her creation would be destroyed and it didn't matter how far back she rewound the Hands of Time, if she ever got her hands on it.

'Makutu is the one we all wish we could banish from the universe,' said Augustus.

All? There's more like her and the old man?!

'But so far' she continued, 'the best anybody has done is contain him.' Augustus circled Jack, running her fingertips across his head.

'If you truly are the one the Order of Foreteller's spoke of then should you be allowed a chance to do better?'

Her sisters sprouted up from the ground and counselled her. After a few moments of calm whispering into one ear and insane screaming and shouting in the other, Augustus held up a hand, the sisters recoiling into the ground, her mind made up.

'The only way we can contain the Lord of Darkness is if we work together, as I and Maxamus did once upon a time.'

This is going better than I could have hoped! She thinks this is her idea!

The old man had never mentioned that both he and Augustus had worked together to keep the darkness contained in the past. Jack had been right all along; the old man and Augustus were both as stubborn as each other, so proud that neither one of them had been prepared to talk with the other and listen to the opposing point of view to work out a solution. It was in that moment that Jack decided he would always listen before he took any sort of action, particularly action that would affect the lives of so many people.

Augustus was not the enemy, but the Lord of Darkness certainly was and that was something they could both agree on.

'If you are who the Order of Foretellers say you are then I would be foolish not to give you that which the old fool holds so dear.'

Jack could barely contain his excitement. He had done it; in a matter of minutes, he had done what the old man couldn't in years and quell the wrath of nature. He had a fleeting thought back to what Mr. Moretimer had told him when they scaled the Evercanever.

Every minute in the Realm of Earth is equivalent to a year in the Realm of Time.

Technically, it had taken him years, but Jack chose not to linger on the minor detail too much.

'But remember, my dear; the winds can change at the drop of a hat and if I am not impressed by what I see from you, they can just as easily blow in another direction.'

Jack held out his hand. After a few uncertain moments, Augustus shook it and a deal between time and nature was struck for the first time in a very, very long time.

- XXXVI -

INTO THE NEST

$\mathcal{T}$O Mr. Moretimer's relief, Jack and Augustus emerged from the Constance, side by side.

'Do not think you have got one over on me, my dear,' said Augustus as she came face to face with him. 'I have an accord with the Thirteenth, not with you. But, for the time being, I am prepared to put our differences aside for the greater good.'

'As am I,' replied Mr. Moretimer.

Jack breathed a huge sigh of relief. 'Now that we are all on the same page, what's the plan?'

'We retrieve the Hands of Time and repair the remaining tears in the Meridian,' said Mr. Moretimer.

'Will that be enough to contain the darkness?' asked Jack.

'If we destroy the clockroach nest to stop them chewing through, then it will keep it here, in the Realm of Time. For how long, I can only approximate, but it will buy you time.'

Mr. Moretimer led the way into the Constance, through the Hall of Fathers, down the winding stone staircase, through the bolted doors and into the lava filled cavern deep within the heart of Mount Evercanever. At the edge of the lava lake, he conducted, and the lake parted, exactly as it had before, which revealed the mine shaft. He led the way across the scorched ground to the grate and opened it once again.

'Master Picklewick,' said Mr. Moretimer, 'now might be a good time to come to terms with your clockroach phobia.'

Jack took a deep breath and followed the old man and Augustus onto the pulley platform which descended into the pitch black below.

When they reached the bottom, Jack could not see a thing which heightened his other senses; the smell was foul, much worse than anything he had ever smelled on the streets, like something putrid had been rotting for a thousand years. A constant ticking sound filled his ears, but he knew it wasn't clocks.

'We must proceed without light,' said Mr. Moretimer. 'As soon as the clockroaches see you, they will come for you. It is the will of the darkness that you are destroyed.'

The old man led the way. Not being able to see anything combined with the constant crunching of clockroaches beneath his feet made Jack feel nauseous.

There must be millions of the things.

With every step, Jack felt the ground move, his imagination running riot as to what he was surrounded by. Every part of his body itched, and he found himself repeatedly slapping his arms and shoulders, like they were crawling all over him, even though they weren't.

Journeys with the old man seemed to take forever and the walk through the mine shaft was no exception. The pitch blackness had a funny way of disorienting the senses.

'We are here.'

Wherever they had come to a stop was vast and cavernous as Mr. Moretimer's voice echoed over and over, on and on, almost infinitely.

'The nest is huge and there are many tears in the Meridian here, far too many for me to repair entirely. But now we are three, we have more of a chance.'

As they moved further forward, the tears in the Meridian became visible and were the only source of light. Despite the huge crack in the summit's surface above, they were so deep down in the heart of the mountain it wasn't even visible. Jack couldn't count how many tears there were but, through them, he could make out little glimpses of the Realm of Earth, parts of London he recognised.

'Avalon,' said Mr. Moretimer, 'I need a storm of biblical proportions; thunder, lightning and a lot of rain.'

'I am sure I can conjure something up, my dear,' Augustus replied.

'Master Picklewick and I will attend to the tears in the Meridian and retrieve the Hands of Time. Once the flooding starts, the clockroaches will naturally seek refuge wherever they can so it is imperative that we stitch up as many of those tears as possible, so they don't find their way into the Realm of Earth.'

'How am I supposed to do that?' asked Jack.

Mr. Moretimer put a hand on his head like a priest blessing a clergy member. He uttered some words beneath his breath that Jack could barely hear nor understand then removed his hand from his head.

'There.'

'There what?'

'When it is time, you'll see.'

Whatever the old man had done, Jack didn't feel any different to how he had thirty seconds ago.

'I may be able to assist in more ways than one,' added Augustus.

'How? Asked Mr. Moretimer.

'When it is time, you'll see, my dear,' replied Augustus, mimicking him.

Jack liked Augustus. He just hoped she would stay true to her word and give him time to make good on his promise. Mr. Moretimer crouched beside him and gave him instructions.

'When we get to a tear, imagine you are conducting your favourite piece of music. If you concentrate and focus hard enough, the threads of time will dance to your tune and you will control it, just as a conductor controls an orchestra.'

So that's what the hand thing is.

Finally, Jack would be doing something truly magical. Excitement coursed through his body as thunder rumbled and lightening flashed.

Augustus's storm began, raging throughout the cavern.

Thanks to intermittent flashes of lightening,

Jack bore witness to the terrifying scene that engulfed him. Augustus stood at the centre of it all, commanding the weather effortlessly from her fingertips. The clockroach nest was huge, just as the old man had said and there were countless numbers of the creatures. The lightning flashes confused them, and they scurried in all directions, unable to focus on Jack. Black clouds formed inside the cavern and rain poured, the greatest monsoon Jack had ever seen. He found it difficult to take his eyes off it.

A monstrous roar sounded, and the cave rumbled. Fire shot up from cracks that appeared in the ground where lakes of lava flowed below. The darkness knew they were there. Just as Mr. Moretimer had said they would, the clockroaches darted for cover from the torrential downpour. As they rushed towards the tears in the Meridian in their droves, Augustus sent huge gusts of wind to blow them away and hold them off. The clockroaches that could not get off the ground quick enough drowned in the water which pooled at the base of the cavern and rose at an alarming rate, quenching the lava and turning it to steam.

'No time to waste!' cried Mr. Moretimer.

As he and Jack traversed their way across the cavern, Augustus followed through on her offer to help in another way; her sisters sprouted from the ground, commanding tree roots which grew and slithered everywhere, creeping, and spreading like Japanese knot weed over the walls of the cavern. Mr. Moretimer watched on as Augustus patched over tears with tree roots, natural bandages to cover the

Meridian's wounds.

'A temporary fix,' shouted Augustus over the roar of thunder. Mr. Moretimer nodded in approval. Jack sensed there was a mutual respect between the two, even if they didn't see eye to eye.

'Come on, time to try out your new gift.'

Jack followed Mr. Moretimer towards a tear and did as he had instructed. He hadn't listened to a whole lot of music but could appreciate the technical mastery it took to compose a full orchestral score. He thought for a moment before he settled on his chosen piece; Beethoven's Symphony No. 5 in C minor.

Perfect.

Given that many music critics suggested the famous "da da da dum" chords at the start represented the sound of fate knocking at the door, Jack could not have chosen a more appropriate piece of music to occupy his imagination. He closed his eyes and allowed his hands to dance and conduct the music in his mind. He became lost in the music, as if he had been transported out of the cavern and onto the biggest theatre stage in London. There he was, right at the front, in total control of the four sections of the orchestra. With a flick of his wrist, he brought the brass to a roaring crescendo and then, with equal finesse, brought the string section peacefully down into a soothing diminuendo. Finally, he felt as though he was doing what he was born to do.

Performing.

When Jack opened his eyes, something was different; everything around him moved in slow motion yet he maintained his usual speed. Time was dancing to his tune. He conducted his imaginary orchestra and with each fine movement of his wrists, bright red flashes of light zipped across the tear like a sewing needle and pulled it closer together.

I'm doing it! It's...it's...magic!

Jack thought about all the fantastic characters he read about in Jules Verne's books but now he was one. No longer would he have to imagine the amazing things they saw and did. He could see and do them for himself.

Like a firework fizzles out, the red light faded, the tear stitching itself up. Jack lowered his arms. Everything returned to normal speed, and he felt as if he had just woken up from a dream.

'Totally tantalising tick-tockery! You're a natural!' Mr. Moretimer smiled, proud and pleased with his apprentice's first completed piece of work. Even Augustus looked impressed. Jack dusted his shoulders off.

'You're looking at the Preposterous Picklewick.'

'No,' said Mr. Moretimer.

'I am looking at the Thirteenth.'

Full of confidence, Jack leapt into action, skipping, and bouncing across the cavern, repairing tear after tear. Much slower than Jack but with just as much enthusiasm, Mr. Moretimer did the same, master and apprentice working side by side. The cavern flooded with rain as Augustus showed no sign of slowing things down. Clockroaches scurried in search of cover. Each time they got to a tear in the Meridian, Mr. Moretimer and Jack denied their escape.

The plan was working but then, out of the blue, Jack heard the voices from his nightmare, whispering everywhere, speaking the strange language.

'**Makutu, Makutu, Makutu.**'

The voices weren't in his head, they were coming from somewhere in the cavern. He glanced around but nobody was there. Mr. Moretimer continued repairing tears and Augustus's storm raged on, oblivious to what Jack was hearing.

The voices were calling to him and only him.

Drawn towards them in a hypnotic state, Jack wandered towards the edge of the cavern, up to his chest in water and drowned clockroaches. He saw a small tunnel burrowed into the rock. The closer he got, the louder the voices became. He tried to turn around and get back to the task Mr. Moretimer had set for him, but something wouldn't let him, like it had hold of him and drew him closer. The water around him swirled and turned jet black.

When he reached the tunnel, Jack saw something he thought he would never lay his peepholes on again.

Edgar.

The teddy bear stared back at him from within the tunnel. Not giving any thought or consideration as to how he had even got there, Jack reached out towards him.

'You're letting him get into your head!'

Mr. Moretimer dragged Jack away from the tunnel and the voices disappeared, as if they had never existed in the first place. Jack snapped out of the trance, but his veins bulged black on the back of his hands and up his neck.

'Look, the Hands of Time!' Mr. Moretimer pointed towards the device which hung precariously on a ledge, a river of lava flowing below thanks to a large crack that had opened up in the cavern. Both he and Jack scrambled up towards it. As they reached the ledge, the voices returned only this time Mr. Moretimer heard them as well.

'He is here.'

Without warning, the cavern shook with an incredible force the likes of which Jack had never felt, knocking him, Mr. Moretimer and Augustus all off their feet. Jack sprinted towards the Hands of Time, blocking the voices out, slaloming through falling stalactites which snapped off from overhangs and plummeted to the ground. He grabbed the device just as the overhang collapsed, falling into the lava below, and returned it to Mr. Moretimer.

'Let's finish what we started and get out of here,' the old man exclaimed. 'We must destroy the clockroaches so that he has no physical presence to occupy.'

'Nothing a little fire won't resolve, my dear,' shouted Augustus, throwing a lightning bolt towards the clockroach nest. As soon as it struck, it erupted into flames. The remaining clockroaches poured out of it as the fire and flames spread across the cavern, setting it ablaze.

Suddenly, Jack was swept up off the ground by an invisible force. Mr. Moretimer grabbed his leg and was lifted into the air with him, whipped back and forth through the cavern. The old man lost his grip and was tossed through the air, clattering into Augustus. Her storm subsided as Jack was sucked through the air towards the tunnel. He struggled and tried to free himself from whatever had hold of him, but it was no use, he was well and truly helpless.

Becoming increasingly agitated, Jack's frustration built inside him. His veins turned black and bulged all over his body. In obvious pain, Jack screamed at the top of his lungs but what happened as a result, even Mr. Moretimer could not have approximated.

A shockwave of seismic proportions exploded from within Jack and ripped through the cavern, obliterating everything in its wake; the clockroach nest vaporised as did the surviving clockroaches. Every remaining tear in the Meridian was repaired and healed completely, leaving nowhere for anything to pass through. Flames hissed, extinguished into steam, as Jack's unconscious body plunged into the water below. By the time he breached the water, the cavern was blanketed by strange black ash particles which showered down from above.

Mr. Moretimer and Augustus looked at each other with grave concern. The old man reached into the water and pulled Jack out. With one hand on Jack's shoulder and the other on Augustus, the scene flickered and faded until the hellish cavern around them disappeared and was replaced by a familiar London street, lined by half constructed buildings and architecture.

Putting the Hands of Time to one side, Mr.

Moretimer turned his attention towards Jack who came to his senses, still groggy.

'Wh... what happened?'

He clutched his head, which thumped like a drum as black veins faded away down the side of his face.

'Later, Master Picklewick,' said the old man, 'now is not the time.'

Content that the imminent threat of Makutu was dealt with, Mr. Moretimer relaxed.

'Speaking of time, my dear...'

Augustus cradled the Hands of Time, taking advantage of the old man's guard being down.

'Avalon, we had an arrangement.'

'No,' replied Augustus, 'we didn't.'

Her fingers danced over the sundial, tempted to turn it.

'We did.'

Augustus handed the Hands of Time to Jack. Back in the right hands, Mr. Moretimer was keen to put things right.

'Turn the dial clockwise, Master Picklewick,' he instructed, 'and keep going until I tell you.' Jack rotated the dial and, as he did, the street magically rebuilt itself. The sand that the buildings, vehicles, and people had become whirled back out of the device and reformed, exactly as they had been.

'Stop.'

Jack did as he was asked. 'This does not put things right in the Realm of Time, however,' the old man warned, 'but that time will come.'

As much as Mr. Moretimer hated to admit it,

if it wasn't for Augustus, Jack would be gone and Makutu would be wreaking havoc in the Realm of Earth. He approached her, rather sheepish.

'Maybe it would be better if time and nature were on the same page.'

'My dear,' Augustus replied, 'that depends on whether your successor is the breath of fresh air I hope he is.' She never took her eyes off Jack as she spoke and he respectfully nodded, a signal to her that he had every intention of honouring his promise.

'I will always be watching,' said Augustus.

'Always.'

She shrivelled away into the ground, leaving Mr. Moretimer and Jack alone in the middle of the street. It was ironic, thought Jack, that nature had gifted him time to make good on his promise of a better world. He thought best not to mention it to the old man but, then again, he would know what he thought anyway. Some things just didn't need to be said.

'Come, Master Picklewick,' said Mr. Moretimer, helping Jack to his feet and making their way back towards Jubilee Walk.

'It is your time.'

- XXXVII -

VIOLET'S CHOICE

*T*HE London night sky was settled and calm for a change as Violet bundled her way through the mounds of drunks, peasants, and beggars. Her nose buried deep in her story, she read the text back to herself but wasn't sure why. She had rewritten the piece over and over, painstakingly checking it for grammatical errors and inconsistencies. She was more than happy with it and knew it off by heart.

What she still hadn't decided was what she was going to do with it.

Reading it a few more times, she hoped, would help her come to a decision before she arrived at the London Times office. It was five minutes to midnight and the printing deadline was nigh.

Since the bombshell dropped by Mr. Moretimer, Violet had toiled and debated what she should do. She wasn't sure she believed the old man. Maybe Threadbare and Mrs. Lovell had gotten to him before she had and paid him off to say what he said. On the other hand, what if he was true to his word? She looked on the back of the story where the mysterious shop owner had written the address down for her. There was nothing there, but she had seen with her own eyes that something had most certainly been written and then vanished without explanation. She had tried tracing over it to see if she could get an imprint of the text but turned up nothing. It was a cruel choice for her; the career she had always dreamed of or the way back to her daughter.

The London Times office loomed ahead. The building she had so desperately wanted to get a foot through the door of had become a sight which now filled her with doubt. She could see Pennyworth through the window, waiting. The person who had given her a second lease of life. Regardless of her decision, Violet knew she was going to lose something she cared deeply about.

When she opened the door, the warmth from inside was welcoming. Pennyworth jumped out of his seat.

'Miss. Flemming!' he exclaimed, 'I wasn't sure you would come.'

Neither was she.

Violet had considered losing herself to a bottle again and scrubbing the whole thing from her memory. So much had happened in such a short space of time it felt like a dream. She even contemplated the possibility that she had died the night she jumped off the bridge and had been trapped in some sort of strange limbo before she moved on to the afterlife.

Stop being so ridiculous, Violet. Everybody knows there is no such thing!

'Did he give you anything?' asked Pennyworth.

'In a fashion,' Violet replied.

'What are we waiting for?'

As giddy as a schoolboy, Pennyworth ran towards Violet, desperate to read the story that he believed would catapult his paper back into the limelight. But, as he put an arm around her, she backed away.

'I'm sorry, I can't let you print this.'

Deep down, Violet's decision had been made the minute Mr. Moretimer made his counteroffer, even if she had just spent the whole evening kidding herself that there was one to make.

It wasn't even a choice; it was a no-brainer.

There was nothing in the world she wanted more than to be reunited with her daughter and if there was even the slimmest, slither of a chance that Mr. Moretimer spoke truthfully, Violet had to take it.

Pennyworth was flabbergasted. 'What? Why? I thought this is what you wanted?'

'Somebody once told me,' answered Violet, 'what we want and what we need are sometimes not necessarily the same.'

Violet avoided Pennyworth's gaze. He knew there was something she wasn't telling him.

'I don't understand. If it's Threadbare you're worried about I can take care of him.'

Violet took Pennyworth's hand. It was warm and comforting. 'You're a good man; I owe you my life and I won't ever forget that.'

Pennyworth felt his chest tighten but it wasn't his condition. Not running the story was pushed out of his mind as what his heart truly desired looked to be on its way out of his life. He had fallen for Violet and had hoped that their relationship might become more than just professional but reading newspapers and stories for as many years as he had had gifted him the ability to read between the lines.

'Will I see you again?'

'I hope so,' replied Violet. She had fallen for Pennyworth too but couldn't tell him. With Mr. Moretimer's bombshell, she didn't need to complicate things further.

'There's just something I need to do.'

Pennyworth looked into Violet's eyes. The tears that stared back at him told him it wasn't a decision she had come to lightly. 'Anything I can help with?' he asked.

'You've done enough for me already.'

Violet smiled and put her arms around him. Pennyworth didn't want to let her go but he knew he wouldn't be able to change her mind. All the way through the embrace, Violet prayed that she was right about Pennyworth; that he was truly a decent man and wouldn't run the story without her blessing. At one time, she would not have trusted him but the longer she stayed there, wrapped in his arms, she knew she had nothing to worry about.

'Thank you.'

The words flowed off the tip of Violet's tongue as the embrace ended. Pennyworth smiled.

'You're welcome.'

Violet walked towards the door, forcing herself not to look back. She took a deep breath, opened the door, and stepped out into another new unknown.

Pennyworth ran towards the window and pondered what might happen. At that exact moment in time, he couldn't care less about the story. He just hoped that he would lay eyes on Violet again. As he watched her disappear down the cobbles, his thoughts returned to the paper. He still had a job to do and a score to settle. He was certain that, if he dug deep enough, he would find something that could bury Alfred Threadbare once and for all, without going against Violet's wishes.

At the end of the cobbled street, Violet could no longer see the London Times.

Out of sight, out of mind.

At least that is what she hoped. She took her handwritten story out of her notebook and turned the back page over, staring at it, willing the text that Mr. Moretimer had written to reappear.

Come on, come on, please let it be true.

Then, just as Mr. Moretimer had said it would, the writing reappeared.

Black ink reformed, letter by letter until an address was visible. Violet was enchanted; there was a magical story to be written about the old clockmaker further down the line. Tears streamed down her cheeks and dripped onto the paper, smudging the ink. It didn't matter; it might as well have been burnt into her skin it was so ingrained in her memory. Not wasting another moment, Violet tucked the paper into her notebook and marched off into the night, the start of an adventure she once feared she might never embark upon but, thanks to the amazing abilities of Mr. Moretimer, she had real hope that she would be reunited with her beautiful Eve, once and for all.

- XXVIII -

AS ONE DAY ENDS, ANOTHER BEGINS

$\mathcal{M}$R. Moretimer stood in his shop and soaked it all in. He had been all over the world in his many lifetimes and seen everything there was to see but the shop was the only place that had ever really felt like home. He ran his fingers across the jam-packed shelves then slumped at his piano. It needed a tidy up on the grandest of scales. Despite the volume of clutter and amazing timepieces, there was one thing missing that just made the place feel empty:

Hanz.

As Mr. Moretimer remembered the amazing memories he had forged there, the interesting people and all the weird and wonderful timepieces that passed through his doors, he had a strange feeling in his bones that he had not felt before.

It was time.

For the last time.

'Probably a good thing, really,' reflected Mr. Moretimer. 'It would take me, oh, I would say, thirty-two days, six hours, twenty-four minutes and nineteen seconds to tidy up all my stock. Approximately, of course. Who wants to spend that long tidying?'

Jack slid onto the piano stool beside the old man.

'Don't feel like you have to tidy up on my account. I'll just fit in where I can.' In all the madness of the past few days, Jack hadn't given any thought to how things would work once he took up the position of Father Time, but he had assumed the old man would be pottering around the shop, showing him the ropes as he learned his new craft.

'There can only be one Father Time, Master Picklewick. Once I swear you in and you become the Thirteenth, my time is up.'

He's...leaving?

Jack hadn't thought for a second that the old man would abandon him. How was he supposed to be Father Time when there was so much that he hadn't yet learned or remembered?!

'But why?'

Mr. Moretimer reflected on his unique past.

'I was human, once upon a time, until I had the honour bestowed upon me and became the great wizard. Once I pass it on to you, you will be transformed from your Neither Here nor There state into the great wizard for there can only be one Father Time. I will become human again and live out my remaining years as I choose, a reward for my service.'

'Could you choose to stay here?'

'We always have a choice, Master Picklewick, but it is your time now. You must find your own way as I did, and as the Fathers before me.'

A sadness built within Jack. The old man had kept him safe, albeit in the most insane, unimaginable manner, and watched over him throughout his life. He had developed an affinity with Mr. Moretimer and he was about to walk away from him with so many questions still left unanswered.

'Your brain will become a sponge and soak up absolutely everything there is to know with each passing moment,' said Mr. Moretimer. 'There are many other powers that come with the role, but the fun will be in discovering them when the time is right for you to do so. You will have a very long time to do that, believe me. The only thing you must remember, above all else, is that time is constant and must remain so.'

Mr. Moretimer's words offered small comfort to Jack. Discovering magical powers was music to his ears but he would still rather have the old man around. It was odd; he had been so independent and self-sufficient in his time on the streets but having finally found something that felt remotely like a home, he wasn't sure he could face it alone.

'What about what happened in the Realm of Time?' asked Jack. 'You still haven't told me.'

Mr. Moretimer had not relished the moment he had to broach the subject with Jack, but the time had come. 'You are the Thirteenth and have great power within you, as both I and Augustus bore witness to in the cavern. Used in the right way, you will achieve great things, but it could make you a conduit for the darkness. It seems to me that both you and he are very much intertwined and, one day, you will have to reckon with that.'

Jack wondered whether it was the black magic his parents used to dabble in that had put him in this situation, through no fault of his own. Mr. Moretimer was keen to change the subject. Jack would learn all there was to learn, in time.

'That reminds me,' exclaimed Mr. Moretimer.

It still amazed Jack how the old man always knew what had gone through his head. He wondered whether that was one of the powers he would possess, one day. Jack's eyes grew large as saucers as the old man revealed a box, wrapped up like a gift with a bow on top. He handed it over and Jack ripped it open.

Edgar!

Jack clutched the teddy bear to his chest. He thought he had seen the last of Edgar. For all the talk of ancient prophecies and saving the universe from all consuming darkness, in the moment, Mr. Moretimer realised that Jack was still just a child at heart with a lot to learn.

He was confident he would, in time.

'Saved from a fiery fate with not a single hair singed or out of place,' observed Mr. Moretimer, pleased that he had successfully rescued the bear in perfect condition.

Well, almost.

When he rescued Edgar, the teddy still lacked an arm but Mr. Moretimer had seen to it that it was fully repaired and restored to the same condition as when Jack first entered his shop. To say Jack was over the moon was the understatement of the century and being reunited with Edgar went someway to soften the blow of Mr. Moretimer's imminent exit.

'Thank you,' said Jack, putting Edgar down on a table.

'No,' replied Mr. Moretimer, 'thank you for what you have already done and for the good that you will no doubt do.' He made his way through the clutter of the shop and beckoned Jack to follow him. Jack slid off the stool and followed, Edgar dangling from his hand, as usual.

'If you choose to take on the honour and responsibility of Father Time, kneel.'

His heart racing, Jack obliged. This was it; not fate or destiny but a direct result of choice and consequence.

'Give me your palm.'

Jack held out his right hand. The old man revealed the Hands of Time and pressed it into Jack's palm, his own hand forming a bond with Jack's as he spoke.

'Since the dawn of time, this device has ticked and tocked, gifting the universe a canvas on which it can paint. With your acceptance, I shall relinquish the responsibility and pass on the honour to you. Do you swear by the Order of Foretellers that you shall watch over time, guard and protect it with your entire being - mind, body and soul?'

Jack nodded.

'I will.'

'Then so it is time.'

Mr. Moretimer closed his eyes.

'I, Maxamus Moretimer, hereby vacate my

position as such and appoint you, Master Jack Picklewick, as the Thirteenth incarnation of Father Time.'

Although it could not be seen by anybody, a portrait of Mr. Moretimer appeared in the previously blank twelfth frame on the corridor behind the curtains. At the same time, in the Hall of Fathers, a stone statue of his likeness constructed itself atop the empty twelfth podium.

Mr. Moretimer was immortalised, just as every other Father before him, a part of history never to be forgotten.

Beneath his Adam's apple, Jack felt a burning sensation which became excruciating. He cried out but, as quickly as it came over him, the pain subsided, and he felt completely normal again.

Mr. Moretimer removed his hand.

'Now you look the part,' observed Mr. Moretimer.

Jack sprinted towards a mirror and laid his peepholes on his reflection. Branded deep into his skin, were the Roman numerals **XIII**, just like the **XII** Mr. Moretimer had burnt into his.

'It is done.'

Out of the corner of his eye, Jack noticed a tiny mark gradually appear on the back of his hand, like an invisible artist was drawing on it.

'What is that?'

'A reminder,' answered Mr. Moretimer. 'You will collect those for the significant moments, just like me.'

'This is going to take some getting used to,'

commented Jack.

'All you have is time,' replied Mr. Moretimer, 'which is the exact opposite of what I now have.'

Jack pulled himself away from the mirror and threw his arms around Mr. Moretimer. The embrace gifted the old man a sense of contentment - free from the commitment of being Father Time, he felt the way he had always wanted to feel.

The way it felt to be a real father.

As the embrace ended, the old man smiled. 'You've just inspired me, Master Picklewick.'

'Is that one of my new powers?'

Mr. Moretimer ruffled Jack's hair. 'You have given me purpose for the finite time I have remaining in this world.'

Jack wasn't sure what he had inspired or even how he had done it; it didn't feel like he had done anything magical, but the old man seemed happy.

Mr. Moretimer hobbled towards the shop exit, frail and unsteady on his feet. He had visibly aged again in the moments since handing over responsibility to Jack and he looked older than ever, which seemed impossible given the number of years he had under his belt. In his current physical condition, one could be forgiven for suggesting he might not even see the end of another week, let alone a year. As he reached the door, Mr. Moretimer reached into his robe and pulled out a key.

'I believe you already know what this is for.'

Jack smiled as he took possession of the key that he had previously stolen. The old man took one final look at his shop.

'As one day ends another begins.'

Mr. Moretimer stepped out onto Jubilee Walk.

'Wait!' shouted Jack. 'One final question.'

'In time you won't need to ask questions,' responded Mr. Moretimer. 'You will already know the answers but, as that is a skill you are yet to master, go ahead.'

Jack looked sheepish. The question had been eating away at his curiosity for some time.

'Why didn't you give Hanz a voice?'

The old man resembled a criminal in the dock, crushed by the weight of guilt in his moment of judgement. After a long period of reflection, a single tear ran down his cheek as he quoted the words Augustus had spoken to Hanz in her captivity.

'The only voice this old fool ever listened to was his own.'

With that, Mr. Moretimer slipped out of the shop and hobbled off into the night leaving Jack to ponder whether he might ever see him again. He was exhausted; the last few days had all been a blur and he had barely slept a wink. He approached his sack of belongings which he had hidden beneath the grand piano and untied it from the stick. He now had somewhere to store his only two possessions in the world. For the time being, he laid them atop the grand piano.

Twenty Thousand Leagues Under the Sea.

I know just the place for you. I wonder if there's a section for fiction.

A pen with the name V. Flemming inscribed into it.

When I get a minute, I'll return you to your rightful owner and apologise.

Jack placed the Hands of Time down beside the other two items then thought better of it. He picked it up and tucked it beneath his arm.

I need some sleep before I decide what to do with you.

He let out a huge yawn and navigated his way through the shop, up the staircase and into the bedroom he had woken up in the first night he came across the shop. When he climbed into the bed and tucked himself in, it didn't feel normal. It would take some getting used to, having only slept in a bed once in the past two years. Even so, it felt nice.

At last, Jack had a roof over his head and wouldn't have to worry about the weather or being mugged and, for the first time in as far back as he could remember, he didn't have a nightmare.

Laid on the bed beside Jack, Edgar had a slightly odd look to his appearance. One by one, stitches popped until a seam opened and a clockroach crawled out onto the bed. It paid Jack no attention as Edgar's seam magically repaired itself and, instead, scurried away, beneath the door and out of the shop onto Jubilee Walk. Scuttling its way along street after street, it stopped outside another door then slipped beneath it, crawling along a very dirty factory floor.

It came to a stop beside a pair of feet, working late into the night, on which were a pair of very expensive shoes. From out of its mouth, a puff of black smoke exhaled and left the insect's body, swirling up into the air. It rose and rose until it reached the nostrils of the person it thought would be best suited to help in its quest to end the Thirteenth prophecy.

With his next breath, the already ruthless and morally vacant Alfred Threadbare inhaled the darkness.

- XXXIX -

A NEW DAWN

*T*HE following morning, Jack woke to glorious rays of sunshine which shone through the shop window. As he stood and rubbed sleep from his eyes, he looked out of the window onto Jubilee Walk. He felt like a new person but there was something he wanted to do before he did anything else.

Bursting out of the shop, he ran all the way up Jubilee Walk and out onto the bustling street at the end of it. Edgar dangling by his side, he commenced with the habit of a lifetime.

'Step right up folks, step right- -'

'I'll give yer threepence to pipe down! Bad enough with the bleedin' sparrows!'

'You know what that means, Edgar.'

Jack threw the teddy bear into the air.

'I'm not invisible anymore!'

To the many eyes watching on, Jack looked like a mad man as he ran circles around crowds of people, shaking their hands and repeatedly throwing his hat into the air in celebration. When he managed to calm himself down, he noticed the young girl he had given bread to beneath the bridge a few days previously. He approached her and she looked at him, unsure of his intentions.

'You ever need a roof over your head, find me at Twelve Jubilee Walk. We're all in this together, after all!' The young girl smiled as Jack skipped back towards the shop. He stood outside and admired it through peepholes full of life. Now it belonged to him, it looked impressive. The sun highlighted the letters on the sign above the doorway, in desperate need of repair:

Mr. Moretimer's Timely Creations.

For several moments, Jack pondered the words that the old man had repeatedly spoken.

Time is constant.

'You know what, Edgar?'

A mischievous grin glimmered across his face.

'I think it's time for a change.'

EPILOGUE

*E*XCEPT for the odd drunken sailor, snoring and unconscious in his own mess, it was completely dead atop the deck of the merchant ship that floated steadily down the Thames. Big Ben marched on towards midnight and the only sounds that could be heard were of water slapping against the hull and the almost hypnotic creaking and groaning of the ship's weathered woodwork.

A hooded man appeared from the port side and shuffled along the deck, a long, white beard trailed down, well below his waist from which various trinkets and pocket-watches hung. The sound of metal clanging on metal accompanied each footstep as the pocket-watches collided against each other. Doing his best to keep his presence a secret, Mr. Moretimer stopped in his tracks. Not a single soul flinched, the ship's crew had consumed way too much alcohol and were out for the count, oblivious. Tired and out of breath, he slumped to his knees.

DONG!

Big Ben chimed as midnight arrived, grabbing the old man's attention. He looked towards the huge clock that stood proudly next to the houses of parliament and marvelled at

its brilliance. It really was an impressive feat of engineering and architecture. Mr. Moretimer fumbled around in his robe pocket and removed something. He opened his fist and revealed something small, and seemingly insignificant.

Not as impressive as you.

A tiny spring, like something from the inner workings of a timepiece, glimmered a glorious gold on his palm in the dim glow of the moonlight. It was no ordinary, run of the mill spring; strangely beautiful, it was unique, in its own way. It was truly...

...one in a million.

As Big Ben sounded for the twelfth and final time, signalling the beginning of a new day, Mr. Moretimer hobbled along the deck towards a galley entrance.

A great place for a stowaway.

The ship meandered along the river until it eventually reached the open sea, where choppy waters lay ahead. Where it was going was anyone's guess but Mr. Moretimer had a very specific destination in mind. He glanced at the golden spring on his palm.

'Don't you worry, old friend.' Mr. Moretimer caressed the spring then tucked it safely away in his robe pocket.

'It's time I did what I should have done a long time ago.'

Like what you just read? Please leave a review on
Amazon and sign up for our mailing list at:
www.harrisneedham.com

Don't forget to ask an adult's permission if you are
under fourteen.

ABOUT THE AUTHORS

Destiny: the development of events beyond a person's control, determined by a supernatural power.

Does such a thing exist?

Many moons ago, two individual paths crossed in a chance meeting. Two minds with the same ambition: to inspire a generation of youngsters at a time when the world was short on inspiration. They believed in the power of stories; the ability to shape imaginations, to influence values and attitudes, and to stretch even the most difficult to reach mind. In a bid to forge unexplored worlds and create unforgettable tales, the two creatives locked themselves away, driven by a desire to be influenced only by their inner voices, nothing else. They wanted to be heard more than they were seen, fully emphasising the power of imagination.

Welcome to the world of Harris & Needham.

www.harrisneedham.com

Jack Picklewick and Mr. Moretimer will return...

...when it is time.